Judy Nunn's career has been long, illustrious and multi-faceted. After combining her internationally successful acting career with scriptwriting for television and radio, Judy decided in the 90s to turn her hand to prose.

Her first three novels, *The Glitter Game*, *Centre Stage* and *Araluen*, set respectively in the worlds of television, theatre and film, became instant bestsellers, and the rest is history, quite literally in fact. She has since developed a love of writing Australian historically based fiction and her fame as a novelist has spread rapidly throughout Europe, where she has been published in English, German, French, Dutch, Czech and Spanish.

Her subsequent bestsellers, *Kal*, *Beneath the Southern Cross*, *Territory*, *Pacific*, *Heritage*, *Floodtide*, *Maralinga*, *Tiger Men*, *Elianne*, *Spirits of the Ghan*, *Sanctuary*, *Khaki Town*, *Showtime!* and *Black Sheep* confirmed Judy's position as one of Australia's leading fiction writers. She has now sold well over one million books in Australia alone.

In 2015 Judy was made a Member of the Order of Australia for her 'significant service to the performing arts as a scriptwriter and actor of stage and screen, and to literature as an author'.

Visit Judy at judynunn.com.au or on
facebook.com/JudyNunnAuthor

JUDY NUNN

the Long Weekend

PENGUIN BOOKS

PENGUIN BOOKS

UK | USA | Canada | Ireland | Australia
India | New Zealand | South Africa | China

Penguin Books is part of the Penguin Random House group of companies
whose addresses can be found at global.penguinrandomhouse.com

Penguin
Random House
Australia

First published by William Heinemann in 2022
This edition published by Penguin Books in 2023

Cover photograph by Garry Hodson/OpenSky Photographics
Cover design by Adam Laszczuk © Penguin Random House Australia Pty Ltd
Internal illustrations by Louisa Maggio
Author photograph by David Hahn/bauersyndication.com.au
Internal design and typesetting by Midland Typesetters, Australia

Printed and bound in Australia by Griffin Press, an accredited
ISO AS/NZS 14001 Environmental Management Systems printer

 A catalogue record for this
book is available from the
National Library of Australia

ISBN 978 1 76134 461 9

penguin.com.au

We at Penguin Random House Australia acknowledge that Aboriginal and Torres
Strait Islander peoples are the Traditional Custodians and the first storytellers of the
lands on which we live and work. We honour Aboriginal and Torres Strait Islander
peoples' continuous connection to Country, waters, skies and communities. We cele-
brate Aboriginal and Torres Strait Islander stories, traditions and living cultures; and
we pay our respects to Elders past and present.

To the memory of Jenny Coleman

CONTENTS

A NOTE FROM JUDY

Hello, and welcome to this eclectic assortment of stories. It's true, unlike many collections, these stories share no particular theme. They do, however, have one thing in common – they're a personal trip into an author's mind. In this case, the mind of one Judy Nunn.

I'm sure all writers play around with ideas for novels and that they constantly make notes – I know I certainly do. These stories are the result of some particular notes having ended up taking on a life of their own. They didn't result in a huge novel, or even become a part thereof as intended. Instead, they demanded a smaller canvas that belongs just to them.

This being the case, I've included a few personal words at the end of each story about its specific source of inspiration, which I hope you'll find interesting.

With warmest regards,

Judy Nunn

THE LONG
WEEKEND

The long weekend was Melanie's idea. Not the long weekend itself, of course, but the way they should spend it.

'No mobile phones, no social media, no computers or devices of any sort,' she said, 'just the five of us alone in the wilderness, living the way people did forty years ago.'

'Sixty, more like,' Tracy remarked drily.

Mel ignored the comment. Trace was always the cynic among them. 'Three days in a remote mountain cabin – communing with nature, hiking along bush tracks, gathering around log fires . . .'

'Burning fossil fuel –'

'Wood's not a fossil fuel,' Eve interjected.

'Polluting the atmosphere anyway –'

'Oh shut up, Trace,' Danny said good-naturedly; she was all for Melanie's idea. 'Go on, Mel,' she encouraged.

'If we leave straight after work on the Friday, we could be up there by seven – it's only a couple hours' drive.'

'A long-weekend Friday?' Tracy again. 'The traffic'll be hell.'

'Then if we're prepared to get up at sparrow's on the Tuesday and come directly into work, we'll have three full days,' Mel rattled on. 'And I tell you what, a full three days up there feels like a week. Even more.'

Tracy's sceptical glance said, *I'll just bet it does,* but in her droll way she was only being amusing. A sophisticated thirty-two, she found twenty-five-year-old Mel's childlike enthusiasm quite endearing.

'At least it did when I was a kid,' Mel concluded.

They all took a swig of their drinks and gazed out at the view from the yacht club's balcony as they gave the matter a moment's thought.

'Do we dare?' Jet was the only one not looking at the view. Glancing up from the Facebook posts she'd been idly scrolling through, she voiced the uncertainty that now prevailed among them – with the apparent exception of Mel. 'I mean, do we *really* dare? I mean, like, you know . . . no *phones?*'

'There's a landline at the cabin.'

'She means no *iPhones,* Mel.' Tracy exchanged a look with the others. Jet and Eve nodded, and Danny, who had so embraced the idea, now dubiously eyed the phone that sat on the table beside her.

'Definitely no iPhones,' Melanie replied firmly. 'That's the whole point.' There was an element of accusation in her tone as she continued. 'That's what we agreed, isn't it? We're all "Zoomed out" – that's what we said. We've had enough of virtual team meetings and events and staring at each other on screens. *"Whatever happened to human connection?"* That's what you said yesterday, Trace. In fact, if I recall, those were your exact words.'

Tracy gave a careless shrug – yes, she'd said that.

'And *you*,' Mel turned to Danielle. 'You said, *"Now that the Covid rules are relaxed, we should get away from it all – just the five of us."* Don't you remember?'

'Yep, I remember.' Danny's acknowledgement, unlike Tracy's, was tinged with a touch of guilt.

'So what's suddenly wrong with Nonna and Pops' cabin in the mountains?' Mel demanded. 'When I came up with the idea yesterday you were all for it. What's happened? What's different all of a sudden?'

'No *iPhones!* I mean, like ... Are you for *real?*' The query in Jet's eyes spoke for them all. A second-generation Vietnamese Australian and the granddaughter of boat people who'd arrived in the country following the Vietnam War, Jet was an interesting mix of contradictions. She was extremely attractive yet surprisingly 'ocker' (as was her brother, who played AFL). She happened also to be fiercely intelligent – at twenty-six years of age Jet was already one of the most highly regarded editors at Albatross Books Australia, which made her turn of phrase at times odd. She didn't talk like someone who worked with words on a sophisticated level. But Jet was Jet, a true original who never conformed to anyone's expectations of her. Except, as it now appeared, when it came to iPhones.

'I dunno if I could live without my phone,' she admitted, meeting the eyes of the others unashamedly. 'I mean, like ... it's a lifeline, isn't it? You'd be severing your connections, wouldn't you? Pretty brutal. And for a whole three days!'

'Brutal is what we agreed yesterday,' Melanie insisted, 'and severing our connections is just what we need.'

The five women all worked for the small but highly successful publishing company, and it was true that just the previous day they'd bared their souls in no uncertain manner. Finally allowed to return to their workplace, they'd decided they were thoroughly *fed up* with the constraints that had been forced upon them working from home, not to mention the unrealistic expectations that could never be realised given the regulations imposed during the pandemic.

At lunch break, gathered in the recreation area over the takeaway meals they'd bought at the food hall across the road from the ABA offices, it had become a real whinge-fest.

'How were we supposed to sell books when the shops weren't open,' Mel had demanded – pleasant, good-natured Mel, who rarely complained – 'readers need to *browse!* They need to wander between shelves and read back-cover blurbs . . .' Mel was an account manager.

Twenty-seven-year-old Danny from marketing had taken up the argument in seamless fashion. 'Exactly!' she'd exclaimed through a mouthful of tacos with double jalapeños, which she still managed to eat with elegance. Stylish and fashionably androgynous, Danny was always elegant. 'And what about the groundwork we put in to dump bins and posters and lightwalls – and for what? No-one was travelling, no-one was shopping.'

'It's all right for you lot . . .' Not to be outdone, Tracy had joined in with a vengeance. 'You haven't had to wrangle imbecile authors incapable of linking up to Zoom. God almighty, what is it about authors! Don't they know the world's gone digital? Electronically useless! Dinosaurs, every one of them!' Even in her exasperation she recognised the need to clarify herself. 'Well, the older ones anyway.'

Tracy actually adored authors, and authors adored Tracy. As publicity director, she loved nothing better than being out on the road with an author, travelling the country, counting the crowds that turned up and the numbers of books they bought, but above all basking in the bond between readers and writers. Book tours really were Tracy's 'thing'. But a virtual tour was something altogether different, and the endless Zoom events necessitating links between authors' homes and multitudinous libraries where technicians were sometimes reliable, sometimes not, had proved a source of immense irritation.

Having had her rant, she dived guiltily into her bowl of kale and tofu salad. Traitorous words. *God, if anyone heard me call authors 'imbeciles' my life wouldn't be worth living.* But she knew she was safe among her mates.

'Whatever happened to human communication,' she grumbled as she gamely gathered up another parcel of kale with her chopsticks. She didn't care much for kale, but maintaining a svelte body like hers demanded she make the effort.

Eve was ABA's fiction publisher, a pretty, petite woman who at thirty-four was the oldest of the group. She had followed on with her own pandemic whinge about home-schooling. With three children under the age of ten the situation had certainly been a challenge. She didn't add the fact that her husband, Jason, had not shared the burden as fairly as she'd hoped he might. In fact, Jase had been a right pain in the arse, but she'd decided to keep that opinion to herself – for now, anyway.

Then another voice chimed in.

'Well, let's face it, the whole world's suffering, isn't it?'

They all halted in their tracks and turned to Jet, who was lounging back in her chair wolfing down a massive hamburger with a side serve of chips that she was dunking in tomato sauce. Slim as a whippet, Jet ate a lot of junk food. 'I mean, we don't have things too bad in Australia, do we?'

The dagger looks from the others didn't bother her in the least. Sure, she was single, no kids to worry about, and as an editor she hadn't had to go through their hellish online experiences, but hers was the voice of reason – they must realise that. Aware of their irritation, however, she was prepared to placate.

'There's a long weekend coming up,' Jet said, flicking her glossy black hair over her shoulders and flashing them an amiable smile. 'We could go on a holiday.'

Her suggestion had been flippant, but Danny had pounced on it instantly.

'Why not? Now that the Covid rules are relaxed, we should get away from it all – just the five of us.'

As a rule, the close ABA female fraternity numbered seven, but two were currently absent. Jodie wouldn't be back from maternity leave for another two months, and Kylie was due to give birth any time now. There was nearly always someone off on maternity leave.

Working in different departments as they did, the women might not have been drawn into such close contact had it not been for Lauren. Lauren, the company's previous publishing director, had bonded the women together right from the start, and with potent purpose.

'Strength in numbers,' she had declared. 'There'll be no misogyny in the workplace if we stick together, my friends. *Unus pro omnibus, omnes pro uno.*'

ABA, having been founded by two brothers, was headed solely by men, and Lauren had been the only female executive with any form of senior rank. A confirmed feminist, she'd used her charismatic powers of leadership to full advantage, although not in a militant fashion.

'Civility at all times,' she would say. 'No need to wage war when a show of strength will suffice.' And she'd flash that devilish grin of hers. 'Strong women are a formidable force, particularly when they share an unbreakable friendship. As we do,' she'd add meaningfully.

The female fraternity at ABA had adored Lauren; she'd been their hero. But Lauren was dead. She'd been dead for just over a year now – a Covid-related death from 'complications' apparently. But what complications? Lauren had been fit and strong, not one of those deemed 'vulnerable' with 'underlying conditions'. And she'd only been forty. How could she have died from Covid? But doctors evidently didn't give out any details apart from 'complications'.

A new publishing director had been appointed, a man this time, but it hadn't altered the bond that had been forged between the ABA women. *All for one, one for all* was their motto, and it always would be. Their friendship remained unbreakable, and Lauren would always be a strong presence in their midst.

Danny now invoked their hero. 'The five of us off on an adventure,' she said. 'Lauren would approve.' With an enthusiastic fist-pump she hurled out several of Lauren's many quotes. "Think large" ... "Live big" ... "Get out amongst it while you can."'

And that was when Mel, fired up, had gone one step further. Her grandparents had a cabin in the mountains, she said, and they'd be away over the long weekend. In fact, they'd be away for a whole fortnight.

'They've booked a railway trip on the Ghan,' she explained, 'Adelaide to Darwin, and they're staying several days either end. Nonna and Pops wouldn't mind us having the cabin for the long weekend.'

'Nonna?' Tracy asked with the arch of an impeccably sculpted eyebrow.

'That's right. She never wanted to be "grandma", and she loves Italy, so we opted for Nonna instead.' Mel smiled fondly. 'Nonna's seventy-five, but she's still frightfully groovy.'

'*Frightfully groovy*', Tracy thought, *how quaint*. There was something so old-fashioned about Mel. Tracy wondered whether this might perhaps be due to her relationship with her grandparents. *Nonna and Pops?* Only Mel would retain the childish titles of her grandparents. Tracy's own grandparents had been Wendy and Pete since she was ten years old.

'She and Pops usually do a river cruise in Europe,' Mel went on, 'but because of the pandemic they've settled on the Ghan. Nonna just loves trains.'

A flurry of excitement ensued as they agreed that a long weekend in the mountains would be a wonderful idea. Eve said she might even be able to borrow her parents' kombi van so the five of them could travel together without having to take two cars.

'How fab,' Mel enthused. 'We'll be just like the Famous Five.'

'The what?' Danny asked.

'Enid Blyton,' she explained as they all looked at her blankly. 'Nonna used to give me a Famous Five book every Christmas. I adored them.'

Of course you did, Tracy thought, *which explains everything.*

Lunch break over, they'd left the discussion there.

And now, the following day being Friday, they found themselves seated at their favourite watering hole. Or rather, it had been before Covid had closed the city. The picturesque little yacht club down the hill from ABA's offices had only recently reopened, and they were seated out on the balcony overlooking the bay.

On arrival, they'd laid claim to their favourite table outside, purchased their bottle of wine with four glasses – plus a beer for Jet, who never drank anything else – and toasted their newfound freedom. Talk soon returned to their plans for the following weekend.

Mel had phoned her grandparents the previous evening, and they were more than happy to loan the group the cabin.

'Nonna said the key'll be under the doormat,' she announced.

'Original,' Tracy remarked.

And Eve had scored the kombi van. 'It's twenty years old,' she warned them, 'but Dad has always kept it in mint condition.' Eve was the eldest of six siblings, and for many years the kombi van had been an essential vehicle for her busy parents.

Then Melanie waxed rhapsodic about the rustic return to nature she envisaged – 'Just the five of us alone in the wilderness, living the way people did forty years ago' – and within only minutes the reality of being without their smartphones hit home.

'But I'll have to be in touch with the kids,' Eve said.

'There's the landline,' Mel replied. 'What's wrong with that?'

Without FaceTime? Eve thought, but she didn't say anything.

'What about Covid check-ins?' Danny demanded with a ring of triumph. 'What if we need to show proof of vaccinations?'

But Melanie had all the answers. 'We won't be checking in anywhere,' she explained. 'There isn't a shop within twenty kilometres of the cabin, and we'll take everything we need with us.' Aware Danny was on the verge of interrupting, she continued, 'You can carry a printout if you're worried. Pops says everyone should be doing that anyway. He says there's too much reliance on mobile phones and that everyone should carry documentation.'

Good old Pops, Tracy thought.

As if to add personal emphasis to the argument, two phones suddenly sounded, Eve's pinging with an incoming text message and Melanie's giving off its tinkly melodic ringtone. While they responded, the others gravitated to their own phones, each scrolling through their own sea of content, particularly Jet, whose phone never left her hand.

'Oh how lovely,' Mel said, a smile lighting her face. Her fiancé, Ryan, had managed to score two tickets for tomor-row's matinee of *Hamilton*. The bookings were heavy and they'd been registered in a queue, but the theatre had just got back to him – cancellations, he explained. He'd be seeing her tonight, but he simply couldn't wait to tell her, knowing how excited she'd be. 'Oh that's wonderful, sweetheart.'

Eve returned Jason's text. Yes, she'd pick up some milk on her way home – apparently they were all out. It'd be Col, of course. He pigged milk straight from the bottle when no-one was watching. *Won't be long,* she tapped. *Home by six.*

Then they resumed the conversation, although Jet's attention remained principally on her phone, which didn't matter in the least – she was a highly efficient multi-tasker.

'So how does Ryan feel about you deserting him for a girls-only weekend?' Tracy asked. Melanie and Ryan were to be married in three months. They were sickeningly in love, but they didn't even live together, which Tracy found odd. *About as old-fashioned as it gets,* she thought, *further evidence of Nonna and Pops?* 'I bet he's not too happy about it.'

'Oh, no, he thinks it's a great idea. He's going to have a blokes weekend. He says we should relish these last months before we tie the knot.' Which was true – as soap opera as it sounded. Ryan *had* actually said that, the reason being simple: they both wanted children and intended to start a family as soon as they'd married.

'How sweet.' Tracy managed to sound her humorously acerbic self while experiencing a pang of envy. 'And Jason,' she quizzed, turning to Eve, 'how's he coping with the idea?'

'Surprisingly well,' Eve said, 'although he's glad we're using Dad's kombi. The long-range weather forecast is fine for the whole weekend, and he'll need the car to take the kids to the beach.'

Jase had actually been most obliging, a sign that Eve had rightly read as evidence of a guilty conscience. He'd so detested homeschooling; he knew he'd left her with an unequal share of the burden. Now that the kids had returned to school, life would be so much easier. Simpler too. He could go back to being a dad instead of a teacher. Jase enjoyed being a dad.

'Why don't I start making up a list of things we'll need,' Jet suggested, thumb still scrolling, eyes still trained on her phone. But Danny had a further matter she wished to discuss.

'Given it's a girls-only weekend,' she said, 'can I bring Val?'

There was a deathly pause.

'No partners,' Tracy replied crisply, aware she was speaking for the others.

'We never said that,' Danny countered with a touch of belligerence.

'It was implied, obviously.' A further pause. 'Oh come on, Danny, be realistic.' Tracy curbed her acidic tone. Danny's girlfriend, Val, had only recently shifted into her flat, so it was to be presumed the two were seriously in love. 'Just the five of us, remember? You said so yourself.'

Danny was aware she was fighting a lost cause, but she was also aware Val wouldn't like her going away with her work mates. Val was fiercely jealous and saw every other female as serious competition, which was perhaps not surprising given the promiscuity of Danny's past. With her short-cropped hair and preference for elegantly tailored trousers and jackets, Danny was fatally attractive to women of her own persuasion. But her ABA mates? Never! Surely Val should recognise that. Danny dreaded having to tell Val she wasn't invited.

'It's hardly as if Val's a *bloke*,' she muttered. 'It'd still be a girls-only weekend.'

Tracy was about to bite back, but ever-practical Eve intervened. Eve was a highly competent peacemaker, due no doubt to the mother in her.

'Val's a partner though, Danny, and that changes the dynamic,' she said pleasantly but firmly. 'No partners means no partners.' And Danny knew she had to accept the decision, which she supposed, after all, was fair.

'So shall I get on with the list then?' Jet suggested, thankful she wasn't part of this whole 'partners' business. She currently had a steady boyfriend, which was surprising, although not so surprising was the fact that she refused to live with him.

'I'll have to give him the flick soon,' she'd recently confided to Tracy, the only other member of the group who remained steadfastly single.

'Why?' Tracy had asked. 'Ben's drop-dead gorgeous, and he absolutely adores you.'

'Yeah, pity about that. I like him too – he's a really beaut bloke, fun to be with, but . . .' A regretful shrug.

'But *what*?'

'He's so dead-keen for us to shack up together, it'd end in disaster.' Jet wholeheartedly embraced both her single status and her bisexuality, 'freedom of choice in all things' being her mantra. 'Before long he'd want to get married and have kids . . . I mean, you know . . .' Another shrug. 'The full catastrophe. Not fair to string him along.'

'Ah. Yes. Of course not,' Tracy agreed.

They'd shared the understanding and camaraderie of the 'single sisters' they were perceived to be – it was certainly the image Tracy chose to project, but in reality the two women were poles apart.

Tracy had played the field for years, flirting with reckless abandon, the men upon whom she set her sights invariably falling under her spell. 'Racy-Tracy' was a term touted behind her back, which didn't remotely bother her, but in truth she secretly longed to have a child, and had for some time.

After starting work at ABA as an ambitious nineteen-year-old, Tracy had watched throughout her twenties as other young women around her got married, physically swelled before her eyes, then took off on maternity leave with waves of well-wishes from often-envious compatriots. None of this had troubled her. Her focus had been upon her career, and she'd risen swiftly through the ranks while enjoying the life of a single woman. She'd partied wildly on Fridays and Saturdays, and over time her *femme fatale* persona had become her cover. She was a successful career woman by choice, not one to be halted like the others by mere *motherhood*. But the conquests had gradually become auditions, which these days were in deadly earnest. Somewhere out there was the right husband–father candidate, and she was determined to find him.

Tracy kept all of this very close to her chest. There was a lot about Trace the other girls didn't know.

'Games,' Eve suggested. 'We'll need games . . .'

They'd covered all the necessities by now, Jet's thumbs tapping away at the list with clinical speed. 'I'll do a printout,' she'd promised upon being reminded she wouldn't be allowed to take her phone with her.

'I can bring Monopoly and Trivial Pursuit,' Eve went on, 'although they're old and bound to be dated. We haven't played them for years.'

'Nonna and Pops have all that sort of stuff.' Mel gave an airy wave. 'They've got jigsaws and Boggle and Pictionary – they've even got an ancient set of pick-up-sticks.' Then, catching Tracy's arched eyebrow, she added with a touch of defiance, 'There's a chess set too, if you must know.'

Tracy held up her hands, a gesture of innocence clearly indicating, *I didn't say a word*.

The forms of entertainment they might favour during their evenings at the cabin had become an essential matter for discussion upon the discovery that their options might be limited.

'*What?* You mean there's no *TV*?' Tracy had been aghast.

'There is, but it's an analogue set with no digital connection, and the reception's pretty bad,' Mel had explained. 'They've got heaps of tapes and DVDs though. Old ones, mainly, from the eighties and nineties, because after that

Pops retired and they spent most of their time on river cruises.'

This news wasn't going down at all well, until Danny piped up, 'I think we should forego television altogether.' And when they turned as one to stare at her, she boldly continued. 'It's in keeping with our purpose, isn't it? To get away from it all? We've been pigging out on TV for the past two years – everyone has. Why not give the whole thing a rest? Besides, we'd only argue about which show to watch.' *Hell,* she thought, *Val and I argue about that every night. Five women could prove a bloody battlefield.*

'Games!' That's when Eve had come up with her suggestion. 'We'll need games.'

Although offered as a bid for peace, the idea had also been a practical one and was quickly embraced.

Ten minutes later, Eve's phone pinged again. It was six o'clock. *Don't forget the milk,* Jason texted, which could also be read as, *You said you'd be home by now.* Time to go.

As the group broke up, Danny left dreading the imminent confrontation with Val. Halfway home she decided to put it off until the following week. There was bound to be angst. *No point in spoiling the weekend,* she thought.

Tracy was popping home to have an early bite and freshen up before setting off to one of her favourite bars. It was Friday night after all. Jet would probably have accompanied her, both women surfing the crowd if Ben hadn't been on the scene, but these days Jet did dinner with Ben on Fridays. Exploring a different upmarket restaurant each week had become their 'thing'. No matter, Tracy thought, there would be other female singles with whom she could mingle while sussing out any possible candidates.

Mel was cooking dinner for Ryan that night, at her apartment. He'd be arriving in just over an hour, but there was no hurry – she had everything under control. Crab linguine with a touch of garlic and freshly chopped chilli, tossed in a robust olive oil and topped with shaved parmesan. The linguine would take only minutes to cook, the delicious 'hand-picked' blue swimmer crab would be from the expensive vacuum-packed carton she'd bought at the fish markets, and the fresh chilli would be homegrown from her pot on the balcony. Mel adored cooking. The dessert was to be a joint childhood favourite of theirs – vanilla ice cream and chocolate sauce (the sort that went crunchy when you poured it over the top). She and Ryan had a lot in common.

He would stay the night and they would make love. Then tomorrow they had the exciting prospect of *Hamilton*, after which he would again stay the night and they would again make love – a toothbrush and shaving kit lived in the bathroom cupboard, and a special drawer in the bedroom housed his fresh socks and undies. They would spend Sunday together, probably going to the markets or a visit to the art gallery, but he wouldn't stay that night. He never stayed on a Sunday night, or any night during the week apart from a Friday. Mel and Ryan's life slotted into a precise pattern, just as their marriage would.

*

Then all of a sudden it was the following Friday. The week had flown by. But Jet's list (printed out with a copy for everyone) had been observed, and they'd kept meticulously to their plans. Boxes of supplies were piled up in the storeroom at work, the arrival of each new contribution heightening their enthusiasm. They were now eager for adventure.

Fortunately, Nonna had instructed Mel that there was no need to bring linen and towels.

'Plenty there, Mellie darling,' she'd said, 'just run them through the machine before you leave. Oh, and don't use the Hills hoist, pet – hang them on the back verandah clothesline, under cover in case it rains.'

On the morning itself they arrived at work early, bringing with them the perishables. Packed in coolers and eskies with freezer bags and ice, they stacked them into the kombi van, which Eve had parked in the coolness of the basement car park, and during lunch break they added the boxes of supplies from the storeroom.

Come the end of the work day, they were all set to take off, and they were excited, albeit some had mixed feelings.

Danny had told Val of the girls-only long weekend just the previous night, after they'd made love and were curled up in bed, the light still on – they always made love with the light on. She'd known it was a gutless move on her part, leaving the confrontation until the very last minute, but she'd dreaded the angst. She was thankful, however, that Val had unwittingly presented the perfect way to downplay the issue.

'You're telling me this *now!*' Val's outrage had been of predictable proportion.

'Why not?' Danny had feigned puzzlement at her reaction. 'You said the other day you were going home to see your folks for the long weekend.' This was surely a justifiable excuse. Danny hadn't been invited to the family home herself, of course. Val had remained in the closet as far as family was concerned, and Danny's appearance was a bit of a giveaway – even to country folk. 'Come on now, baby,' she said reasonably, 'you won't even be around.'

'You're right. I won't.' Val tossed her hair huffily and sat up, staring straight ahead at the image of herself in the mirrors of the built-in wardrobes. She refused to meet Danny's eyes. 'I won't be here when you get back.'

'You what?' *A tad melodramatic, surely.*

'You heard me. I'll move out while you're away with your *girlfriends.*'

'They're not my *girlfriends*, they're my *work buddies*, for God's sake.'

'They're *women,* Danny!' Val turned, hurling the accusation right in her face. 'You can't be left alone with women, you can't help yourself . . .'

'These are women I *work* with, baby.' Danny kept her tone calm in an attempt to soothe. 'I don't sleep with the women I work with . . .' Which wasn't altogether true. She and Jet had had a brief fling a couple of years ago. Just a one-night stand in recognition of the fact they found each other hugely attractive, but they'd agreed that sleeping with work buddies wasn't a wise call.

'You're going to have to start trusting me, Val,' she went on. 'These are my friends who happen to be female. You are the woman I live with.' Then she added in all seriousness, 'And you're the only woman I've ever asked to move in with me. Surely that means something.'

She kissed her lover gently, and although the kiss was not returned, she was relieved that Val didn't pull away. 'Now, let's get some sleep.'

Things remained tense in the morning, but nothing more was said, and as she left for work, the overnight bag and wine cooler kit all too conspicuous, she hoped she wouldn't be coming home to an empty apartment. *Ah well,* she thought philosophically, *that's what happens when you decide to commit. There's definitely something to be said for staying single.*

Tracy had met an interesting man the previous Friday. He sold 'off the plan' real estate, which she considered perhaps a bit dodgy, but he was extremely handsome. This was a prerequisite very high on her agenda, as she wanted a good-looking child, so the father-material was promising. But husband potential? He'd obviously wanted to sleep with her – well, why wouldn't he? They were in a bar, it was a Friday night, and they'd shared amusing online dating experiences, so he was obviously searching just as she was. But when she'd refused to accompany him to his flat 'for a drink', saying it was past her bedtime and she was going home, he'd asked her out the following week. A very good sign.

'I'm away this weekend,' he'd told her, 'viewing the layout of a new high-rise up the coast. Back on Monday. How about dinner, say, Wednesday?'

'I never go out during the week,' she'd replied, which was true. Playtime was always reserved for the weekend. Next Friday then, Greg had asked, or Saturday if she preferred? Either would be fine by him. He'd suggested a particularly trendy Japanese restaurant that just happened to be a favourite of hers. While discussing food they'd discovered they both loved Japanese. Very promising.

'Can't,' she'd said, 'I'm going away with friends for the long weekend.'

'Ah. Pity.'

She'd be in town the weekend after that, though, she'd told him, and she'd given him her phone number.

'I'll call you,' he said.

'Do,' she replied with a captivating smile.

Tracy didn't regret being unavailable this long weekend. Or so she told herself. *Good idea to keep him on ice,* she decided, *test his staying power. All part of the game.* But now, as the gang set off for the car park, she was hoping like mad that he'd call.

They all admitted feeling strangely naked as they waited for the lift that would take them down to the basement. They'd left their mobile phones locked up in the office, or so they'd promised each other. Mel, however, raised last-minute doubts about Jet. If anyone was likely to cheat on the deal, it would have to be her.

'You swear you don't have one with you?' Mel demanded.

'I swear. Honest. You saw me lock it in the drawer.'

But Mel remained suspicious. 'You have two phones, Jet, one for work, one personal, and –'

'And they're *both* locked away, I swear.'

'Perhaps we should do a strip search,' Danny suggested with a mock leer, and the others laughed.

The lift arrived.

'Actually, I'm sort of looking forward to being without a phone now,' Jet said thoughtfully as the lift descended. 'In a sick kind of way, if you know what I mean.'

They didn't.

'Severing all connections the way we are . . . Well, it's a bit like dying really, isn't it?' No comment, but she didn't appear to be seeking one. 'I mean, life as we know it is about to be taken away from us,' she went on. 'At least, that's the way it feels to me. Like your umbilical cord has been severed, you know?'

The others exchanged glances. Jet had voiced her serious misgivings only the other week, now she seemed to be relishing the prospect of 'severing all connections'.

'Like you've been cut off from your supply,' she continued, 'from the lifeblood that feeds you. Like you're floating about on your own, disconnected from the world. Weird, don't you think? I mean, really, *really* weird.'

Nobody had a rejoinder to that.

'*You're* weird,' Danny said, and they stepped out into the underground car park.

As they walked to the kombi van, Eve was wondering whether she'd miss the kids, and secretly knowing she wouldn't, further wondered whether she should feel guilty. *No, bugger it,* she told herself. *I deserve this break. Over to you Jase.*

She climbed into the driver's seat, Mel taking the front passenger seat beside her. The other three hauled open the sliding door to sit directly behind them, the supplies piled on the last row of seats and in the rear storage space.

'We're off,' Eve said, starting the engine and backing the van out of the parking bay. 'Buckle up.'

Eve was the only one permitted to drive the old kombi van. She'd had firm instructions from her father.

'No one else is to take the wheel, Eve,' he'd said. 'You're a very good driver, and I trust you implicitly, but I don't know the skills of your friends, and I want no accidents. You are to be solely responsible.'

'Sure, Dad,' she'd promised.

'I don't know where the hell I'm headed,' Eve now admitted, pulling out of the car park and turning left. 'There's no GPS in this old thing.'

Seated behind Mel, Jet piped up triumphantly. 'There, you see, that's *exactly* what I mean. Cast adrift. No help. No lifeline.' She held up the claw of her hand, as if clutching a phone. 'No connection, you see?'

'Shut up, Jet,' Danny said.

'No, no,' Jet insisted, 'don't get me wrong, I find it exciting. Creepy, but exciting. Travelling blind like this. No electronic influence, no artificial intelligence. Just us and the physical world we're living in. Kind of primitive, don't you think? Spiritual even.'

'Mel knows exactly where we're going,' Eve said. 'Don't you, Mel?'

'"Course I do. Straight ahead for the next twenty kilometres till we get to the highway,' Mel replied as if to emphasise the point. It was why she was seated in the front after all.

Tracy gazed out the right side of the rear passenger window, trying to recall his name. Greg, yes, she remembered that, but the surname? She really should have asked if he had a business card. But then perhaps not. That would have appeared too eager.

'With daylight saving we should get there before dark,' Mel said. 'It's only a couple hours' drive.'

She was clearly destined to be proven wrong, however, when half an hour later they found themselves stuck in a gridlock that showed no sign of moving.

'Long-weekend Friday,' Tracy commented smugly. 'Told you the traffic'd be hell.'

'Bit of a bummer,' Danny complained, 'arriving in the dark with all this gear and no torches.'

'You didn't read your list, did you?' Jet's comment was more an accusation than a query. 'I stipulated torches and cameras.' She'd noted down any equipment that was normally provided by smartphone apps.

'Who owns a torch these days?' Danny retorted. 'Or a camera for that matter?'

'I have both.' It was Mel's turn to be smug. She even took a pencil torch from her coat pocket and waved it in triumph.

'There's a torch in the glove box too,' Eve said.

'We're moving,' Tracy remarked as the car in front started to inch forward.

An hour later, when they'd reached the outskirts of the city and had taken the turn-off Mel indicated, the traffic was starting to thin. But only a little, and dusk was already gathering.

'It'll be pitch bloody black by the time we get there,' Danny grumbled, but no-one took any notice as Mel handed around two packets of crisps.

'Barbecue or sea salt,' she cheerily offered. 'Take your pick.'

Mel's attitude remained chirpy throughout, determined as she was that this long weekend should prove memorable. They were going to Nonna and Pops' after all, revisiting the halcyon holidays of her childhood. What could possibly be better?

'I brought along six puzzle book collections,' she said brightly. During their discussion on games, they'd been in agreement: they all loved crosswords. Besides, being such a group activity, crossword puzzles would prove ideal. Mel had taken it upon herself to purchase an ample supply.

Danny was still in the mood for a whinge though. 'Did you make sure they have Sudoku?' she asked darkly, perhaps hoping to catch Mel out.

But she couldn't.

'Yes, yes, Sudoku for you as agreed, and cryptic crosswords for Jet.' As always, little fault could be found with Mel's ability to organise.

'Oh my God, that's rap,' Tracy barked. 'Switch it off, switch it off!'

Eve had turned on the kombi's radio, the volume just loud enough to distract her from the bickering. She quickly tuned the dial to another station.

'Justin Bieber.' Jet voiced her instant approval. 'I like him.'

'I don't,' Tracy said.

At that point another stalemate presented itself. They hadn't brought up the subject of music, had they? Everyone's personal playlist was stored on their phones, and Spotify was obviously out of the question.

'Nonna and Pops have heaps of CDs,' Mel said. But the prospect of Nonna and Pops' CD collection did not hold great appeal.

'There's a radio at the cabin,' Mel offered.

'ABC only,' Tracy replied sharply.

'What's wrong with silence?' Jet suggested. 'We could live without music for a few days. Listen to the elements instead.'

'Not a bad idea,' Danny agreed, and harmony once again reigned.

Then finally they were wending their way up the mountain, still following a line of the city exodus, though an ever-thinning one as other holiday-makers peeled off the highway towards various destinations. It was dark by now, and despite an occasional gap in the traffic Eve continued to drive slowly. They were encountering pockets of mist here and there, and although the moon shone brightly from a cloudless sky, the visibility was not good.

The higher they travelled the mistier their surrounds became, the pockets of mist joining up to form one continuous soupy grey. They'd turned off the highway by now and, with less traffic around, Eve switched the headlights to high beam, but that only made her vision worse. She hunched over the wheel, peering into the fog of the night.

'Should only be about a half an hour till we turn off to the left,' Mel said. 'Glen Road. It's usually deserted.'

They very nearly missed the turn-off, despite the fact that Mel had undone her seatbelt and wound her window down in order to lean out and gaze into the bushland ahead.

'There!' she exclaimed, startling them all. 'There, there, Eve! Turn left! Glen Road!'

Eve turned the vehicle into the even gloomier back road. Just as well she'd been travelling slowly, she thought, or they would have driven right past it.

'We're about ten k's from the cabin,' Mel announced, winding her window back up. 'We need to look out for a dirt road off to the right. Won't be long now.'

I bloody well hope not, Tracy thought. She'd be needing to pee soon. The toilet break they'd taken at a gas station had been well over an hour ago, and given the potato crisps they'd been eating – Mel had produced another three packets – she'd drunk nearly two bottles of water.

'Wow,' Mel said, 'in all the years I've been coming up here I've never seen it this thick.'

The mist, which had by now become fog, encircled them, blanketing them with seemingly deliberate purpose, as if wrapping them in a shroud.

'Eerie,' Danny said.

'You're not wrong,' Jet agreed. 'Spooky.' She peered through the side window at the world that swirled outside. 'But somehow exciting too, don't you think?' Jet seemed to be engaging with the experience on an altogether different level.

'Can you see okay, Eve?' Tracy asked, feeling on edge. She couldn't see a thing herself.

'Not really. Just trying to stay on the road.' Eve was hunched even more intently over the steering wheel, squinting into the gloom, following the hazy blur of the headlights.

'Favour the right,' Mel instructed. 'We're on a ridge that drops off to the left.'

'Oh great. Now you tell me.' Eve tried to sound jovial, aware they were all nervy, but she obeyed the instruction and stuck to the right, hoping there was no vehicle coming from the other direction.

They lapsed into silence as they made their way through a ghostly, grey-white world. Occasionally there'd be the slap of bushes on the side of the van, warning Eve that she'd veered a little too far to the right, and she'd make the adjustment.

What happened next, no-one knew, but in the instant it did they all thought it was a head-on collision. And, in a way, they weren't wrong. The kangaroo, a large grey buck, had bounded out from the right and smashed into the windscreen, its body tossed from the bonnet up over the cabin to land in a bloodied mess behind them. All they'd seen through the miasma had been the blurred shape of something looming out of the fog, immediately followed by an almighty crash. Eve had instinctively over-corrected and wrenched the wheel to the left. And then they were tumbling. Tumbling over and over down the rocky slopes of the ridge.

The jangled chaos seemed to go on forever. The cacophony that engulfed them, the crashing and smashing – inside the vehicle, outside the vehicle – their entire existence spiralling into madness, was lasting forever. But in reality it was barely twenty seconds before the van came to rest upside down in the gully ten metres below, everything suddenly and ominously silent but for the hissing of a broken radiator.

Mel came to her senses, lying on her back. She sat up to discover, miraculously, that she wasn't wounded – at least not as far as she could tell. But where was she? Where was the van? She stood and ferreted for the torch in her pocket. Switching it on, she surveyed the murky world that surrounded her. She was in the gully. And there was the van. She could see the hazy outline of its shape barely five metres away. It was resting on its roof, front wheels still spinning. Her door must have swung open at some stage; she must have been flung from the vehicle as it rolled. Of course. She hadn't had her seatbelt on, had she?

She took several paces towards the van. She could see the front passenger door now. Yes, it was open, but it was buckled in on itself, a crumpled heap of metal. It was impossible to see inside. God, she'd been lucky! But what about the others?

She moved closer, dreading what she might find, and held her torch up to one of the van's side windows. She peered through.

Oh dear God! She was sickened by the sight. There was blood. She was looking through to where Jet was sitting, and she could barely see anything for the blood. Jet was hanging upside down and there was just her matted black hair pasted upon the glass. *Oh God! Oh God!*

She moved to the next side window, and in the narrow beam of the pencil torch she could make out the rest of the van's interior. There was no sign of movement. She could see each of them where they hung motionless in their seats, Eve hunched forward, clutching the steering wheel; Tracy and Danny, heads flung back; Jet and all that blood . . .

She screamed out their names as if in doing so she might wrench them back to the world of the living.

Oh God, they can't be dead, she thought as she grabbed the handle of the sliding door and hauled on it with all her might. *They can't be! They can't be!*

'Eve! Tracy! Danny! Jet!' She kept screaming their names but the door wouldn't budge. And everything remained so deathly still. Just the low mechanical murmur of the van's front wheels could be heard as the spinning began to slow.

Panic gripped Mel. She had to get help. Her friends were dying in there. The cabin! She must get to her grandparents' cabin and phone the police. She started feverishly clambering back up the ridge. They were only a few kilometres from Nonna and Pops' place. She knew this area well. Of course she did. Heavens above, the trekking she'd done with her older brother during their childhood! She and Chris must have covered every bush track in a twenty-kilometre radius of the cabin. *I'll be there in no time*, she told herself, all the while her mind begging, *Don't die! Don't die!*

She started along the road then considered whether perhaps she should cut through the bush. But given the poor visibility, was that wise? Of course it was, she decided. Much quicker. And speed was of the essence. *Don't die! Don't die!*

The trek through the bush seemed surprisingly easy. Was the undergrowth less dense than she remembered? Was it the adrenaline pounding through her? But after what felt like an age, she started wondering why it was taking so long. Her watch had stopped, obviously damaged in the accident, so she had no idea of the time, which didn't help matters. But surely she should have reached the cabin by now. The fog was a complication, but even through the haze and dark of night she'd recognised in the torchlight two bush tracks she knew. One, well established, had been a favourite of hers and Chris's. It led down to a rock pool, which in the rainy season even boasted a small waterfall. She recalled how she and Chris had thought it their personal discovery, a secret place no-one else knew of. They must have been around eight and ten at the time.

Images flooded her mind. Images so vivid. The two of them stripping down to their undies, braving the icy water of their very own pool. Standing under their very own waterfall, mouths open, drinking in the crystal-clear water that belonged just to them. *We were explorers,* she thought, *explorers who'd discovered our own magical paradise.* She even found herself smiling at the memory, her mind having momentarily blanked all else, or so it seemed. The rock pool had turned out to be no secret at all but a popular picnic spot for any number of locals who knew of its existence – which was, of course, why the track was so well-worn.

How Nonna and Pops had laughed when they'd recounted their 'discovery', she remembered. But she and Chris had made other discoveries. Trees that demanded to be climbed, tracks that led to panoramic views of the valley, caves that made perfect cubbies. She could see each and every one of them. She was there, nestled in the branches of that tree; there, looking out at that valley; there, hidden away in that secret cave.

With her mind wandering the past, Mel's panic had subsided altogether. She felt strange – very strange – light-headed and dizzy. Was she concussed from the accident? Did that explain why it was taking so long to get to the cabin? She wasn't even using the torch anymore but instinctively following the tracks that she knew – or rather the tracks she thought she knew. *Have I been walking around in circles?*

She stood motionless, testing her sense of direction. *The main road would be back that way,* she told herself, *and the dirt road to the cabin should be just ahead.* Even as she gauged her surrounds, she swore she could see through the night and the mist and the bushland, a flash of head-lights some distance away. Right where she'd just assessed the road to be. *Damn, I should have stuck to the road – I could have flagged that car down. But I'm close*, she told herself. *I know I'm close now – very, very close.* And she continued onwards with renewed purpose. She must not let her mind stray again.

Still, it seemed to be taking so long, and try as she might her mind kept straying. She was finding it difficult to concentrate. *It has to be concussion*, she thought, *and maybe shock as well.* She mustn't give in, she mustn't faint or pass out. She must get to the cabin and phone the police.

Then, without realising, she found that she'd unconsciously stepped from the bushes and was on the dirt road. *I'm here!* she thought, surprised.

Panic once again set in as she quickened her pace, rounding the curve to where she knew the cabin would be sitting in its picturesque clearing off to the left, the road continuing on to other remote properties in the area. It had taken her so long to get there; she could only hope she was in time to save her friends. *Don't die*, her mind was once again chanting. *Don't die! Don't die!*

She halted, staring ahead in amazement. The cabin was right in front of her, but what was going on? It was ablaze with lights, and parked out front was a police car and an ambulance. What further catastrophe could have taken place on this horrendous night?

She ran up the short driveway and onto the verandah. She could hear voices in the front lounge room. A man's voice, authoritative. A woman crying, other voices more muted. The door was ajar. She pushed it open and stepped inside.

She remained frozen in the open doorway, unable to believe the sight that confronted her. There they were, the three of them: Danny, Eve and Tracy. Danny, her face drained of colour, was sitting in a hardback chair at the table, her broken arm being treated by a paramedic, another paramedic assessing her vital signs on a laptop. Eve and Tracy were seated on the sofa, both looking bruised and battered, Eve with a comforting arm around her friend, who was weeping uncontrollably. In fact, Tracy was bordering on hysterical. Watching them, Mel thought in a strangely detached way how odd it was that Trace was the one to weep and lose control. Racy-Tracy, who always played things so tough.

A middle-aged police officer with a hint of a paunch was standing near the sideboard delivering orders, sharply and efficiently, into his handheld radio. The situation, he said, was more serious than it had sounded from the triple-zero call, which had apparently made little sense due to the caller's hysteria.

'We'll need a rescue unit and another ambulance,' he ordered. 'The vehicle rolled down an incline and two of their group may be seriously injured or possibly dead.'

Mel wondered how on earth no-one seemed to register her presence, standing where she was in the open doorway.

'What's happening?' she asked, mystified. 'What's going on?'

But they didn't appear to hear her. She stepped into the room, but still everyone seemed too preoccupied to notice.

The police officer continued to address his handheld radio. The unit and ambulance were to take the turn-off onto Glen Road and proceed roughly eight kilometres, he instructed. The crash site was to the left. He would meet them there.

As he barked directions, his eyes were on Eve, who nodded.

Eve had calmed down enough now to assure Senior Constable Reynolds that she would be able to guide him directly to the site. When the three women had climbed to the top of the ridge, she had noted in the light of her torch the damage inflicted where the vehicle had left the road – mashed trees, flattened bushes, a minor rockslide . . . *Nothing short of a miracle we're alive*, she'd thought. And she'd timed their hike to the cabin. *Someone has to be in control, with Danny groaning in agony and Tracy hysterical.*

When they'd reached the cabin and she'd telephoned triple zero, however, she'd been incoherent, or so it seemed. She'd tried desperately to explain where the crash site was, where the vehicle remained, where her friends lay wounded, perhaps even dead. She'd felt herself becoming hysterical when the emergency operator kept demanding, *Where are you telephoning from?* The operator's calm was maddening. *What is your current location?*

Eve had forced herself to recall Mel's exact directions. 'Ten kilometres along Glen Road,' she'd said. 'A dirt road leads off to the right. We're in a cabin and my friend has a broken arm, but my other two friends . . .'

'Remain where you are,' the operator had said. 'Help is on its way. Please turn on all outside lights to ensure you are clearly visible.'

His instructions now completed, Senior Constable Reynolds clipped his handheld radio back onto his belt.

'Let's go,' he said.

Eve winced as she rose to her feet. Probably a mistake to have sat in the first place, she realised – her whole body was racked with pain.

'You sure you're up to this?' Reynolds asked with a touch of concern. He was a good cop, a good man.

'Yes, I'm quite sure,' Eve said firmly.

Gutsy little number, he thought as he led the way through the open front door.

Mel watched, still mystified, as they walked right past her.

'Eve,' she said, and reached out her hand. But Eve neither heard her nor felt the touch of her fingers.

Mel turned from the room and followed them into the night.

She watched as Eve and the officer climbed into the police car. And she watched as the car took off, headlights cutting through the mist, conjuring the bushland eerily into focus. They were going to the crash site. Well, she would go to the crash site too. She would find out just exactly what was going on. She started to follow the vehicle.

Again, she seemed to be in some sort of time warp, her mind straying, distracted. The police car was no longer in sight, but she was travelling. Travelling through the bush, effortlessly, yet with a purpose. She was going back to the site.

And then she was there. She didn't know how, but she was there in the gully. She could see the kombi van, upside down, its front wheels no longer spinning, all deathly still. She could hear the sound of sirens from far away. Police? Ambulance? *Both*, she thought. *He'd called for both*.

Up on the ridge a car's headlights were approaching. She heard the vehicle do a U-turn. Two people alighted, one carrying a torch. Eve and the police officer.

'There,' she heard Eve call. 'Down there.'

A powerful beam of light was directed from above.

That was when Mel saw herself. Quite clearly. In that instant, the mist miraculously disappeared, and on the rocky ground before her lay her broken body, twisted in grotesque fashion, five metres from the van.

She gazed down at herself. The distant sirens grew louder. She stood motionless, bewildered. *How could this be?*

But she was not alone. From out of the shadows stepped Jet, who joined her in the pool of light where the mist had cleared.

'I've been waiting right here,' Jet said, 'waiting for you to come back. Didn't want to leave without you.' She held out her hand. 'Come on. Time to go.'

'Go? Go where?'

'I don't know. But we're about to find out.'

Mel took her friend's hand. Jet looked so serene, so pretty, so beautifully unscathed.

'Find out what?'

'I don't know that either.' Jet smiled. 'But we'll find out together.'

They turned to go.

'Don't look back,' Jet said.

And, the sirens growing ever louder, they walked together into the fog that slowly closed in around them, claiming them for its own.

A WORD FROM JUDY

I can't recall exactly where I was when I encountered a truly scary fog, but it was somewhere in the UK, possibly Scotland or Wales, and I was in my early twenties, which means it was a long, long time ago.

I was in a car (not driving, as I didn't have a car in those days) with a couple of other people (can't even remember who they were) and we were travelling through mountainous country when a thick fog came from out of nowhere and blanketed us entirely. It was an incredibly eerie sensation! As we crawled through this virtual 'pea souper' a scenario presented itself – someone is killed in an accident caused by a fog but, not knowing she's dead, is unable to contact the living. This scenario didn't actually come to me as a story at all, but rather a TV script – very visual. I think I saw it as an episode of The Twilight Zone, *which in those days was a telly series with a supernatural theme.*

Anyway, it's stayed with me all these years, so it obviously made an impression – here I am, half a century later, putting it to paper.

THE WARDROBE

I bought the old house in '75, I was just twenty-two at the time. It was tiny. A relic of yesterday. Hard to believe it was mine. I hadn't planned to buy a house – I was footloose and fancy free – but I know, as I look back over the years, that that old house was my destiny.

When Grandma Rose died and left me a modest inheritance, it came as quite a surprise. As far as I'd known, old Grandma Rose hadn't been a wealthy woman.

There were five other grandchildren to be considered, so it wasn't a vast amount, but in '75 ten thousand dollars was not a sum to be sneezed at. Particularly not if one was a young, struggling journalist. A 'freelance' who commanded no more than the standard fee of eighty dollars a story and who scored, on average, two assignments a week. In fact, I doubted whether I would see such a lump sum ever again in my life.

The money was accompanied by a personal instruction, sharp and to the point: 'Write that book, Margaret.' Grandma Rose was as concise in death as she had been in life. The old lady had died in her sleep at eighty-nine years of age, so there was little to grieve over, but I would miss her sorely.

In the meantime, I was left with a dilemma. Ten thousand dollars. What to do with it? I was guilt-ridden with the certain knowledge that the book I'd always said I was going to write would not be forthcoming. Well, not immediately. One day perhaps, but Grandma Rose's legacy confronted me with the fact that there was no point in my galloping off to a crumbling villa in Tuscany or a bohemian studio loft in Montmartre and dedicating myself to my art. What art? Now that I had the means, I was forced to admit that there was no book. For three years there'd been endless notes on scrappy bits of paper, but still there was no book.

I was depressed and rather wished that Grandma Rose had kept her money and I'd kept my romantic delusions. Then I took myself to task and set about addressing the problem. Ten thousand dollars. What to do with it? Not writing the book as instructed was bad enough, but to squander the money . . . That would be unforgivably disrespectful to Grandma Rose.

'Buy a house,' my friends advised me. 'Ten thousand's enough for a deposit, and then you won't be wasting all that dead money on rent.'

Despite their nagging, I didn't give much serious thought to becoming an owner of property. Having lived a hand-to-mouth existence for the past four years, never knowing where the next story was coming from, I found the prospect of heavy debt terrifying.

I have to confess however, that real estate signs suddenly became more prominent. Through the windows of buses and trains, bright yellow 'For Sale' signs dominated my peripheral vision. And 'Auction, Open for Inspection' popped up regularly where it had never been before.

On my twice weekly token jogs through Paddington ('four times a week, minimum,' my fitness fanatic friend Sandra lectured me) I'd slow down when I saw 'Raine and Horne, 3 bdrm, lock-up garage, spacious backyd', or 'LJ Hooker, 2 bdrm, ensuite, open pl living, sundeck with views'. Bloody stupid, I told myself, a lifetime of debt. And I'd jog on.

Then one day I saw it. In a grubby little lane in an inner-city suburb. I was on an assignment at the time. Walking purposefully down Ann Street in my best linen suit – my 'reporter's uniform' – and feeling good. No wonder, I'd been commissioned by a fashion magazine to write a thousand-word 'retrospective' article on Surry Hills and the early rag trade days, and the editor had offered double the standard fee.

I'd done my morning's quota of interviews so I decided to explore the suburb. Field research, I told myself, but it was really an excuse to stay away from my typewriter – it was such a lovely day.

I wandered around the colourful backstreets and up the hill, finally arriving at the old Clock Hotel on Crown. Then I turned the corner into Alexander Street and there it was: the tiniest terrace house in the worst condition with a sign that read, 'For Sale. Renovator's dream. Ideal first home for imaginative buyer.' The house looked a wreck, but it was within my price range.

My recent library research told me that it was one of the early workers' dwellings. Probably built in the late 1850s.

Around the time when Surry Hills was transformed from
a fashionable suburb of mansions and paddocks to a
network of alleys and laneways lined with rows and rows
of tiny, two-storey brick terraces to house the workers in
the new and thriving factories.

Despite its derelict state, the house was quaint and picturesque with its rusty lacework balcony and ragged grey
slate roof. But there was more to its appeal than architectural charm and a sense of history. There was something
personal. It beckoned. It compelled me to look inside.

Well, I told myself, an inspection wasn't binding. A quick
tour through the house would satisfy my curiosity, I didn't
need to buy it.

'You can't go wrong with this little gem, she's a steal,'
the real estate salesman said as he tried the front door
for the third time with yet another wrong key. Yes, yes,
I thought, already wishing I hadn't got into this.

'Needs a bit of work, of course.' Yes, I'll bet, I thought.
'Deceased estate, old lady died six months ago and her
sons want to make a quick sale.'

Key number four fitted. He turned it. 'Watch where you
walk, the floors are a bit crook.' He opened the door and
I stepped inside.

There was a moment's respite from the sales pitch while
the man jangled his keys behind me. Key number four had
jammed in the lock.

I was in a tiny room. The afternoon sun streamed through
the front leadlight window, catching the dust particles that
hung in the air. An old wooden hallstand with brass fittings
stood beside the door, and to the right was a mantelpiece

and an open fireplace framed in pretty blue and green tiles, a number of them cracked. A small iron grate sat within the fireplace, and on the slate hearth before it was a blackened old pair of tongs and a coal shuttle.

I crossed and knelt to inspect the fireplace. There was coal in the grate, and in the tray beneath were several inches of fine, grey ash, the residue of a number of cosy fireside evenings, I imagined.

'Yes, these days people pay a fortune for mantelpieces like that.' The man had finally conquered his keys and was standing beside me. 'And those little tiled fireplaces are all the go now. Come on, I'll show you the rest of the place.'

I followed him into a room of identical proportions but it seemed even tinier. A quarter of the space was lost to a narrow wooden staircase against the left-hand wall. It was two feet in width and led to the upstairs bedrooms. A small four-seater wooden dining table dominated the room. It was old and scarred and well-loved once. There was no other furniture, although it would have been difficult to fit in anything more than a couple of dining chairs.

'Kitchen's next,' the salesman said and he led me through the door. 'The stove's an old one but it works a treat. Kookaburra. Gas, of course.'

I made a show of inspecting the old 'Kookaburra' – he obviously expected me to – but it wasn't the stove itself that impressed me. It was the cleanliness. Beneath the fine film of dust there was not a speck of grease. I opened the oven. Scoured. Spotless. Nobody kept an oven that clean. The stove stood in the corner of the kitchen and, in the two-inch gap between the wall and the side of the old

Kookaburra, I could see the connecting pipes. They were thick with the congealed grease and grime of a lifetime's meal preparation, and I pictured the endless frustration for the hand that could never reach those pipes.

I followed the salesman up the wooden staircase to the bedrooms. He was into his pitch again, 'best buy in town', 'great opportunity', 'young person like you', but I wasn't listening.

Although the light was gloomy on the staircase and the uncarpeted stairs were steep and narrow, in climbing them I had a sense of sureness and safety. A shallow well was worn in the centre of each step and, beneath my hand, the railing was solid. Smooth and cool to the touch.

The bedroom at the top of the stairs was bare but so tiny it could contain no more than a single bed and perhaps a small chest of drawers.

'Bit on the small side,' the salesman admitted and proceeded quickly on. 'Think you'll like this, though. Come and look, the front bedroom's a little beauty.'

It was indeed a pretty room. The plaster walls were painted cream, the same as the rest of the house, but the ceiling was molded in a floral design. Leaves entwined with roses and daisies, and, in the corners, sunflowers and poppies. French windows opened out onto the balcony with its rusty iron lace. The sun shone through the windows' leadlighting, dappling the walls. With neither furniture nor dressing, it was a feminine room.

But there was furniture. Just one piece. Who could fail to notice the wardrobe in the far corner? It didn't belong somehow. It was too big. Too square and bulky.

Not ugly, but intrusive. It belonged in a different sort of room. A masculine room.

'How come there's furniture in the house?' I asked. The first words I'd spoken throughout the inspection.

'Deceased estate,' the salesman explained. 'If the relatives don't want it, it goes with the place. Happens quite a lot.'

I nodded. 'Of course.' I hadn't known that. But then I'd never bought property before. And suddenly, jarringly, I realised I was going to buy the house.

As I stepped out onto the balcony and looked at the street below, his voice followed me.

'The old lady had two sons; their wives came along and took what they wanted. Chairs and the fridge and stuff. Don't know why they didn't take that old hall stand – those things fetch a price these days. Too old-fashioned they said, and the table too small. And this wardrobe, well . . .' He shrugged. 'How the damn thing got up here's beyond me. It won't fit through any of the doors. Must have been hauled up over the balcony.'

I didn't say anything but looked down the road to the corner where the rows of terraces marched down Arthur Street. 'I can get the stuff carted off if you take the place. For a modest fee,' he added.

The sun warmed my face. 'No, leave it here.' Then I realised what I'd said.

The man sold me the house for twenty grand. It seemed a good price. And I couldn't be bothered pretending to haggle, I was too euphoric to care. There was only one thing in the world that mattered: the little old house was mine.

'But it's a dump,' Sandra said. 'An absolute dump. Good grief, Nance, what have you done?' (My Christian name being Margaret and my middle name Anne, it's a mystery how I came to be nicknamed Nancy. I can't even recall whether it evolved from early family or school days but evolve it did and, although I've never particularly liked the name, I've allowed myself to be stuck with it.)

'You haven't really bought the place!'

'Yes,' I said firmly, 'I have.'

'Surely it's not too late to back out.'

'Yes,' I said, 'it is – the gas and electricity are on and the phone's –'

'Oh that doesn't mean a thing, you can still –'

'No, I can't. It's too late to back out and I won't.'

'Shit.' Her muttered oath was one of resignation and I breathed a sigh of relief.

'It was cheap,' I boasted. Sandy was good with money, surely that would impress.

'I should bloody well hope so.' We were in the downstairs front room and she prowled about testing the floor's weak spots, of which there were many. 'You realise you'll have to replace this whole floor.'

I nodded. 'The builders are coming next week.'

'And what about the roof?' Before she'd come in she'd given the house a good 'going over' from the street. 'Half the slates are missing.'

'Yes,' I said, 'the roof people are coming next week too.'

'So it'll be ages before you can move in.' She wandered through to the dining room, still stamping the floor with her designer sandshoes. 'This room's just as bad; it'll have to be done too.'

'I'm moving in tomorrow.'

'You're *what?*' Her face was a mask of horror.

'Well, not totally, of course,' I added. 'But I want to camp here while I scrub things back, paint the kitchen and bathroom and stuff.'

'Where will you sleep?'

'I've got a fold-up bed.'

'But they'll be replacing the floors.'

'Not upstairs. Upstairs is in very good condition.'

'But the roof. What if it rains?'

'Then I'll come downstairs for goodness' sake. Shut up, Sandy. Please!'

We'd progressed through the kitchen ('That stove's ancient,' she muttered) and I held my breath as she walked out the back to the bathroom. As with most small early terraces, the bathroom did not feature in the original design. A hundred and twenty years ago, people bathed in their bedrooms from large china bowls on small marble-topped washstands.

According to the real estate agent, it was some time in the '20s when the weatherboard shack had been added. There was just enough space for the enamel bathtub and the small handbasin, no more. And a tin medicine cabinet with sliding mirror doors hung from the wall. There was no lavatory, but a wooden outhouse at the end of the narrow courtyard.

I jumped in quickly before Sandy could comment on 'the dunny down the back'. 'I'll build a whole new bathroom, I swear, one day when I can afford it. Now just wait till you see upstairs,' I added. 'You'll love the master bedroom.'

When the house inspection was finally over and Sandy had left for the gym, I was glad to be alone, just the little old house and me. I didn't do anything. I sat on the floor by the fireplace and thought of ... nothing at all. But I remember, as if it were yesterday, my feeling of sheer bliss. There was something so good in that little old house that it touched my very soul.

I moved my gear in early next day. Just the camp bed, linen and some cooking utensils – enough to boil a kettle and fry an egg – and, of course, the cleaning and painting supplies.

Then I started to explore the house in more detail. There were so many things I'd overlooked (which Sandy most certainly wouldn't have). A severe shortage of three-point plug outlets, poor water pressure, the lavatory cistern that kept flushing unless one manually adjusted the ballcock. None of which mattered, of course.

I made a cup of tea and wandered around, touching the walls and the stairs, 'just being there', the painting and scrubbing forgotten. (That was typical of me in those days, motivation was not my strong suit.) Then I wandered upstairs. I supposed I should have at least carted the bed up with me but, no, that could wait, plenty of time.

I looked at the wardrobe in the corner. I should have accepted the man's offer to take it away. Getting rid of it was going to be hell. I opened the French windows and stood on the balcony. Amazing to think that they'd hauled the thing up and over the railing. Maybe it wasn't as heavy as it looked.

I went back inside and opened its doors. One half of the wardrobe was bare hanging space. The other was open shelves. And, to my amazement, the shelves were full, stacked neatly with blankets and linen. The blankets were old and threadbare – the grey military kind you buy at St. Vincent de Paul's – but they were clean and smelled of mothballs. The sheets, bleached white and carefully mended in places, were crisply ironed into squares.

I spread a blanket on the floor and carefully, one by one, lifted the contents out of the wardrobe, marvelling at what was there. Tea towels and pillowslips, bath towels and tablecloths, all worn but in pristine condition. I went through the wardrobe shelf by shelf and, when I came to the very last one, I found two pieces of hand crochet – one navy, one pink. Hot water bottle covers, I presumed 'his' and 'hers'. And, behind them, at the very back of the shelf, something wrapped in tissue. Quite a large parcel. I lifted it out, set it down and gently eased back the paper. On top was a christening gown. Cream lace. Very old and in perfect condition. And it rested on top of a man's dressing gown. Wool, the old-fashioned sort, in big maroon checks with a satin tassel tie.

I sat back on the floor and looked at the love and the care laid out on the grey army blanket. Who'd lived here, I wondered. I so wanted to know. Love pervaded this house, I'd felt it the moment I stepped inside. Who were they? Who was she? Who'd tended the Kookaburra stove?

'Deceased estate,' I remembered the salesman said. 'Old lady died six months ago, her sons want to make a quick sale.'

Then I noticed the open wardrobe door – the one on
the other side. There was writing there, figures and dates,
some difficult to read. Whoever had written them had
had trouble with the pen, but they'd laboured to make an
impression in the wood and, even where the ink ran out,
the words had been indelibly inscribed:

Elizabeth Jane, 2nd Jan. 1922.
Stephen Harold, 25th Feb. 1925.
James Robert, 9th Mar. 1930.

And then, below these dates:

8th Nov. 1948, my beloved Harry died.

There was nothing after that.

I looked at the dressing gown. Harry's surely. And the
other names and dates. Children? A daughter and two
sons?

I packed everything neatly back into the wardrobe, just
the way it had been. Then I rang the real estate man.

'Yes, the old lady had been a widow for a long time,
I believe. Don't know anything about a daughter. One
of the sons lives in Surfers Paradise. High-rise real estate.
Loaded. The other one's here in Sydney. Jim Roper. He's
the one who put the house up.'

Roper. Yes, I remembered the name on the contract.

When I asked the man if Jim Roper would like to collect
his mother's personal belongings from the wardrobe, his
answer was immediately dismissive. 'Oh no, he wouldn't

want any of that junk. The wives went through the place with a fine-toothed comb; they said there were some old blankets and stuff. Just chuck it out or give it to the Salvos.'

I was bristling with anger as I replaced the receiver. I didn't know which pair I disliked most, the sons who hadn't bothered to check through their mother's belongings or the daughters-in-law who had and considered it 'junk'.

During the week that ensued I didn't have much time to ponder the matter. Workmen came and repaired the roof and builders came and replaced the floor, and I worked hard on my magazine assignment amid the chaos.

Then, suddenly, it was over and the house was my own again. Peaceful. I still hadn't got around to painting the kitchen and bathroom. I think I knew I never would, although the five-litre cans of paint stood accusingly in one corner.

I did, however, move in my motley selection of furniture, mostly acquired from second-hand shops. The removalists left it piled in the downstairs front room, and I stood there wondering where to start. The main bedroom, of course – it was where I'd been camping out after all. The chest of drawers would have to go up there and I could finally stop living out of a suitcase.

I cursed myself for not having had the presence of mind to ask the removalists to cart some of the heavy stuff upstairs, but those sorts of things always occurred to me too late and the men had seemed only too eager to leave. I'd have to get a friend to help. Damn. During my week's encampment, I'd become very proprietorial about the house – I didn't want anyone else there.

'Just until I've done the place up,' I insisted to my friends, although it wasn't really that. I don't know what it was, but whatever it was, it was annoying Sandra. 'You're becoming a bloody recluse,' she grumbled. 'We only want to help.'

Maybe, if I took the drawers out, I could cart the chest up by myself, I thought. I measured it; I measured the width of the stairs (I'd have to drag it up sideways); and I measured the wardrobe and the front bedroom to see where everything would fit. The wardrobe would have to be shifted. Only a yard or so. And, yes, I could do that by myself too, I decided. If I shuffled it.

I started shuffling. It wasn't difficult. And, inch by inch, between my feet, a cardboard box appeared. A slim, flat cardboard box, grey with layers of dust.

I lay on my stomach, cheek pressed against the floorboards, and peered beneath the wardrobe. There was another box, or what appeared to be another box, a little smaller than the first. I pushed it out the other side with a broom handle and checked if there was anything more. There wasn't.

With an old tea towel, I wiped the layers of dust from the boxes. The smaller of the two turned out to be a biscuit tin. An Arnott's biscuit tin with a picture of a once gaudy parrot on its now faded top. It was rusted solid, the lid immovable, so I sprayed it with anti-rust compound and set it to one side. Then I opened the cardboard box.

Its green 'marble' design reminded me of the Laminex-topped table we had when I was a child. The box had a lift-up lid and looked as if it had originally contained office stationery, ledger paper or such.

There wasn't much inside. Something that looked like an old bank deposit book and half a dozen official papers.

I opened the bank book. Columns. Amounts on the right and dates on the left. Each amount was for three pounds seven and tuppence ha'penny and each was dated fortnightly throughout the year of 1918. It was in the name of Corporal Harold James Roper. And, folded up in the last page of the book, there was a separate piece of paper. The Australian Army's notification of the honourable discharge of Corporal Harold James Roper.

So Harry had been in the army, the First World War, and he'd left nothing but the barest of records. He obviously wasn't much of a memorabilia hoarder. How frustrating.

I sifted through a couple of insurance policies dated 1919 and came to a letter from the Australian Immigration Department. It was dated 12th September, 1920, and it informed Mr. Roper that application for the entry of his fiancée, Miss Emily Tonkin, had been approved. Beneath that, a letter from the P&O shipping line:

Dear Mr. Roper,
We are pleased to inform you that passage has been
secured for your fiancée, Miss Emily Tonkin, aboard
the SS 'Orontes' due to depart Southampton
5th December, 1920, and scheduled to arrive in
Sydney 7th February, 1921.

I sat back on the floor and looked at the wardrobe. The doors were slightly ajar. I pushed them wide so that

I could see the writing on the inside and the folded linen on the shelves.

So her name was Emily, I thought. Emily Roper, née Tonkin. It was Emily who had tended the Kookaburra stove and recorded the dates of the births of her children and the death of her husband in the old wardrobe.

It was Emily and Harry Roper who had lived in the little old house.

I turned my attention again to the cardboard box. Only one paper remained. It was folded and, when I picked it up, I felt a weight inside. I opened it. A medal. Plain. In bronze. And the paper was an army citation that read:

Action for which commended.
On 24th April, 1918, between the junction of the
rivers ANCRE and SOMME, near HEILLY, this
N.C.O. and men were linesmen attached to the
8th Australian Field Artillery. The enemy put down
a heavy bombardment of gas and heavy explosives,
and all telephone lines were cut. These men at
once set out to get communication with batteries.
The lines were broken in dozens of places, and the
bombardment continued for eight hours, during
which time these men were exposed to the heaviest
shell fire. They eventually succeeded in getting
communication with batteries and it was only with
unflagging energy, dauntless courage and devotion
to duty that this was accomplished. (Sgd; 3. Monash,
Major General, G.O.C. 3rd Aust. Divn.
Military Medal was awarded to Harold James Roper (Corp)

By now I had no idea of the time of day, lost as I was in Harry and the past. But, as I closed the French windows to keep out the draught, I was surprised by the chill, dusk air. I turned on the overhead light and, one by one in sequence of dates, spread the papers out on the floor. Then, armed with a screwdriver, I attacked the Arnott's biscuit tin.

When, after a fifteen-minute battle, the lid finally gave way, I was not disappointed. Letters. There must have been over a hundred jammed into the tin. But neatly. Still in their envelopes and in bundles – one small and three large – each tied up with a slim blue ribbon.

The smaller bundle was addressed to Miss Emily Tonkin of 23 Warrane Road, Halstead, Essex, England. The larger bundles were all addressed to Mrs Harold Roper of 21A Alexander Street, Surry Hills, NSW, Australia.

At the bottom of the tin, beneath the letters, were two christening photos, each in a miniature silver frame. Both babies were wearing the same christening gown – the gown that now lived in the wardrobe. Where was the other baby, I wondered. There should have been a third christening photo.

I opened the first few letters from each bundle, intending to sort them into sequence in order to follow the events of Emily's life. But no sorting proved necessary; Emily had done that for me. The letters in the smaller bundle were from Harry during 1919 and 1920, and those in the larger bundles were from a woman called Margaret Leigh and they dated from 1921 on.

I settled down to read. I had no compunctions about what I was doing, no underlying guilt at the thought that

I might be prying. Strangely enough, I had the feeling that Emily would like me to know about her.

Harry was a lazy correspondent for whom writing was a chore. But, far from being hurt, Emily apparently nagged and teased him mercilessly.

It is all very well for you to chide me for my shortcomings, my dear, but I have difficulty in expressing myself through my pen. The ease with which you find the right words and place them in the right order is a talent I shall never possess. And the pleasure you attain from so doing is a pleasure which totally eludes me.

The next letter was dated two months later, during which period Emily had obviously written to him a number of times.

You have every right my dearest to take me to task for the time elapsed between my letters, but never for the brevity of the letters themselves. After all, it is not the lines upon the paper you must read, but the spaces in between.

The banter between them continued and the more I read of Harry's letters, the more I cursed him for not having saved Emily's. Damn you, Harry, couldn't you have saved just a few? Two? *One* even?

There were times when Harry did commit himself to paper. When he genuinely had something to talk about. 'I have found our house,' he wrote joyfully.

*Oh, my dearest girl, how you will love it. In fact, it
reminds me of you. It is neat, petite, quaint, loving and
has great strength of character. Forgive me for perhaps
waxing a little overly lyrical but I am envisaging
your excitement upon seeing it and, as usual, your
excitement is contagious.*

Harry could certainly express himself when he wished
to but, as Emily well knew, he was just bone lazy most of
the time.

He even had the grace to admit it. A letter several
months later stated,

*I may have been a little lax in my correspondence
(yes, yes, all right – lazy), but I have been far from
lax or lazy in my efforts to accelerate the bureaucratic
process. The man from the Immigration Department
assures me the papers will be through any day now
and I have already approached the P&O shipping line
for dates and details.*

I opened the last of Harry's letters. It was written in his
customary lighthearted vein but, when I got to the end, he
took me totally by surprise.

*Emily, My Dearest,
I count the weeks, the days, the hours until I see you.
You are in my heart and I pray that, until the very last
breath I take, you shall always be by my side.
Your loving husband to be,
Harry*

I looked at the letter and felt a sudden pang of conscience at having read it. I returned it to its envelope and, as I was retying the blue ribbon around the small bundle of his letters, I glanced up at the open wardrobe door.

8th Nov. 1948, my beloved Harry died.

A tear blurred my vision. Harry's prayer had obviously been answered. Emily had indeed been by his side until the very last breath he'd taken.

I was tired, I decided as I wiped away the tear. Tired and overly emotional. I hadn't eaten, I was cramped and cold from sitting on the floor – I should go to bed. I could leave Margaret's letters until tomorrow. But they sat there looking at me. 'Mrs Harry Roper', they read. By now Emily was married. Maybe I'd read just the first few. I opened the top envelope.

Dear Emily,
How strange to be addressing you as 'Mrs Harry
Roper'. My dear friend, I am so happy for you.
I am happy for you both. Do give Harry my very
best wishes. Although we only met on those several
occasions when I returned to Halstead, I liked him
very much and it is obvious he loves you dearly.

Yes, I have heard that Sydney is extraordinarily
beautiful and I am delighted that you are so taken by
the city. But then I am not particularly surprised – you
seem to delight in your surrounds wherever you are.
It is possibly your greatest charm and one I quite envy

*from time to time. Personally, I find so many places
and people tedious.*

*The house sounds picturesque but, truly, you must
have the bathroom built as soon as possible. It sounds
positively heathen bathing out of bowls and buckets.*

Margaret went on with a bit of a whinge about her job
at the library and the London summer.

*Thank goodness autumn is coming on, I do so hate
the heat. How you are going to handle your first
Australian summer is beyond me. I shall think of you,
my dear, when I return to Halstead for Christmas.
I shall think of you as I nestle before the log fire in
mother's front sitting room and look out at the blanket
of snow and the old elm tree we used to climb all those
years ago, remember?*

*Oh, Emily, I do miss you so and I do wish you
every happiness in your new life.*

*Your loving friend,
Margaret*

On to the next letter (I'd read just two more, I promised
myself). It was dated 24th November, 1921.

*Emily, My Darling,
What thrilling news! And of course I am deeply, deeply
honoured that you should ask me to be the child's
godmother. I have posted you a gift, which I have had
specially made. It will reach you well before the event,*

but I am not going to tell you what it is. Oh, my dear,
I am so excited.
*   And the bathroom! Well, about time! You will*
certainly need a bathroom with a baby on the way.

I skipped through the rest of that letter and went on
to the next. Margaret's present had arrived. It was the
christening robe, of course!

My Dear Emily,
I am so glad you like the robe. Yes, it is beautiful,
isn't it? I had it specially sent from France. It is of
handmade Chantilly lace and will last from generation
to generation. The sons and daughters of your own
children can be baptised in that very same gown, my
darling. Just think!

I did think. I thought of the sons' wives who had
explored the wardrobe. I thought of the sons themselves,
who must have been told of the robe.

I lifted the parcel out and laid back the tissue paper.
There it was. In cream lace. Sitting on top of the old
dressing gown. I stroked the satin ribbon and lifted the
scalloped hem in my fingers. It was beautifully made.

I felt a shiver run down my spine. Was it the ghosts of
the wardrobe? No, I was cold, I told myself. Freezing, in
fact. Although it was early spring, the night held a wintry
chill. And so I put on Harry's dressing gown. It was warm
and clean and smelled of mothballs, and it seemed the
natural thing to do.

Then I curled up on the floor with the next letter, promising myself that it must be the last. Take yourself to bed, Nance, for God's sake. It's nearly one o'clock in the morning and there must be at least forty or fifty more letters to go, they'll keep till the morning.

My Dearest Darling,
What can I say? There is nothing, of course, nothing I could say could possibly ease the burden of your sorrow. But you must be strong. For Harry's sake as well as your own.

Is it of any comfort to tell yourself that your little girl simply didn't awake? That she slept peacefully on and knew no pain? Oh, Emily my dear, I feel so far away and so powerless when I do so long to help.

So that was why there was no christening photo of Elizabeth Jane. Emily's first child had been stillborn.

I finally went to bed. I was too tired to eat and too tired to shower. I stripped off to my T-shirt and lay with the covers around my chin, my mind awash with thoughts and images, and I wondered whether, indeed, I was too tired to sleep.

But I wasn't. It must have been minutes after my head hit the pillow that the thoughts and images became dreams.

The slim, shadowy figure of a girl – I couldn't see her face. She was climbing a tree. A huge tree, possibly an elm. The girl had to be Emily, surely. And there was another girl with her. That had to be Margaret. Emily called her name, laughingly. 'Margaret!' Over and over. And, gradually, the image of Margaret became me.

Then we were in the old house, sitting together in the downstairs front room, a cosy fire crackling in the grate. And, as we talked, Emily's image slowly became clear to me. But she was no longer a young girl. Her hair was white and I watched her gnarled hands as they busied themselves with the hot water bottle cover she was crocheting. I couldn't see her face.

'It never ceases to amaze me how cold a Sydney winter's night can become,' she was saying. 'Not as cold as Halstead, I'll grant you, but they come as a surprise nonetheless.'

Then she turned to me. 'You must write that book, Margaret,' she said suddenly. And it was the face of Grandma Rose. 'You owe it to me to write that book, my dear.' It was said kindly enough, but it was an order. 'I want to see your words in print. A published author. That would be something to be proud of, don't you think?' She put down her knitting and stared into the fire.

'Writing is such pleasure, do you not agree? The English language is so rich.

Out of us all
That make rhymes,
Will you choose
Sometimes –
As the winds use
A crack in the wall
Or a drain,
Their joy or their pain
To whistle through –

Choose me,
You English words?

'Do you remember?' She turned to me. 'I sent you a copy all those years ago. Edward Thomas.' She smiled and the face was no longer that of Grandma Rose. This had to be Emily.

It was a beautiful face. The eyes, although faded with age, were alive, exhilarated. 'Edward Thomas,' she repeated. 'To think that Harry knew him – a man who wrote a verse like that.' Then she turned back to the fire. 'It was always my favourite poem.'

Other images followed, but they all became a blur and I awoke the next morning with nothing left but the shadowy figures of the girls in the tree, fragments of the poem and the old lady's face as she smiled at me. But that face was not a blur. Emily's smile and the life in her eyes were strongly etched in my brain.

I made myself shower and eat a proper breakfast, and then the telephone rang. Again and again. The magazine editor, Margot. *The Sunday Times* with an assignment for next week. But my mind wasn't functioning on a normal level. I was haunted by the image of Emily and the fragments of the poem that hung in my memory.

Finally, I took the telephone receiver off the hook. The poem. I had to find the poem. Words. It was about words. And it was by Edward someone. Hopeless, I thought. How many English poets were there called Edward someone. Then I remembered. Harry knew him. A contemporary of Harry's. Well, there was a starting point.

Less than an hour later, at the library, I found him. It was incredibly easy. Flicking backwards through an anthology of English poets dating from the year Harry returned to Australia, 1918, there he was. Edward Philip Thomas, a list of his works, and the poem was called 'Words'. He had been killed in action at Arras in April 1917. Had Harry served with him in the Great War? Is that how he knew Edward Thomas?

I found the poem itself in a collection of war poets and, as I read it, a shiver ran down my spine. I had never before in my life read or heard of this poem. That is, not until last night. Now every word of the opening stanza Emily had quoted returned to me, and I could once more hear her gentle voice:

'Out of us all
That make rhymes . . .'

I went home and noticed that I'd left the telephone receiver off the hook. I wondered briefly whether I'd lost a job as a result and then I thought, damn it, and I left it there. Upstairs, I opened the Arnott's biscuit tin and sat down with Margaret's letters.

I savoured every word as, hour after hour, I lived Emily's daily existence. She obviously wrote of everything and anything except the loss of her baby girl, and Margaret tastefully kept her letters in the same lighthearted vein.

Dearest Emily,
A gas stove! My dear, you hadn't even told me you'd
been stoking wood fires all this time. Unthinkable

horror. And a 'Kookaburra'. How delightfully
humorous. Mind you, I have discovered a picture
of a kookaburra in my encyclopedia and it is such a
fearsome-looking creature. Do they really laugh?

And then the wardrobe . . .

Oh, My Dear Emily,
How hysterical. To think that the first argument you
and Harry ever had was all about a wardrobe. I am
quite sure it is a hideous wardrobe and that it quite
ruins your lovely bedroom, but Harry's tenacity in
getting it up there is to be admired. The picture you
paint of his intricate pulley system and the neighbours
risking life and limb to assist in the exercise is hilarious.
And yes, I can imagine Harry's fury when they tore
out the balcony railing, but you really shouldn't have
laughed. Anyway, as you say, you are stuck with it now,
so you may as well make the best of it.

It was shortly after the wardrobe episode that Margaret
admitted to having a beau. Well, more or less. He was
a lawyer, she said. His name was Geoffrey Brigstock.
He was a very conscientious young man and he studied
regularly at the library.

Geoffrey's diligence was obviously a facade. The truth
was he was smitten with the librarian. Not that Margaret
said so herself. For someone so forthright she was
uncharacteristically shy about her admirer, which led me
to believe that she was equally smitten with him.

Dear Emily,
Yes, I do dine regularly with Geoffrey but I refuse to be
drawn into discussion about him. I am sure his invitations
are merely a courtesy in return for the assistance I have
given him with his research at the library.

Then she rapidly changed the subject . . .

I have received the poem you sent. I agree, it is quite
an inspiration for anyone with a love of the English
language, particularly one such as yourself . . .

Gradually, over the following year, Geoffrey's name
featured more and more regularly in Margaret's letters,
and Emily obviously badgered her for details. Then finally,
in a letter dated 20th June, 1924,

My Darling Emily,
It has happened. Geoffrey has proposed to me. Last
night, in fact, and I simply could not wait to tell you.
My dear, I have not been 'keeping you in the dark'
as you suggested in your last letter. I have simply not
been daring to hope. I love him so much that I have
not dared to believe that he could love back. And, oh
Emily, he does!
I am the happiest woman alive. Just as you and
Harry found each other, I have found my perfect love.
And now I promise you, my dearest, incorrigible
friend, I shall admit my innermost secrets to you and
you may tease me as mercilessly as you wish . . .

It was the following year, shortly before Margaret's wedding, that she wrote:

My Dear Emily,
What a lovely, lovely present. How do you manage
to crochet as beautifully as you write? The little poem
accompanying the antimacassars is exquisite. I intend
to have it read out at the ceremony.
*   But, my darling, your news is the best wedding*
present of all. I am so happy for you.
*   Emily, forgive me if I am being insensitive – I cannot*
help but ask. The fact that you inform me of your
news so close to your confinement, is it because you
are frightened? Please, please, my darling, do not be.
You are strong and healthy and you will have a strong
and healthy child, I know it.

The letters that followed were joyful. Margaret returned from her honeymoon, as in love as any woman could be, to discover that Emily had given birth to a boy at four o'clock in the morning on the 25th of February and that Harry had been most inconvenienced by the hour of his son's arrival.

I sense that as he smoked four cigars and drank a half
a bottle of cognac, Harry cannot have been quite as
inconvenienced by the hour as you would have me
believe, my darling,

By now my involvement in the world of Emily and Margaret and Harry and, indeed, Geoffrey, who was also proving interesting, was total. It was early afternoon but I couldn't bear the thought of stopping to make a sandwich, or even a cup of tea. I read on. And on and on.

Geoffrey was made a junior partner in his law firm and was doing very well. He bought a house in South Kensington and the antimacassars looked beautiful on the new lounge suite.

Baby Stephen was walking and talking, and Harry tried to pretend that he wasn't a doting father but he spoiled the boy rotten. Then the news of another impending birth. James Robert was born on the 9th of March, 1930. Late afternoon, five o'clock, a far more civilised hour.

Evidently Margaret and Geoffrey were unable to have children:

Emily, My Dear,
The copy of James's christening photograph arrived last week. Already I have had it framed and it stands on the mantel beside Stephen's. I look at them both in the christening robe and feel so proud of my godchildren. How I would love to hold them in my arms!

My dear, I sense a certain reluctance to discuss the children in detail as you used to do, and I can only surmise that you are being protective of me. Please do not be. If it is God's will that Geoffrey and I do not have children, then so be it. It makes Stephen and James even more important to me and it gives me great pleasure to hear of every first step, every first word, every first tooth. You are my family, Emily. You always have been. And now your children are too.

Not one to dwell on regrets, Margaret obviously poured all of her energies into Geoffrey and his work. Geoffrey was now a senior partner and shareholder in the firm and Margaret created her own career working alongside him in the Central London offices of Brigstock, Gracy & Tomlinson, Solicitors. Theirs was evidently a very close and very cerebral relationship.

> *He says I am indispensable, not only to him, but to the firm. I am now on full salary, and I must admit that it makes me feel very modern and very liberated.*
>
> *It is strange, is it not? At school you were always the career conscious, emancipated one and I was content to anticipate a life as a wife and mother somewhere along the track. How we would have laughed had someone told us those roles would be reversed. But we both lead happy, full, rich lives with husbands we love who hold us dear. We are to be envied, Emily.*

I was halfway through the third and final bundle of Margaret's letters and I found myself starting to worry. I was running out of correspondence and I was only up to 1934. Emily had died in 1975 – what had happened to them in the years between? They hadn't had a falling out, surely. Not Emily and Margaret.

I read on, compulsively, praying that nothing untoward had happened. War was declared. Both women breathed sighs of relief that their men were now too old to be a part of it (Geoffrey had also served in the Great War) and they

commiserated with those who were destined to lose their
loved ones.

> Yes, my darling, I know the cause is an 'essential' one
> and you are right when you correct me. 'Worthwhile'
> is too weak a word to apply – it is indeed the essence
> of good which must overcome the essence of evil but,
> oh Emily, what a price to pay! Like you, from the
> safety of my nest, my heart aches for those women, the
> daughters and sisters and mothers and wives who must
> go through what we went through all those years ago.
> And the men who must brave it! It is so cruel. There
> is certainly some comfort in being forty years of age,
> midway through the possible loss of our husbands and
> sons, but that does not help the others, does it?

It was seven o'clock in the evening and, once again, the
air was chill and, once again, I put on Harry's dressing
gown. There was a sick feeling in my stomach. Only a half
a dozen or so letters were left . . .

> My Darling,
> Please do not worry about me. There is no danger in
> London.
> The war rages across the Channel and, although the air
> raids sound regularly, they are false alarms and people
> do not take them too seriously.
> Rationing is taking its toll, of course, and many are
> suffering deprivation, but spirits are high and everyone
> believes it is only a matter of time.

In the next several letters Margaret tried to make light of any personal hardship in order not to worry Emily. And then I came to the very last letter. My heart was in my mouth. I was loath to open the envelope. Despite the warmth of Harry's gown, the night air had chilled my bones. I switched on the little two-bar radiator and walked around to release the cramp in my leg. I stepped out onto the balcony and looked down at the streets of Surry Hills. So many of these terraces were just the same as they would have been in Emily's day.

I breathed the air and prepared myself, the night was not cold at all. Then I went inside and opened the envelope.

There was something enclosed in the final letter. It fell to the floor at my feet. A photograph, two teenage girls. Happy, healthy, smiling faces. I picked it up and stared and stared – I'd seen that face before. Those eyes, that smile, belonged to her. The old woman I'd met in my dream. The girl on the right of the photograph was Emily Tonkin-Roper.

I turned it over and read on the back 'Halstead School for Girls'. And the date, also written in Margaret's hand, 'Nineteen Hundred and Twelve'.

Dearest Emily,
Remember this? I've long since lost the copy of the
school magazine in which it was published. But I
found this photograph as I was doing one of my
rare spring cleans. How proud we were, heading the
debating teams with such vigour. And, of course, in
summation, you annihilated me. Such innocence seems

a lifetime ago. Little did we know then that the Great War was just around the corner, and now here we are in the midst of this new horror.

I can no longer lie to you. Of course you read it in your newspapers. They have started to bomb London. The air raid sirens are no longer false alarms. Whole areas are reduced to rubble and it is fearful to see.

But, oh Emily, the bravery which rises above the fear is inspirational and I am so proud of my countrymen. Not only do people rally to help one another in moments of crisis but everyday life goes on. Services continue. Workmen brave the blackout to perform menial tasks. A plumber arrived only the other day to tend to our kitchen sink and, when the siren sounded, he said, 'Blast Hitler', and continued his work.

And several weeks ago we attended the West End theatre. (A performance of Noel Coward's Cavalcade, which was most enjoyable.) When a siren sounded halfway through the second act, an interval was called for those who wished to go to the bomb shelters and then the actors simply went on with the play. The people of London are thumbing their noses at Hitler, and I know that such spirit will win out and that good will triumph. It is remarkable. Prime Minister Churchill is quite right. This is our 'finest hour'.

Your loving friend,
Margaret

And that was it. The last letter. No more. Had Margaret been killed in the bombing of London? I could only suppose so. There was nothing else in the Arnott's biscuit tin and I felt empty. Bereft. Margaret was gone. Geoffrey was gone. There was no more news of Harry and Emily and the children. What had happened since 1940?

I resolved to find out. But where to start? Geoffrey's law firm! Of course! I sifted back through the letters. There it was. Brigstock, Gracy and Tomlinson. I dialled directory assistance and, in no time at all, the helpful woman on the end of the line found me the number.

I looked at my watch. Nearly half past eight – that would make it around ten-thirty am London time, I thought. Good.

'I'm enquiring about a Mr. Geoffrey Brigstock,' I said to the very cultivated voice on the end of the line. 'I wondered whether –'

'Mr. Brigstock is in Singapore and he shan't be back for a week.' There remained, beneath the woman's carefully rounded vowels, the faintest tinge of her cockney origins. 'Might he contact you?'

'Oh. No. Thank you.' I was so delighted to discover Geoffrey was alive that I wasn't sure what my next step should be. 'I'll write to him,' I said finally, and I took down the address the woman gave me.

Yes, a letter would certainly be easier, the words must be chosen with care. How exactly did one say, 'I have just finished reading the letters your wife wrote to her best friend for twenty years and I want to know what happened to the two of them'?

It was surprising to discover that Geoffrey was still working. I'd presumed he was around the same age as

Emily and Margaret – that would put him well into his seventies, but perhaps he'd been younger.

It took me a good two hours to compose the letter and, even then, when I awoke in the morning and re-read it I spent a further hour on rewrites.

After I'd been to the post office, I wandered about the streets of Surry Hills making enquiries. Emily had lived in Alexander Street for over fifty years; the locals must have known her.

It was disappointing. The locals certainly knew *of* old Mrs. Roper from 21A, but apparently nobody had known the woman herself.

She appeared to be a creature of habit. She went to the butcher's and the greengrocer's on Saturday mornings, and every Friday late afternoon she settled her weekly account with the newsagent.

I thought I might be getting somewhere when I chatted to the exuberant little Italian woman who ran the corner store. 'Thirty years I been live here,' Mrs. Panozzi boasted in her thick Neapolitan accent. 'Me and my husband the first Italians live in Surry Hills. All the rest, Greek.' Thirty years. Perfect, I thought, she would have known the younger Emily. But, again, it was a brick wall.

'Oh, very nice, very nice lady,' Mrs. Panozzi assured me, 'but she keep to herself, you know?'

It saddened me to think that the latter half of Emily's life might have been empty and miserable. Following Margaret's death or disappearance in 1940, she had only eight short years until, on the 8th of November, 1948, her 'beloved Harry' died – had hers been a sad existence for the ensuing twenty-seven years?

Then I recalled my dream. And the exhilaration in the old woman's eyes as she spoke about the poet Edward Thomas – 'To think that Harry knew him – a man who wrote a verse like that.' No, a spirit and a mind like Emily's could never lead an empty, sad life. But what had happened? What had she done with the rest of her days?

At nine o'clock the following Friday night, the telephone rang.

'I do so hope this isn't too late to call.' The voice was British. Male. 'But I just received your letter and I simply couldn't wait.'

'What letter?'

'Oh, I'm most terribly sorry, it might be a good idea to introduce myself, mightn't it? I'm Geoffrey Brigstock . . .'

Geoffrey Brigstock? Impossible. This wasn't the voice of a man in his seventies. This was a young man's voice, and a rather goofy-sounding one at that.

'My turn to apologise,' I said. 'I think I might have picked the wrong Geoffrey Brigstock. You see –'

'No, you picked the right one, you were just ten years too late. My father died in '65 . . . Hello? . . . Hello, are you there?'

I finally found my tongue. 'You're Margaret and Geoffrey's son?'

'Yes.'

Margaret's son? Impossible. I wondered fleetingly whether he'd been adopted but, even as my mind raised the question, the answer followed.

'My mother was eight and a half months pregnant when she died, so you can understand how important the discovery of her letters is to me. She was killed in the bombing of London, you know.'

I remained speechless. So Margaret had finally conceived. Why didn't she write and tell Emily?

I was sure I knew why. Margaret had given up the possibility of ever conceiving, and when the miracle occurred she was too terrified to announce it for fear of tempting fate – for fear that she might experience Emily's own horror of a stillborn child.

'I can't tell you how excited I am at the prospect of reading her letters,' Geoffrey Brigstock was saying, desperate for a reply.

'Yes, of course,' I answered at long last.

'I've only known of her from my father, you see. So to read her own words would be a marvellous experience. I wondered whether –'

'Yes, of course,' I said. 'I'll post them to you immediately.' I chastised myself for feeling loath to part with the letters.

'I have an even better suggestion – so long as you don't think it's too intrusive,' he added hurriedly. 'I go to Singapore regularly on company business – we have an office there – and I wondered whether I might visit you. You described their friendship so beautifully, I would love to see Mrs. Roper's house. Would you mind?'

Mind? I'd be delighted, I thought. To meet Margaret and Geoffrey's son! And he didn't sound that goofy, really, just very eager.

'What a lovely idea,' I said. 'When will you be here?'

He told me that he'd arrive within the next month, that he'd let me know the date in a week or so, and he refused to allow me to meet him at the airport.

'Wouldn't think of it,' he insisted. 'I'll ring you next week. Thank you so very, very much. Goodbye.' And he rang off.

I cancelled an appointment the day Geoffrey Brigstock was to arrive. Doing so would probably cost me a job, but I couldn't be bothered. I was too excited.

'Nancy,' he said, his handshake firm and friendly. 'Geoffrey Brigstock. How do you do?'

He was a nice-looking man. About thirty-five. And he looked rather like his voice. A cocker spaniel, I thought. A little bit goofy, keen, eager. Margaret would have liked him, I felt sure.

He loved the house. I showed him the Kookaburra stove and the wardrobe and the christening gown – all the things that Margaret talked of in her letters. Then, over a cup of tea, he told me of his father's life following Margaret's death.

'He never married again. After the war, he opened the company branch in Singapore and that's where I spent most of my childhood.'

We were in the front room by the fireplace. He put his teacup down on the coffee table and gazed into the empty grate.

'You mentioned Halstead in your letter. There are two Christmases I recall quite vividly. When I was nine and ten. Two years in a row we returned to spend Christmas with my maternal grandmother. It snowed one time and I was so excited, I remember. She spoke of my mother a great deal, well, rambled really – she was old and her health was not good. She died the following year and we didn't go back after that.'

I could see quite clearly 'the log fire in mother's front sitting room' and 'the blanket of snow' and I wondered whether Geoffrey had climbed the old elm tree.

Now was the time, I thought, and I lifted out the biscuit tin.

'I'll make you another cup of tea and leave you to yourself,' I said.

'Well, if you don't mind,' he answered hesitantly, 'I'd rather like to take them back to my hotel room.' He looked at the three bundles of letters I'd placed on the table. 'I have a feeling I'll sit up through the night.'

He left a half an hour later and I found myself wondering again and again how he would react to hearing his mother's words.

I wasn't disappointed.

'I can't tell you how grateful I am,' he said when he returned the following afternoon. 'What a wonderful thing, I feel as if I know her.'

'Yes, that's the way I felt.' I nodded.

'And Emily. You're quite right. We must find out what happened to Emily. What a pity my mother never kept her letters. Well, of course, she probably did and they were destroyed in the bombing – just about everything was lost, I believe.'

Suddenly I had an ally and it felt good. Geoffrey was just as keen as I was to discover the lost half of Emily's life.

'Simple,' he said. 'Harry's solicitor. Emily would have retained the same firm, I'm sure.' He grinned. 'And solicitors know all about their clients, believe me.' So much for the eager cocker spaniel – when Geoffrey was inspired he really got down to business. 'Ring your own solicitor and find out who handled the exchange of contracts on the house.'

I did. And he was quite right.

Colmer & Mitchell was a small family firm. Old man Colmer had handled the original sale of the house when Harry had purchased it in 1920, and Colmer the son explained to me that he himself had handled the sale of the deceased estate upon the death of Emily Roper.

Before I could think of a probing question, Colmer the younger went on to say, 'And of course I still handle the estate of Emily Tonkin.'

'Emily Tonkin?' I was totally nonplussed. 'What estate?'

'Her book has been kept regularly in print for over twenty years now.'

'Her book?'

'Yes. Published in 1955. Her collection of poems.' A pause while he waited for me to say something. I didn't. 'She was a poet, didn't you know?'

Two days later, I tracked down the book in a small shop in Kings Cross.

'Oh, yes,' said the spindly woman behind the counter, 'among true poetry lovers Emily Tonkin is quite popular, particularly with the older set.' She went on to explain that the publishers printed a limited edition each year, usually in the autumn.

'Two copies please,' I said, wishing that she would hurry up.

I walked to the fountain at the top of The Cross, sat on a bench and looked at the book. A slim paperback volume. *Riches*, it was called. 'The story of an ordinary life' by

Emily Tonkin. I wanted to laugh and cry all at the same time. I flicked through the pages. There was a poem called 'Margaret', there was a poem called 'Harry', there was a poem called 'My House'. I didn't read them then and there. I wanted to be alone. Just Emily and me.

Geoffrey wasn't at his hotel. He was probably out on a book search himself. We'd decided to split up on our hunt for Emily's poems. I left the copy I'd bought for him at the reception desk.

Back home once more, the phone off the hook, I settled down by the wardrobe. And, curled up in the spot where I'd read of her life, I opened Emily's book.

On the very first page was the dedication:

For Harry, who taught me that love
Is the very last breath that we take.
The breath that we share and then, beyond.
To the richness we leave in our wake.

I heard her voice. And I continued to hear her voice all through that night as, page after page, Emily spoke to me . . .

It's nearly twenty years since all of that happened and the little old house is no longer mine. I'm married now – I live in England and my name is Margaret Brigstock. (Although my friends still call me Nancy.) But Geoffrey and I kept the wardrobe and everything's stored inside. There's the cardboard box and the biscuit tin. And the hot water bottle covers and Harry's gown. And, wrapped in tissue, the christening robe, which has been worn three times since then.

I'm no longer a struggling journalist – these days my work's in demand. And, though I never did write that epic novel, I think Grandma Rose would be proud. Because I did become an author of sorts. I did see my words in print. I wrote a story and I called it 'The Wardrobe', and Emily guided the pen.

A WORD FROM JUDY

The setting of this story is not fictional at all. Many years ago, I bought a small terrace house in Surry Hills, Sydney. It was a deceased estate, old and dilapidated. The elderly woman who'd lived there had recently died, and her middle-aged sons had put the house on the market. A few items of furniture had been left, including an overly large and rather ugly wardrobe.

That wardrobe – or rather what was in it – had a profound effect upon me. There was a man's woollen dressing gown, very old but in pristine condition, folded and wrapped in tissue paper. There were hand-crocheted his-and-hers hot water bottle covers in pink and blue. There was a silver-framed photograph of two small boys, obviously brothers, about four and six, taken – it would appear – sometime in the 1930s. And there was a rusted biscuit tin, inside which was a history: personal items, memorabilia, letters from a bygone age, all very touching.

This was poignant stuff and I was deeply moved, but I was also puzzled. What about the sons who'd put the house on the market? Why hadn't they come to clear out their mother's memories? I called the real estate agent, and

*he said that one of the brothers' wives had collected all she
felt was necessary and left the rest of the 'junk'.*

*Pretty shocking, wouldn't you agree? Sheer gold for a
writer though. I adored creating 'The Wardrobe', which
is purely fiction, but inspired by what I found in that little
old house.*

THE OTTO BIN EMPIRE

EMPIRE

Clive's Story

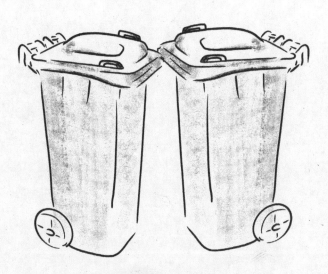

It was Madge who came up with the term. The site had always been referred to among the locals as simply 'The Corner', although it wasn't really a corner at all, just a dozen or so big plastic rubbish bins, the collective property of the old suburb's tiny and impoverished terrace houses that sat under the flyover down near the docks. But one day when Clive, who'd only recently joined the eclectic group that gathered there, had inquired why they'd chosen this particular spot, Madge had waved a hand about airily, referring to the manufacturer of the wheelie bins.

'No reason at all,' she'd said. 'This is just one place among hundreds in the Otto Bin Empire.' Then she'd dragged heavily on her roll-your-own and given one of her chesty chortles, and Clive had laughed along with her. The fact that he'd 'got the joke' had forged an instant bond between the two, for Madge was proud of her wit, and justifiably so – she was a clever woman.

The term had been steadily passed along the grapevine of the inner-city homeless after that. Even those who didn't understand the reference to the Ottoman Empire, and to be truthful most didn't, approved of the title. They were now part of an empire, and they liked that fact. The pools of wheelie bins that littered the city's pokier suburbs and cluttered the lanes behind high-rise apartment blocks had always been popular gathering places, forming practical leaning posts and tabletops as they did, but there was a subtle difference now. The humble Otto Bin had taken on a new form of dignity.

For Clive, Madge's term came to register something more significant than the amusing remark he'd initially taken it to be. As more and more he found himself drawn to 'The Corner', firstly for Madge's company, then for the companionship offered by some of the others, he realised for the first time that he was actually one of them. He was one of the homeless and therefore a member of the Otto Bin Empire.

He'd known for two months that he was a person without a home. A pathetic figure perhaps, a forty-five-year-old whose worldly possessions were housed in a mothy backpack and who roamed the city's streets and parks seeking out nooks and crannies, sleeping in the bedroll he carried slung over one shoulder. But he'd never thought of himself as officially 'homeless'. He was not one of those displaying a cardboard sign declaiming a state of homelessness and begging on street corners; he was not one of those openly scrounging through the contents of public litter bins and gathering cigarette butts that had been ground into the pavement. Nor, thank God, was he one of those lost souls talking gibberish and guzzling who-knows-what, possibly methylated spirits, from a bottle in a brown paper bag. *They* were the homeless – the lost, the

mentally ill, the alcoholics and junkies, the all-round seriously discombobulated. *I'm not one of them*, he'd think.
*I'm just a bloke going through a period of adjustment, I'll
be back on my feet soon.*

He didn't know exactly when that would be because
he didn't give the matter a great deal of thought. For the
moment he earned enough to scrape by doing odd gardening jobs and a bit of handyman work now and then. Some
days he'd walk for miles into the leafier outer suburbs
where houses boasted gardens – he enjoyed walking – and
other days he'd stick to the ritzier city suburbs, choosing
the wealthy homes whose once-meticulous landscaping
appeared in need of a little attention. He rarely asked for
work outright, he found he didn't need to – most oppor-
tunities presented themselves through casual conversation.
That's the way things had started out anyway.

'You want to be careful doing that,' he'd said as he'd
watched her through the ornate iron railings of the house's
front fence. She was ten metres or so away, a matronly
woman focussed upon her task, kneeling on the grass
methodically trimming the dead flowers from a plant that
took up quite an area of the sizeable garden bed.

She'd turned and looked over to him where he stood in
the street, surprised but not annoyed by the comment, for
he'd been polite. In fact, she seemed to be waiting for him
to go on.

'You really should be wearing gloves,' he'd said.

'Why?' she'd asked.

'Because the latex from the Euphorbia is toxic,' he'd
explained. 'That white sap on your hands,' she'd obediently

looked down at the milky fluid on her fingers, 'if you inadvertently get that in your eyes, you'll be poisoned. Very painful.'

That's all it had taken to initiate conversation about gardening, and conversation had led to casual employment. Mrs Cookson, for that was the woman's name, had even become a semi-regular client. He called around about once a fortnight these days, and she always had a morning or afternoon's work for him.

The conversational tactic as a form of introduction had proved so effective that Clive adopted it as his modus operandi. He always chose women, aware that he made a favourable impression upon them, even in his currently reduced state.

'Have you tried Epsom salts for your gardenias?'

'I beg your pardon?' Seated in her wicker armchair on her front verandah enjoying the mild spring weather, seventy-three-year-old Florence McPherson had looked up from the book she was reading.

'Epsom salts,' he'd called once again, 'have you tried them on your gardenias?'

'No,' she'd called back, 'why on earth should I?' Florence had been mystified not only by the comment but the appearance of the man who stood on the other side of the low stone wall. He was pleasant enough and quite well spoken, but he was dressed like a vagrant. And Epsom salts? What could he possibly mean?

'The leaves on your gardenias are turning yellow,' he'd said, no longer raising his voice. Now that contact had been established there seemed no need. The street – a cul-de-sac in a pleasant, middle-class neighbourhood – was silent, deserted, and they could hear each other perfectly.

'Yes, they are rather, aren't they,' she'd replied, looking down at the gardenias that lined the path to the front gate. She hadn't noticed their yellowing before. She enjoyed the garden, but the upkeep had always been Cyril's domain. She didn't know anything about plants, nor was she particularly interested in finding out.

'A magnesium deficiency,' he'd explained. 'Epsom salts should do the trick. Add it to the soil, one teaspoon to one gallon of water every two to four weeks.'

'What a good idea,' she'd said, deciding that she certainly preferred the gardenia leaves green. 'I'll tell the boy the next time he comes to mow the lawn.' Since Cyril's death the 'boy', who was really a young man in his mid-twenties, called in once a month to cut the grass and do the weeding.

'If you have some Epsom salts in the house,' Clive had offered, 'I could do it for you now.'

She had and he did.

After that Florence became another of Clive's semi-regular clients. When there was nothing in the garden demanding attention she would make sure she had some handyman job at the ready. She enjoyed chatting with Clive. He was far more interesting than the boy who mowed the lawn or the cleaner who visited weekly. He never talked about himself though. They occasionally discussed life in general – current affairs, perhaps politics – but for the most part the topic was books. Florence loved reading and so apparently did Clive

Whoever-he-was. She never discovered his surname. He never offered it so she never asked. When she'd inquired how he came to know so much about plants, he'd simply said that he'd once had a gardening business, and then he'd changed the subject. She'd decided the pursuit of any further information might be risky. She had no wish to deprive herself of his company.

Clive had been selling himself short. The 'gardening business' to which he'd referred had been, and still was, a highly successful enterprise. Barnett Creative Landscape Design & Maintenance was now managed by his wife (soon to be 'ex') and their accountant, who'd been running the business side of things for years. In fact, Clive rather doubted his skills were being missed at all. Rosemary was an expert landscape designer and the company, which the two of them had created close to twenty-five years ago, employed any number of skilled gardeners. Barnett Landscaping was indeed well-known in many circles, and during the months since his fall from grace Clive had assiduously avoided those properties whose lavish gardens had been the result of his personal labours.

Florence McPherson was not the only one intrigued by the mystery of Clive. Madge often wondered about her new friend's background. *Intelligent bloke*, she thought, *good-looking, clean-shaven, keeps himself presentable, obviously visits public toilet blocks for his daily ablutions. What's he doing on the streets?* But she didn't ask of course. She never did. Some of those who gathered at The Corner liked telling their story to anyone who would listen, but for the most part a person's past life was their own business, and this was respected. Besides, she'd known others like Clive. Men, women too for that matter, from respectable middle-class backgrounds who, for reasons financial or personal, were forced to a life on the streets. Some even led a homeless existence by choice. Funny that. She had the faintest suspicion Clive might be one of those. *Oh well*, she thought wryly, *every member of the Otto Bin Empire has a story. We're a diverse set. You've got to give us that.*

Madge actually *wasn't* homeless, but she considered herself one of the Otto Bin Empire nonetheless, and no-one would have contested the fact. Approaching sixty, a tough, burly, good-hearted woman and mother-figure to many, she lived in one of the tiny bed-sitters nearby that were rented out to people on the poverty line. Many a cold winter's night had seen Madge's floor space on offer to someone in need, but for those new to the art of survival on the streets, of even greater importance was Madge's advice.

Madge knew the location of every soup kitchen and emergency shelter in the city, and she had contacts everywhere. There was DOCS for the runaway abused kids, the Red Cross and St Vincent de Paul for clothing and supplies, the Wesley Mission, *The Big Issue* and many other charitable organisations that could, in their varying ways, be of assistance. Everyone knew, or they were quickly told, that Madge could point them in the right direction, but no-one knew a thing about Madge's personal background. They would have been surprised if they had, for it included a stint in prison where she'd served three years of a seven-year manslaughter sentence. But that was another story, one which, like Clive, Madge was not prepared to share.

Once Clive had accepted the fact that he was homeless, he fitted in rather well at The Corner. Madge was without doubt the principal attraction; they never seemed to run out of conversation. Occasionally he'd arrive with a book he'd bought for her during his regular forays around the second-hand bookshops, or he'd accept her offer of a hearty lunchtime soup from the latest batch she'd cooked. But as time passed Clive discovered others at The Corner whose company he enjoyed. There was Oskar, propped at the end wheelie bin each morning, but never there during the afternoons. Middle-aged, of dark and brooding appearance with a beard peppered grey, Oskar was always referred to by the locals as 'the Pole', but not without affection. Getting to know Oskar took some time, however, as he rarely initiated conversation, his head buried in the newspapers he spent his life collecting from rubbish bins and park benches. He'd wheel them about in a shopping trolley along with the rest of his belongings.

Clive came to the conclusion that Oskar was inherently shy, which made it all the more amazing that Oskar was the one who provided the habitués of The Corner their major form of entertainment. An afternoon in the park, gathered at the sidelines of the giant chessboard supplied by the city council for the general public's amusement, was a favourite pastime for those who knew Oskar. They would watch as the Pole walked the squares of the board with great deliberation, placing his waist-high pieces unhesitatingly where they belonged. It was magical. The Pole won every time.

Then there was Benny, who sold *The Big Issue* outside Woollies six days a week. Tall, scrawny, minus several front teeth and always sporting a scruffy Tigers football cap, Benny was an ex-junky with a mental disorder of which he seemed rather proud. 'I'm bipolar,' he'd happily announce. Benny loved to chat. He'd never been diagnosed bipolar, but he'd heard the term bandied about and had decided to label himself as such. Madge was very protective of Benny who, although well into his forties, was endearingly child-like.

'I'm not sure whether he was born that way,' she confided to Clive, 'or whether years of substance abuse has addled his brain, but I admire the way he's got his act together. He's been clean for four years now, and all because of *The Big Issue* – that's something to be proud of.'

Clive always bought a copy of *The Big Issue* from Benny, and on Sundays they'd sit on one of the two benches in the nearby pocket-sized park and do the crossword together – the quick clues of course, never the cryptic. Clive would invariably come up with the word, but on many occasions he'd manage to contrive things so that Benny thought *he* had . . .

'It's on the tip of my tongue,' he'd say, clicking his fingers and feigning frustration. 'Sounds like . . .' He'd all but spell the word out for Benny, who would bellow the answer and bounce up and down on the bench, grinning with gap-toothed delight.

Then of course there was Madge's personal favourite, Sal. Sal was eighteen, a runaway with a drug habit she refused to see as a problem and which she supported through prostitution. Madge had taken Sal under her wing from the outset, doing everything she could to get the girl off the streets. But Sal had rebelled. She was having a damn good life, she'd said, better than she'd ever had living under the same roof with that prick of a father, a comment that had led Madge to draw her own conclusions. Now, a year down the track, she'd given up any attempt to reform the girl for fear of frightening her off. Madge was all too aware she could be of far greater assistance if she remained an ally, offering Sal what she needed above all else: friendship and genuine affection.

Clive, too, was drawn to Sal, although he sensed the tragic figure that lay beneath the bright facade she presented on the afternoons she turned up at The Corner.

'Hello, Madge. Hello, Clive.'

If they were present upon her arrival she would always single them out, giving Madge a warm hug, blowing Clive a flirtatious kiss, before lighting up a smoke and starting on her takeaway coffee. Bright and breezy, she would initiate chats with all those who had become family to her. But her company, despite being pleasurable, presented a dilemma for Clive. She reminded him altogether too much of his daughter, or rather his daughter as she had been seven years ago – Jodie was now twenty-five, engaged to be married, her life all in order.

Sal was intelligent and pretty and fun, but if she continued upon her current path there appeared only one way she was likely to go, and Clive didn't want to think about that.

Jodie was intelligent and pretty too, but she was no longer fun, at least not with her father, and Clive didn't want to think about that either.

'What you've done to Mum is unforgivable,' Jodie had hissed over the phone. Those were the days shortly after he'd left Rosemary and taken to the streets; the days when he hadn't admitted he was homeless; the days when he'd answer the phone that vibrated in his top pocket, even though he'd turned it to silent and vowed to ignore it. He could never help checking who was calling though, just habit, and he didn't respond to work colleagues or friends, but when the caller proved to be daughter Jodie or son Joshua, he felt compelled to answer. Well, in those days he had. He'd long since turned the phone off and it lived in the bottom of his backpack. The battery would be flat by now. He had the requisite lead and could easily have charged it at one of the Neighbourhood Centre's outlets. But he hadn't.

'I presume you're shacked up with her, whoever she is and wherever she lives, neither of which I give a damn about personally, but you could at least do the right thing by Mum,' Jodie had continued, her anger pulsating in his ear.

'And what exactly would that be, Jodie?' he'd asked calmly. 'Your mother kicked me out, remember? She had every right to, of course, and I don't blame her, but she made it quite clear she doesn't want me back. If I attempted to make contact I'd be interfering in her life.'

His composure had only increased his daughter's anger. 'But no-one knows where you are, for God's sake. Josh says you won't tell him either.' Jodie was a young woman who liked to be in control and her anger was born of frustration, the current situation having rendered her powerless. 'You can't just disappear from the face of the earth – it's irresponsible.' No reply from her father exasperated her further. 'You do realise that, don't you, Dad? You're shirking your responsibility!' More than accusatory now, she was damning. 'You're running away, that's what you're doing!'

'Yes,' he'd agreed, surprised that the answer really might be that simple. 'Yes, I believe you're right.'

That was when Jodie had finally exploded.

'Well, stay with your girlfriend, see if I care, but don't bother turning up at my wedding. I don't want you there, do you understand me? Josh can give me away. You're no longer my father.' She'd hung up then, and Clive had had the feeling that she'd probably burst into tears afterwards. He regretted the fact but felt incapable of doing anything about it. The apparently irreparable schism that now existed between him and his daughter only heightened his sense of being adrift in a world of his own making. There was nothing he could do about anything really.

Josh wasn't as condemnatory as his sister. Twenty-seven-year-old Josh had tried very hard to be the voice of reason.

'Look, Dad, I know the marriage is over and you're not coming back,' he'd said over the phone, 'and I know that's the way Mum wants it. But to break all ties with everyone ... I mean with us, your own family ... with your friends and your business ... Hey, man, no-one knows where the hell you are ... I mean, that's not healthy ... You need some form of human contact ... Well, I know you've got your new girlfriend,' he'd added hastily, 'but you get where I'm coming from, don't you? I mean, you can't just leave your past behind. What say we meet up and talk about this, eh? Just you and me, what do you say?'

Clive had smiled as he listened to his son: 'I mean', 'hey, man', 'what say' ... There were times when Josh sounded distinctly American. It was his job of course. Joshua was an exceptionally bright IT man and had recently been appointed head of marketing at a major publishing house. Given the change from print to electronic media that was still moving at such a pace, he was revolutionising the company's website and electronic marketing methods, the new whiz-kid on the block – no wonder there was an American sales pitch to his manner. *Good for you, mate*, Clive had thought fondly.

'I'm not breaking all ties with you, Josh,' he'd said, 'that's not my intention, I promise. It's not my intention to break all ties with Jodie either, although I don't think she realises that. It's just that I need to be on my own for a while.'

Do any of them realise I really do mean 'on my own'? he wondered. *They all seem to presume I'm living with Barbara. Well, let them*, he decided.

Telling the truth was not an option to Clive. God forbid it might appear a bid for sympathy or a plea for forgiveness, both of which were the last things he wanted.

He accepted entire responsibility for his current situation. Besides, Barbara wouldn't have wanted him to shift into her life. He wouldn't have wanted to shift into hers either, such an option had not occurred to him once. All ties had been broken with Barbara too. She was another whose calls had gone unanswered, and it hadn't taken long before she'd stopped ringing. Their relationship had been a six-month casual affair, pleasant dalliances that suited them both, just like the other affairs he'd had throughout his marriage. A weakness, of course, but he'd rarely been able to resist a woman who made it obvious she found him attractive. There had been no conscious intent on his part, he'd never sought out women for the purpose of seduction; things had seemed simply to happen. In the early days when he and Rosemary had still shared a passion, she'd seen his infidelities as betrayal and threatened to leave him. He'd practised discretion after that, escaping detection for the most part, or so he'd thought, and as they'd drifted into the complacency of middle-age he'd assumed that whenever she suspected a brief affair was afoot she was content to turn a blind eye. He'd been wrong. This latest fling, only recently discovered, had pushed Rosemary over the edge. And who could blame her?

'How long's "a while"?' His son's voice had jolted Clive from his reverie.

'I don't know, Josh. I truly don't know.'

A pause. 'What are you going to do about the business?'

'Oh, I think your mother's more than capable of handling things,' he'd replied. And she was, of course. The business had been Rosemary's from the start – Rosemary's idea, Rosemary's passion, even Rosemary's money. She'd invested the entire $50,000 left to her by her grandmother in order to get them started. The company's very name, 'Barnett Creative Landscape Design & Maintenance', was of her invention. A bit fancy in his opinion, he would have preferred simply 'Barnett Landscaping'. They'd worked equally hard to get the business up and going, it was true, and the company was registered in both their names, but Clive had always considered it Rosemary's. He wanted no part of it now. He wanted to turn his back and walk away from it all.

'So how long will this go on, Dad? I mean, when do I get to see you?' Josh's 'voice of reason' now held an element of impatience that he made little effort to disguise. 'I mean, when do you intend to get back in touch with the real world?'

'I'll get back in touch when I've sorted myself out, mate, I promise,' Clive had said, although even as he did something deep inside told him he wasn't at all sure he could honour the promise.

They'd said their goodbyes and that was that.

Over the ensuing weeks Josh had phoned several times and the conversation followed similarly frustrating lines. Jodie, too, had made further contact, but not verbally, preferring instead to send text messages damning her father. Finally, Clive had turned his mobile phone off altogether, dumping it in the bottom of his backpack. He'd thought of throwing it away, but some sixth sense had warned him not to.

As time passed and he came to accept his homeless state, Clive was surprised to discover that his life had taken on a bizarre form of routine.

There were those whose gardens he tended on a semi-regular basis and who he'd come to know – Mrs Cookson and Mrs McPherson (who insisted he call her Florence) and several others besides. There were Saturday afternoons watching Oskar the Pole play chess and Sundays doing the crossword with Ben. There were those occasional afternoon chats with Sal, whom he suspected had come to view him as something of a father-figure, and of course there was Madge, whose conversation never ceased to stimulate.

His world seemed strangely complete, without threat or demand, and he was forced to admit that perhaps he didn't really want to 'sort himself out'. Perhaps he preferred being adrift in a world free of all responsibility other than that of survival. His daughter had been quite right when she'd accused him of running away, he'd decided. He was too cowardly to try and resurrect a new life. Upon coming to this conclusion, he didn't particularly like himself, but before long, and without too much difficulty, he'd managed to shrug off a sense of worthlessness and embrace his mindless routine.

Then one day something happened to break the routine, something quite mundane.

He'd finished a morning's work for Florence, painting some kitchen cupboards that didn't really need painting. He'd told her as much, but she'd insisted they be done. The kitchen would be neater that way, she'd said, and besides, she'd be able to get rid of the unsightly tins of leftover paint that had sat in the garage ever since Cyril's death. Clive had wondered why the unsightly tins needed to be got rid of at all as the garage was never used; it wasn't even seen by anyone from what he could gather. But he'd been grateful for the work. With autumn on the wane, gardening jobs were harder to come by, and as the weather had grown colder he'd incurred extra expenses: a warm fleece-lined jacket, several pairs of thick winter socks, a woollen beanie and a spare army blanket, all purchased from St Vincent de Paul. The regular nightly nooks of his choice were not as cosy these days, but he had determined not to seek refuge in one of the shelters for the homeless – that was the domain of the truly needy, and he was not one of those.

After leaving Florence's, he'd bought three steaming hot meat pies on his way to The Corner – one for him, one for Madge and one for Sal, just in case she was there. If she wasn't then he'd eat two. As it turned out she was, and the three of them had stood around their Otto Bin, downing their pies with liberal serves of tomato sauce from the bottle Madge had fetched from her bedsit. She'd also fetched a longneck of beer in a brown paper bag. 'What's a pie without a beer,' she'd said, and she and Clive swigged from the bottle while Sal stuck to her takeaway coffee. Sal didn't drink, not even beer.

When they'd finished, the women lit up their cigarettes – Madge one of her roll-your-owns and Sal one of her tailor-made Dunhills. While they chattered away Clive ceased to listen and drifted off, gazing distractedly out at the street that led down the hill to the docks, his mind a blank. And that's when he saw her.

She was an attractive woman, in her early to mid-forties he guessed, and wealthy by the look of her: shoulder-length hair stylishly highlighted; dark glasses that he presumed to be Gucci because they looked so like the pair Rosemary had; and a well-cut beige suit, obviously designer label, with a knee-length skirt showing off a fine pair of legs. She was striding purposefully up the hill in the sort of high-fashion shoes few women could manage, and that was what caught his eye above all else. He did so like a woman who could strut her stuff in high heels. Frankly, he'd never known how any of them could, but it seemed so few were able to master the art these days.

But even as he admired her assured gait, he realised that something wasn't quite right. *She's a bit wobbly*, he thought, *and it's not because of the shoes*. He smiled to himself as he realised the problem. *She's pissed, that's it. I bet she's been to lunch at The Pier. She wouldn't have been drinking at one of the dockside pubs, that's for sure, but there's no two ways about it, she's pissed.*

Then, as the woman neared the Otto Bins and was less than ten metres away, she suddenly fell. One of the heels wobbled a little too much, her ankle gave way, and she landed in an awkward heap on the sidewalk.

The several others congregated at The Corner, including Madge and Sal, didn't see her fall, but Clive leapt instinctively to her aid. Within seconds he was beside her, helping her to her feet.

'I'm fine, thank you, really, I'm fine,' she insisted, gathering up her Louis Vuitton shoulder bag and the Gucci glasses that now lay on the pavement. But she was nonetheless forced to accept his assistance as, in struggling to her feet, her ankle once again deserted her.

'I think you might have a sprain,' Clive said, 'better come over here and sit down.'

'Yes, yes, all right.' Wincing with pain and accepting his support, the woman allowed herself to be led, limping heavily, past the Otto Bins to the tiny communal park with its patchy grass, its several scrawny trees and its two wooden benches, both badly in need of a coat of paint.

They sat side by side on one of the benches.

'I think we should take that shoe off,' Clive suggested. He made as if to do so, but she froze.

'Thank you, that's very kind, but I can manage,' she said tightly.

Sarah was shocked as, for the first time, she took in her rescuer and her surrounds. The diminutive, litter-strewn park; the man in the worn flannel shirt and lurid tartan beanie who looked like one of the homeless; those people lounging about the wheelie bins barely twenty metres away, one clearly a hooker, the others obviously vagrants.

Instead of taking off her shoe, she fumbled in her shoulder bag for her mobile phone. 'I appreciate your help, really I do,' she said, hoping he would recognise the dismissal in her tone and return to the company of his friends. 'You've been most kind.' The mobile was now in her hand. 'I'll call a cab, please don't trouble yourself any further on my account.'

Clive had read correctly the woman's horrified realisation of the company she was in, which rather amused him, but he'd read a great deal more besides. He'd been right, she was drink-affected, but she was also upset, very upset. *She's been crying*, he thought, noting the smudges of mascara under her eyes. *In fact, she's doing everything she can to keep herself together right now.*

He pulled off the woollen beanie, which he knew wasn't a good look. 'You'll still need help to get to the cab when it arrives,' he said, hoping he didn't appear quite so threatening or ludicrous minus the beanie. He was thankful that at least he'd had the presence of mind to cut off the pom-pom. 'And honestly, you need to get rid of that,' he added, looking down at the high-cut shoe and her ankle, which was already visibly swollen.

That was when Sarah received a further shock. *My God, what an attractive man*, she thought. The realisation made her want to cry again, or perhaps she wanted to laugh, she wasn't sure which. How insane. The whole day had been one massive shock. Damien taking her to lunch at The Pier, their favourite restaurant, only to tell her the affair was over. After a whole year! She'd even thought there might be a future for them together; in fact, she'd desperately hoped that there would be. But no, he'd decided to 'move on', the polite way of saying he was bored now. And he'd left the announcement until dessert! Then her mad sprint from the restaurant, ignoring the cabs sitting at the rank, deciding to walk off the effects of the wine, striding up the hill as she had. He'd made no attempt to follow of course. And now this? Falling arse over tit in the street, being rescued by a dero who, in divesting himself of his awful beanie, had revealed himself as attractive. *The mousey secretary letting down her hair and taking off her glasses – 'my God, but you're beautiful' – how clichéd is that?*

She let out a strange sound that might have been a yelp of laughter and leaning down obediently removed her shoe.

'You wouldn't happen to have a cigarette, I suppose?' she asked as she straightened up and delved in her bag for a tissue to stem the tears that once again threatened.

'I don't smoke, but yes, I can find you one.'

She watched briefly as he crossed to the wheelie bins, to the two women who were observing them closely – the hooker, little more than a girl really, and the other a beefy, grey-haired woman of around sixty in a truly dreadful cardigan. She quickly averted her eyes, dabbing at the tears, wiping away the mascara that she knew must have run. *How embarrassing*, she thought. *No, more than embarrassing, how utterly humiliating.*

He returned with a packet of Dunhills and a Bic lighter. 'There you go,' he said, offering her the open packet. 'Sal's happy for you to take a couple if you like.'

'No, one will do fine, thank you.' She took a cigarette, he lit it for her, and she watched as he walked back to the bins, returning the packet and lighter to the girl. *A gentleman to boot*, she thought wryly, *this really is the most insane day*. She gave the girl a thank-you wave, which was acknowledged, and then once again looked away.

He returned to sit beside her. She took a hefty drag of the cigarette.

'I haven't had one of these for three months,' she said as she exhaled, studying the plume of smoke with fondness, as if revisiting an old friend. 'I thought this time round I'd finally kicked the habit, but it's been one hell of a day, so . . .' She shrugged, feeling dizzy from the instant nicotine hit, which was thankfully distracting. 'I'm Sarah,' she said, 'Sarah Martell.'

'Oh, like the brandy,' he replied pleasantly, hoping to put her at ease, she appeared very tense. But she made no comment, and he presumed she hadn't understood. 'Martell Cognac?' he offered.

She had registered the reference, but it had been of no interest and her attention remained concentrated on the cigarette. Sadly, the dizziness had passed, and with it the pleasant distraction it had offered. The cigarette was now just a cigarette.

Clive studied the woman as she studied the plume of smoke rising in the autumn air. He felt sorry for her. She seemed so sad. Then she turned to him.

'What's your name?' she asked.

'Clive.'

She smiled, which came as a surprise to them both. 'How deliciously old-fashioned,' she said. 'My grandfather's name was Clive.'

'Really?' He returned the smile. 'I had an elderly aunt called Sarah.'

A moment rested between them, a familiar moment. This was the way men and women flirted. *How ridiculous*, both thought. Then she picked up her mobile.

'I'll ring for that cab now,' she said. 'What's the nearest crossroad? They're bound to ask.'

He told her and she made the call. 'Next available,' she said, 'shouldn't be long.'

She sat back, dragging again on her cigarette, knowing she'd get the cab driver to stop on the way home so she could buy a packet. *Meant to be*, she thought, Dunhill was even her brand.

'Who are you, Clive? What do you do?' The question was no doubt offensive to the man – he was probably unemployed, on the dole, possibly even homeless. But he was unfathomable, a mystery; she wanted to know at least something about him.

The question *was* presumptuous, but for some reason Clive wasn't offended. In fact, he was quite prepared to offer an honest answer.

'I'm a jack-of-all-trades,' he said. 'I do bits and pieces around the place. Some handyman stuff, but gardening mostly. I know a lot about gardens.'

'Really?' She took instant notice. 'I have a very large garden that needs regular attention,' she said, which was quite true. She lived in one of the wealthier suburbs and the house she'd been granted in her divorce settlement five years previously sat in lavish surrounds.

She slipped a hand into the side pocket of her bag, producing a business card. 'Here's my card,' she said.

He took it from her. 'Thanks, that'd be fine. I'll pay you a visit.'

She dropped her cigarette butt onto the stubbly grass and ground it out with the toe of her shoe. Among the surrounding litter it seemed stupid to seek out an ashtray or bin. 'Do you have a number where I can reach you?' Again a seemingly ridiculous question, but one she felt compelled to ask. 'I'll ring and let you know when it's convenient to call around.'

'I do as a matter of fact, yes.' He gave her his mobile number and she entered it into her list of contacts.

She didn't ask for a surname. Oddly enough, that really *did* seem impertinent.

Then . . . 'I think that's mine,' she said as a cab pulled up at the kerbside.

Clive turned, gave the driver a wave and Sarah collected her things.

'I'd take off the other shoe if I were you,' he suggested.

She did so, and in stockinged feet with his arm about her she limped the twenty or so metres to the car.

Madge's eyes followed them every step of the way. Sal's attention was elsewhere now, she was chatting with two of the regulars several bins away, but Madge's ever-observant eyes had been taking in everything.

'Thank you, Clive.' Sarah offered her hand. 'You've been very kind.'

They shook. 'My pleasure,' Clive said.

The cab drove off and he returned to The Corner where, from behind one of the Otto Bins, he retrieved his backpack. He delved an arm into it and, ferreting about at the bottom, eventually came up with his mobile phone. He tested it – dead as a dodo of course. He'd get it charged up right away.

'You're back in action I see,' Madge said, referring to the mobile, which he'd told her some time back he'd con-templated throwing away.

'Yep, why not,' he said with a smile. 'See you, Madge.' Gathering his gear together and slinging it over his shoulder, he set off for the Neighbourhood Centre.

But Madge had been referring to far more than the mobile. *He'll be leaving us soon*, she thought, watching him go. She'd miss him.

Funny, isn't it, she thought. *There doesn't seem to be anything at all wrong with Clive, but he's a lost soul, just like the rest of us. Good that he's found a niche for himself, or at least that he will shortly, but I wonder how long it'll last? Wonder if he'll come back to us when it's over?* Madge had the strangest feeling that he would, that Clive was a true member of the Otto Bin Empire.

A Word from Judy

'Clive's Story' was the first to be written in my series of 'Otto Bin Empire' short stories, which will be published in the not-too-distant future. There are several more yet that I must write in order to round out the collection, but I'm pleased to introduce the concept here. Or rather for Clive to do so. Here's how it all came about.

One day, several years ago, Bruce (my husband, actor/ writer Bruce Venables) and I were walking down Bourke Street in Sydney towards the harbour. As we reached the flyover at Woolloomooloo we passed an alcove with a collection of wheelie bins that belonged to the nearby row of rundown little terrace houses. There must have been at least a dozen or so bins, and leaning on them as table-tops was a motley group of people – some drinking takeaway coffees, others swigging from longneck bottles in brown paper bags, all chatting most companionably. They appeared homeless but were happy here with their own community, in this place, where it was obvious they regularly gathered. I remembered reading an uplifting article about how groups of destitute people supported each other, and I thought there might well be many such gatherings like this around wheelie bins.

We slowed down as we passed by, and I knew Bruce was thinking along similar lines.

'The Otto Bin Empire,' I murmured.

He stopped. 'Where'd you hear that?' He was obviously impressed.

'I just made it up,' I replied, piqued that he should presume it wasn't original.

'The Otto Bin Empire. That's very clever. Can I use it?'

'No, you cannot,' I said. And that's when I decided to write my series of Otto Bin Empire stories, if only to stop him nicking the title. Because the title itself was my initial inspiration.

Unfortunately though, as I embarked upon research I found I'd painted myself into a corner with the use of the title. I wanted my stories to be set in any large city in Australia, so I dropped all reference to 'the harbour', which would have placed 'The Corner' (as it becomes known) in Sydney. Instead, I referred to the enclave as being 'down near the docks'. Oops. I quickly discovered that 'Otto Bin' is a manufacturer's brand name, and although I and many of my friends use it as a common term for a wheelie bin, this usage doesn't apply generally – most of Australia wouldn't know what the heck I was talking about. I decided, however, that it was too good a title to lose, so I persevered in order to make it work (which I hope it does).

CHANGES

I don't dwell on growing old. What's the point? There's bugger-all you can do about it. But turning sixty gave me pause for thought. Decade birthdays tend to have that effect upon one, don't you find? Although I suppose it depends on how old one is. Some of my friends found thirty confronting. Good God, why? I revelled in turning thirty. I found forty a big one, I have to admit, but once I'd got over it, the fifties were a breeze. And then came sixty. And the sixties have finally ushered in a whole new world.

My name is Jacqueline, generally known as Jackie, and to those who are closest, Jac. I'm sixty-five and I find myself amazed by the change that has come over me – the change that has literally transformed my life. I've been thinking about changes a lot lately. Which is hardly surprising, given my current circumstances.

To be quite honest, I don't know why I'm writing this, or even to whom I'm writing it. Perhaps to no-one, perhaps to everyone, perhaps just to myself, but I'm strangely compelled to recall a lifetime that has led to the most surprising change of all – the new me.

Mind you, I've always been one to embrace change. Indeed, the decade of my twenties was one of constant change. I went to London to further my career as an actor, took a refresher course at RADA, did some English repertory and BBC, then two-and-a-half years later when my work visa was up returned to Australia, promptly gave away acting and became an assistant TV director at the ABC. All before I was twenty-five. By the time I was thirty I'd made the move into independent film production and was working freelance. Not in a career-driven, obsessive way, but simply because I'd learned the ropes by then and was an efficient person to head a production office. A far more sensible and reliable way to make a living, I decided. But this was, of course, a living that still demanded change, moving from company to company, location to location.

The only element in my life that appeared to remain constant was my poor choice of men. Or at least the poor choice of those with whom I formed anything approaching a 'relationship'.

The first was Gareth, in London. Gareth was an actor. Now, as a practical person it has always been my firm opinion that actors should never have affairs with other actors. A one-night stand or a brief fling, certainly, but something serious? Something ongoing? No. Wrong. Too much ego and career competition not to mention the insecurity suffered by most actors. I'm sure many reading this will want to throw a dozen perfect showbiz relationships or marriages in my direction, but sorry, doesn't work for me.

Gareth was unbelievably handsome and had the most glorious voice. (I've always been a sucker for voices – still am.) And oh, that smile! Our affair was magical, lasting a whole eighteen months, which was a very long time for me in those days. He was not only drop-dead gorgeous, he was fun to boot, and I could have sworn I was desperately in love. However, when my work visa was up after two-and-a-half years and I had to return to Australia, I discovered that I was not. You see, in order to keep me in the country, Gareth wanted to marry me. He even suggested we have a child to seal the deal. *Whaaat!*

I didn't want to marry. I didn't want a child. During that brief period of my life all focus had been upon my acting career, and, as I mentioned previously, all actors are by nature preoccupied with self. It was a pity, in a way, because if I *had* wanted a child, Gareth would have been the perfect choice. We would have made a beautiful child. I was rather good-looking in those days, and Gareth, believe me, was one hundred per cent pure Adonis.

Given that statement, I feel I must break into this tale of my youth with a brief observation from more recent times. Well, of course I must. This is a story about changes after all.

I bumped into Gareth just a year or so ago. Oh my goodness, what a shock – I didn't recognise him at all. When this man fronted up to me at a book festival in Melbourne, I had no idea who he was. Age had bloated him. He was bulbous-eyed and mottle-skinned, and so toadlike that when he opened his mouth I half expected a croak.

'Hello, Jacqueline.' (He'd always called me Jacqueline.)

The voice, however, was disconcertingly familiar, and when he smiled the toad all of a sudden bore a vestige of the prince he'd once been.

'*Gareth?*' I asked.

'The same,' he said, and as the smile broadened, for one brief second he actually was – the prince, I mean. But only for one very brief second. After that it was all downhill.

Following the book festival event (a panel discussion with screenwriters on the transition of novels to movies, in case you're interested), we went out for a cup of coffee, as old friends do. That was his idea – I would far rather have gone to a pub myself – and while sipping lattes we caught up with the trajectory our respective lives had taken, or rather the trajectory *his* had. I heard everything about his wife and his children, all four of them, each of whom he was inordinately, and justifiably it appeared, *proud*. In fact, he'd come 'all the way down here' specifically for the christening of his daughter Priscilla's youngest child. 'Prissy', as she was known, had married an exceptionally wealthy man with mining interests in Western Australia. He also had a property investment company in Melbourne – or perhaps it was a home furnishings company, I can't remember which – but Gareth talked a great deal about real estate and interior design, so it could have been either, or even both. By that time I wasn't paying much attention. I was too busy thinking how surreal the whole situation was. I am not a superficial person – truly, I'm not. I could have adjusted to my glorious Gareth becoming a toad. But a *boring* toad? Oh, how tragic are the changes wrought by age.

In case I'm running the risk of sounding bitchy, I'll tell another brief story here along similar lines, but this time against myself.

I recently called up a link on Facebook. I have to admit I'm not a great fan of Facebook; I use it mostly to keep in touch with the kids. Kids! Good grief, both girls are over thirty, and Mandy's about to have her second baby, but you know how it is – they always remain kids, don't they. Facebook's become very handy since I moved north, an excellent way to communicate with family, but as a form of social media in general it holds little interest for me. That is, until about a month ago, when I came upon a link that a vaguely recalled old chum Vera had posted with pictures of long-ago drama school graduates in their final-year productions. I couldn't resist calling it up to see if I was there, and of course I was – twenty years of age and in all my glory, playing Nina in 'The Seagull', gift of a role.

Apart from giving it a 'like' and a thanks to Vera, I didn't offer any personal comment, but plenty of other people did – not just a wander down memory lane either, but a veritable highway of reminiscences. And one response was directed specifically to me. A name I recognised in an instant: Rupert, acting course, same year as me. I'd heard ages ago that he hadn't lasted long in the theatre, but had given up acting to become an insurance broker, which I'd found strange at the time because he was a rather dashing fellow. Anyway, Rupert had been a fleeting beau of those passionate and heady drama school days. This is what he said:

Hello there, Jacqueline, Rupert here, long time
no see. I recently caught you on YouTube being
interviewed about the use of computer graphics in
movie production, which I found most interesting.
But oh boy, was I happy the other day when I called
up Vera's link to our drama school pics! How
wonderful to see you the way I remember you! God,
you were a looker, Jac! With fondest memories and
love always. Rupe.

Yes, just a wee bit of a crash to earth. So, you see, poor old Gareth wasn't alone in suffering the ravages of age.

Rupe was actually the first person to call me Jac. Prior to that I'd been Jackie, which my ridiculously old-fashioned, strait-laced Aunt Margaret absolutely loathed.

'So vulgar, Jillian,' she'd say disapprovingly to my mother. 'I don't know why you allow it. You know how I detest diminutives.'

But Mum, who sailed unruffled through any threat of confrontation, would just give an easy-going shrug. 'She likes being Jackie,' she'd say.

Aunt Margaret was a ghastly, embittered spinster born of another age and continuously critical of Mum's parenting. 'Just because Jacqueline is an only child,' she'd scold, 'there is no need to cosset her the way you do, Jillian.' (*Cosset?* I don't recall ever being *cossetted*). 'Spare the rod . . .' she'd add with an ominous shake of the head.

But Mum would remain unfazed. It was difficult to believe she and Aunt Margaret were sisters. Mum was always a true free spirit, a bit of a rebel even.

When I came home to Perth for the Christmas holidays that year, having hooked up with Rupe at drama school in Sydney, I thoroughly enjoyed introducing Aunt Margaret to my new name.

'It's even worse now, Aunt Margaret,' I said as the family gathered in preparation for the full-on baked dinner disaster in thirty-plus degree heat. 'I'm called Jac these days.'

'But that's a *boy's* name!' *And a rather common boy's name at that,* I could tell Aunt Margaret was thinking.

'Not really, I've left off the "k".'

Even greater horror. 'You mean you *sign* yourself that way? You actually *write* your name in that manner?'

'Yes. I think it's rather catching.' *Poor old Aunt Margaret,* I remember thinking, *if she joined the modern world she'd be known as Meg, or perhaps even Maggie.* The mere thought of calling her Aunt Maggie made me want to laugh in her face, so I changed the subject. 'Oops, time to baste the turkey,' I said and dived off to help Mum in the kitchen.

Aunt Margaret was twelve years older than her youngest sibling, Jillian (who was never Jill or Jilly, of course), and probably the very force against which Mum was rebelling. There were two brothers in between – my uncle James (never Jim) and my Uncle David (never Dave) – and Aunt Margaret bossed them all around mercilessly. I barely remember my grandparents, who died when I was nine, but I do recall they were of the 'children are to be seen not heard' brigade, a remote presence, and I suspect Margaret had been encouraged to play the disciplinarian from an early age. Perhaps I should have felt sorry for her, but I didn't. I simply revelled in the fact that my mother refused to embrace the ultraconservatism of her upbringing. She was never loud, never belligerent, but in her own mild, inoffensive way, she chose the path of a nonconformist, to the point where at times she could even be a little outrageous.

For example, a year or so after I arrived back from England I actually *did* meet a man with whom I thought I could settle down, perhaps even marry. But when I shared this fact with Mum she was so dismissive of my feelings that I was shocked. Truly shocked.

'Oh no, dear, you'll never marry,' she said airily. 'You're not the marrying kind.'

Now I ask you, how confronting is that? From your own mother! And bear in mind that this was in the days when every mother presumed her daughter would marry, and every mother ached to have grandchildren.

'How do you know I won't?' I demanded. (Unlike Mum, I was never short on belligerence.) 'You haven't seen me for ages. I might have changed.'

'Really?' She looked as if she didn't believe for a second this was possible, but true to form she made no attempt to argue the point. 'Ah well, in any event, Phil won't be the one.'

'Why not?' I was further taken aback. Phil and I were living together; he'd moved into my flat barely a month after we'd met. I adored him and he adored me. Everyone knew it, including Mum.

'Because *Phil's* not the marrying kind, dear.'

Another below-the-belt remark, which also came as a huge surprise because I knew she liked Phil enormously. The two of them had hit it off the moment they'd met.

'Mum, this is Phil,' I'd said when we'd collected her from the airport. She'd flown over to Sydney for a week's holiday while Dad was at a series of conferences up north. (He was an engineer with the WA main roads department.) 'Phil, this is my mother, Jillian.'

'G'day, Jill,' Phil said, 'good to meet you.' (Jill. Yes. How Aunt Margaret would have cringed.) 'Jac's told me all about you.'

Mum beamed as they shook hands. 'She's told me all about you too, Phil. You love poetry, I believe.'

'I do.'

That night the two of them stayed up till three o'clock in the morning, drinking red wine and reading poetry from the many volumes Phil had to hand. I found it great fun for a while and contributed myself (who doesn't love poetry, or red wine for that matter?) but I petered out around midnight and went to bed, leaving them to it.

Now here we were a week later, with Mum about to return to Perth, and she's quietly but categorically telling me Phil's 'not the marrying kind'. She didn't mean to be hurtful of course – I don't think she even realised the comment had the capacity to hurt. She was just stating things the way she saw them.

'You'll have your time cut out with this one, Jac,' she went on. 'You won't be able to keep him under your thumb like the others.' Again, there was no criticism intended, and she wasn't giving advice. It was just another remark.

'What on earth does *that* mean? I don't *keep them under my thumb!*' Outrage lent ice to my tone, and I had an awful feeling I was sounding like Aunt Margaret.

'Of course you don't, dear. Not intentionally. But you must admit you do prefer to live life on your terms.'

'I thought you liked Phil,' I said, still on the defensive.

'Oh I do, darling, I do. I like him enormously. He's a lovely fellow, grand fun, and I hope you'll both be very happy together for as long as it lasts.'

We left things there because, frankly, I couldn't think of anything else to say.

Mum's mystifyingly 'bohemian' side seemed to spring from somewhere deep within; there was no evidence of where or how she might have acquired it. The truth is she appeared more in tune with my generation than her own. For instance, she'd voiced no disapproval at all of the fact that Phil and I were living together. (Just imagine what Aunt Margaret would have said!) And way back, when I was a teenager vaguely pondering the prospect of losing my virginity to my first steady boyfriend (at the respectable age of seventeen, I might add), she not only seemed to sense my indecision but was way ahead of me.

'I think we might put you on the pill, dear,' she said. 'Best to play things safe at your age.'

I recall it was Phil who rather astutely summed Mum up, although I also recall my initial reaction was somewhat piqued.

'I reckon our Jill's got a bit of the gypsy in her,' he'd said as we drove back from the airport, having seen Mum's flight off.

'How do you mean?'

'I mean that if she'd run away with a gypsy instead of marrying a respectable bloke who works for the government she'd be perfectly happy strumming a guitar by a campfire.'

'She's perfectly happy with my father, thank you,' I replied primly, staring ahead at the heavy traffic that had almost come to a standstill.

'Course she is.' He glanced at me and grinned his gorgeous, lopsided grin. 'She told me George plays the piano beautifully.'

'And he does.' I turned to give him an icy stare. 'Self-taught, what's more. Can't even read music. Plays everything by ear. Dad only needs to hear a song once on the radio and he can sit down and play it.'

'Yes, she told me all that too.'

There was a humorous twinkle in his eye and I realised how stuffy I'd sounded. *God forbid, could there possibly be a bit of Aunt Margaret in me?*

'Sorry,' I said, 'didn't mean to sound stuffy.'

'Yes you did.' His gaze returned to the road, the traffic once again on the move. 'You were defending your father. I respect that. I'd like to meet George one day; he sounds like a good bloke, your dad.'

'He is.'

Phil never did get to meet Dad. We broke up a year later, and when we did Mum's words came back to haunt me. *'You'll have your time cut out with this one, Jac. You won't be able to keep him under your thumb like the others.'*

Was that why we broke up? I remember wondering. I really can't recall how or why we did, but Phil was definitely the one that got away. The one I actually didn't *want* to get away, which was unfamiliar territory for me. As a rule, when an affair was on the wane – and this was usually around the one-year mark – a mutual agreement to call it a day would come as something of a relief. This time, however, it came as an unwelcome surprise. Phil felt the need to move on, he said, really nicely, really caringly. (But that was my line, wasn't it?)

'You probably feel the same way, don't you, Jac?'

'Yes. I do. You're quite right.' (What else could a girl say?)

'But it's been fun, hasn't it?' (That was my line too.) 'We've had a really great time together.'

'Yep. It's been really great fun, Phil.'

In my past, this scene had always been played in reverse, which meant Mum was spot-on when she'd said I prefer to live life on my terms.

I shed a tear after Phil left, but quickly told myself, *Oh well, time for a change. Time to move on.*

And move on I did – from disaster to disaster.

Oh no! Not another actor! When will you learn! I told myself. Actually I hadn't known Ralph was an actor when we'd first met. I thought he was in the hospitality industry. He was a very handsome maître d' in a very fancy restaurant frequented by the upper echelons of the ABC (I'd been invited along by my boss as a bit of a treat), and he was so assured and stylish that I presumed he was the manager, perhaps even part-owner. He turned out to be neither. He was a glorified waiter, chosen to perform as host because of his looks and his ability to play the role. As we all know, many waiters are actors 'resting' between jobs, and Ralph had very cleverly chosen a venue where he might bump into ABC directors and producers. I didn't discover this until after we'd been sleeping together for a whole two months. He was disappointed to find I couldn't open up avenues of employment for him.

Six months later. A writer. A serious intellectual. I'd decided to avoid good-looking men and head for mental wizards instead. I found one in the form of Ian, who was hugely stimulating. We'd stay up half the night talking. Or rather Ian would do the talking while I sat rapt, listening attentively and hopefully learning. This was the time I was branching out from the ABC into independent film production, and I wanted to gather all the knowledge I could.

Ian certainly didn't pass for handsome. Not that he was ugly, just unremarkable. Except for one thing: he was extraordinarily hirsute. I swear you could see his whiskers grow. I said of him once, intending to be funny in a droll sort of way, that he needed to shave twice a day in order to find his mouth. We were at an awfully camp lunch where everyone was being witty, and I thought it was an amusing bit of repartee, but he found the remark so offensive that he grew a beard and a huge moustache just to prove he didn't care. I slowly came to realise Ian lacked a sense of humour, which is probably why we lasted only four months.

There were further affairs interspersed with bouts of celibacy, until finally at the age of thirty-one I met another man who I actually felt I could marry – or rather settle down and live with, because marriage itself wasn't of ultimate importance. He was a New Zealander named Joe, and he was a DOP (director of photography, for the uninitiated). Recalling the Phil fiasco, I said not a word to Mum, choosing to wait instead until Joe and I had agreed to 'give it a go' before dropping the bombshell.

'Want to come to Sydney next month, Mum?' I asked over the phone. 'Joe and I are getting married in the backyard.'

I swear I heard her jaw crash to the floor on the other end of the line.

Mum had already met Joe, and so had Dad; I'd brought him home to Perth the previous Christmas. He'd even met the dreaded Aunt Margaret at the customary family gathering.

'Joe . . .' She'd sniffed her disapproval upon introduction. 'That would be short for Joseph, I presume?'

'No,' he'd replied pleasantly, 'just Joe.'

God, I loved him for that.

Joe and I had been an item for a whole nine months by then, and we'd even moved in with each other – a little semidetached house in Bondi.

'My, my,' Mum had remarked when I told her we were living together. 'My, my *indeed*.' She was neither impressed nor was she being censorious, but obviously thinking, *Bold decision when it's only got a few months to go*. She knew my affairs faded at the one-year mark.

Now here we were, a good six months later, about to 'go the whole hog', as they say. Certainly it was only a backyard job – no church, no lavish wedding gown – but we'd hired the celebrant, written our personal vows, chosen our Shakespearean sonnet and lined up a quartet of muso mates to play our special selection. All of this showed a very deep commitment on our part: we were deadly serious.

Joe's parents flew in from Auckland – Marge and Des, an awfully nice pair but with truly alarming Kiwi accents, which took me by surprise because Joe's accent was very understated. Mum and Dad flew over from Perth and all four, who got on famously, I'm pleased to say, booked into a posh hotel for the week preceding the wedding.

Dad was a little nonplussed when I showed him the backyard, which was quite a nice backyard in my opinion – not landscaped, admittedly, but large enough for the gathering of forty we intended, with a cute potting shed at the rear and choko vines growing along the lattice fence to the side.

'I'm aware outdoor celebrant weddings are quite the thing these days, Jac,' he said hesitantly, not wishing to hurt, 'but do you think perhaps you should look at changing the venue to a park, or . . .'

I stood firm. 'No, Dad, we love the backyard, and our friends do too.' (There'd been many a party thrown in that backyard.) 'Our mates are going to decorate the choko vine and the potting shed. It'll look really great.'

He gave in with good grace, as he always did – George was a real gentleman – but he insisted on paying for the catering (and doubling the bill in the process – the spread was truly fantastic), which made him feel a whole lot better.

'Well, well, well, I never thought I'd live to see the day,' Mum said. 'You getting married, just fancy that.' She was shaking her head in disbelief, but, as I was showing her my wedding outfit at the time, I wasn't sure if it was incredulity at the forthcoming event or disapproval of my choice of bridal wear.

'What do you think?' I asked. I was proud of the ensemble. Carla Zampatti no less, and I never bought designer labels in those days. I still don't, actually – except for the girls' weddings, of course; I splurged on both of those. For my own backyard ceremony I'd bought the most beautiful cream satin blouse to go with a perfectly cut black pencil skirt. Zampatti at her best. I can't begin to tell you how classy it was.

'Lovely quality, dear,' Mum said, although she appeared to have some vague misgivings. 'Very smart indeed.'

'*But* . . .' I goaded her, daring her to tell me the truth, which I shouldn't have, because she always did.

'But,' she said thoughtfully, studying the outfit spread out on the bed, 'it's perhaps just a *tiny* bit reminiscent of the ladies who work at David Jones, don't you think?'

I took a deep breath. 'David Jones' colours are black and *white*, not *cream*,' I replied tightly.

'Of course they are, dear,' she agreed with a smile and not the slightest element of guilt or apology, 'and those ladies always look so smart.'

Following the wedding (which I considered perfect, by the way), Mum went a step further.

'Isn't it strange,' she quietly mused as the two of us stood in a corner hoeing into the *croque-en-bouche*, 'how such a quaint little ceremony can be so legally binding?'

I ask you, what can you say to someone who speaks their mind so openly and innocently and with such downright honesty? Mum drove me mad, but oh god how I loved her.

Marriage led to a host of changes, which rather surprised me, as I'd presumed life would trundle along the comfortable course Joe and I had been travelling for the past year or more. We'd become very good friends by then. Both of us being in the business of film, we understood and were interested in each other's work. We respected and trusted one another when a production called for us to be apart. In fact, I think periods of separation are very good for a marriage.

I remember an overly romantic, recently wedded friend waxing rhapsodic about the added 'sparkle' matrimony would lend to our partnership.

'Oh, Jac, darling,' she enthused, 'you and Joe used to drink out of glass, but soon you'll be drinking out of crystal.'

Really, have you ever heard such puerile rubbish! (Deborah was an actor, and a highly theatrical one at that.)

As it turned out Deb was wrong. Glass and crystal played no part in the changes that followed our marriage. But Joe's desire to have children did.

I'd never really thought about babies. I'd been blissfully unaware of my biological clock, even while many of my contemporaries were popping out offspring at an alarming rate. Babies had simply never been high on my list of priorities. But they were on Joe's. And having consented to

marriage at the age of thirty-two, I considered it only fair
that I should accept responsibility as the vessel of choice.
We decided I'd go off the pill, but I have to admit I secretly
hoped it would be some time before I'd conceive.

It wasn't. Amanda was born virtually nine months later,
and Rose came along eighteen months after that. Life had
changed forever.

Rose's birth had been a difficult one, with complications, which meant that after a brief burst of fecundity
there would be no more babies, leaving me feeling terribly
guilty.

'But what about a boy for you to play footy with?'
I asked Joe tearfully. (Yes, I actually did come up with a line
as banal as that, but I was emotionally unstable at the time.)

'Girls can play footy too,' he said. (You see why I loved
him?)

Joe really didn't seem to mind not having a son. He
loved his girls unreservedly, and was a far better dad than
I was a mum. Fatherhood came naturally to Joe, whereas
motherhood and I seemed to lack a vital connection.

When Rose turned one and was at the early toddler
stage, we took the girls to Perth for Christmas. We'd
decided to acquaint them with their maternal grandparents first – the following Christmas we'd take them to
New Zealand to meet Marge and Des.

There was, of course, the inevitable introduction to
the appalling Aunt Margaret, who considered 'Rose' an
eminently suitable name, but insisted upon calling Mandy
'Amanda', which thoroughly confused the child. In the
early days when Mandy had started to speak, she'd been

unable to pronounce 'Amanda' so 'Manda' had quickly become 'Mandy', and she'd been Mandy ever since. But not to Aunt Margaret. Even when I told her how and why 'Mandy' had come into being, she stuck to 'Amanda'.

'It's high time the child learned her own name,' she announced in that superior, pseudo-aristocratic tone of hers. Truly, she was a caricature from a Victorian novel – something Thackeray might have written.

I had enough of the protective maternal instinct in me to hate Aunt Margaret at that moment, and when she died two years later (in her early seventies) I wasn't particularly sorry to hear the news. Nor did I feel the least shred of guilt for the lifetime of antipathy I'd felt towards her. In fact, little Rose becoming Rosie was probably a deliberate finger to Aunt Margaret.

During our trip to Perth that year, Mum proved a godsend. I confided in her the painful truth that I hadn't dared share with anyone else: I wasn't a natural parent; I didn't particularly *like* babies, and sometimes I even felt alien to them.

'Look at Joe,' I said as we watched him rolling around on the lawn with the girls. 'He's an absolute natural. I'm not,' I admitted, shamefaced. 'I'm a terrible mother.'

'I know dear,' she said sympathetically. 'So was I. But don't worry, it's perfectly normal.'

I stared back in complete disbelief.

'Well, for some women it is,' she added, 'and you and I obviously fall into that category.'

But she'd misinterpreted the reason for my reaction. 'Rubbish!' I exclaimed. 'You were a *wonderful* mother.'

'No I wasn't, Jac. You just *think* I was. I couldn't stand you as a baby. I've always disliked babies. Whenever some doting mother thrusts a newborn at me and says, 'Would you like to hold the baby?' as if she's offering the most precious gift imaginable, I always say, 'No thank you, I'd rather not.'

Good grief, that's true, I thought. *I've seen you do it.* 'Yes, you do, don't you,' I said, amazed. 'I always thought you were joking.'

'I wasn't. My reaction was the same when it came to you, dear – I really didn't enjoy holding your squirmy little body. I breastfed you, as one must, and I did my share of nappy changing, which was only fair, but George was always the one who played baby games. Bathtime was your father's duty too. George liked bathtime. I didn't.'

'But I clearly remember from a very early age,' I said, still with a sense of amazement, 'that you were a splendid mother.'

'No, dear, you just *think* you remember. Most people are convinced they remember things that they don't really remember at all. Why, I distinctly recall being eighteen months old myself.'

She got that distant look in her eyes; her mind was travelling somewhere else.

'I remember clear as a bell standing in a little playpen, rattling the wooden bars and yelling "lolly . . . lolly . . . lolly" at the top of my voice until Margaret would come along and pop a lolly in my mouth. I did it on a daily basis and it worked every time.' She smiled fondly. 'Dear Margaret, she always came to my call.'

Dear bloody Margaret! I thought but made no reply, waiting for her to continue the memory. Instead, she snapped back to the present.

'However, I wasn't really remembering at all,' she continued. 'Years later, Margaret showed me a photo she'd taken of the raucous toddler that was me – head flung back, mouth wide open, rattling the bars of its cage. She told me a lolly was the only way to keep me quiet. "And once you'd discovered the trick," she said, "there was no shutting you up."' Mum shook her head, again fondly. 'Poor dear Margaret was handed the load of parenting at such an early age.'

'So you see,' she went on briskly, 'it was only the photograph I was remembering, not the occasion itself. Most people are like that, including you, dear. You would have no recollection at all of what a terrible mother I was when you were little. Just as Mandy and Rose won't remember what a terrible mother you are.' (How typical of Mum to be able to say such a thing and remain inoffensive.) 'Believe me, you'll enjoy your girls far more when they start communicating on an intelligent level. And that's the part Mandy and Rose will remember. Just as you do of me.'

I can't tell you how relieved that conversation left me. In just a matter of minutes, I'd been freed of the sure-fire belief I was an unnatural monster.

'Every woman has to find her own way of mothering, Jac,' Mum concluded. 'Nobody teaches you how to be a parent.'

And they didn't in Mum's day, nor in mine for that matter. But they do these days, don't they? There are all those books and internet sites out there, dictating to young women how they should go about parenting. Not just advice either, but rules writ in stone, and they have to follow those rules or risk being crucified on social media. I feel sorry for young mothers today. Everyone's telling them how to be a parent.

Mum proved quite right. It wasn't long at all before the girls became a source of great interest to me, due no doubt to their communicative skills, as she'd suggested, but also to the fact that I'd stopped agonising over what a bad mother I was. I actually adored listening to my little girls chatter away and offer opinions. And they had such different personalities! Mandy was so serious and Rosie so funny – how come I hadn't noticed this earlier?

But despite my newfound enjoyment, I still went back to work as soon as was humanly possible, which was the moment I could get Rosie into preschool. This wasn't quite the 'done thing' in those days. Mothers were expected to devote themselves to parenting during their children's younger years, and I risked being judged, but I really didn't care. Work was who I was, and I told myself the girls would surely be better off with a happy mother than an unhappy one. Besides, Joe so adored parenting; he was more than happy to take up the reins.

In fact, so dedicated to fatherhood was Joe that his life underwent a complete transformation. In order to avoid lengthy times away on location, he accepted a position with Film Australia. I don't think he found the job tremendously stimulating, because it involved quite a bit of desk work, but it kept him in Sydney and that, to Joe, was the most important thing. When I was on a production that took me away from home, he had the girls all to himself.

Some juggling was required in the early years, particularly getting the girls to and from kindy, but by the time Rosie joined Mandy at Bondi Primary we had things down to a fine art. This was principally due to the arrival of our new neighbour, Natalie. Talk about luck!

Natalie had recently shifted into a cottage just three doors down from us. (Yes, we were still ensconced in the same little semidetached house with the backyard, the potting shed and the choko vine. We'd actually ended up buying the place, even adding an upstairs extension – two bedrooms and a bathroom.)

Nat was a lovely person with a lovely nature. A rather homely looking young woman of around thirty, she had a son Mandy's age who attended Bondi Primary, and we soon came to an arrangement that suited us all. Nat would pick up the girls when she fetched Ben from school and entertain them at her place until Joe got home. We paid her, naturally, and I know the extra cash was a bonus because she was a single mum and doing things hard. *Hard?* That's putting it mildly! Her husband had been killed in a car crash when Ben was only two. Poor thing, just imagine! After the accident, she'd lived with her parents for a few years, and when Ben reached school age they'd bought her the little Bondi cottage, so at least she didn't have to pay rent. Nat would also babysit for us when necessary, and we all became the best of friends. The girls liked her enormously, and Ben, who'd been a lonely little boy, loved having other kids around.

Then all of a sudden Rosie was eight and Mandy going on ten – things were cruising along, our girls growing up beautifully. Oh, those were magic times. I have to admit several years later that the onset of puberty (and the girls were early developers) wreaked a certain degree of havoc. Their hormonal roller-coaster rides careered into my menopause, and god there were fights. How poor Joe put up with it is beyond me. But we managed to weather the storm and after a year or two sail once again into relatively calm waters, which is just as well because up ahead lay further trials that were far more difficult to navigate.

The first of these was Dad's death. The shock of it. A heart attack. In his sleep. Mum had sent him off to the spare room because he was snoring, and when he didn't come back to bed the following morning she went in to discover him curled up, quite peacefully. She thought he was asleep, but he wasn't.

It was so unexpected. Dad had never had any heart issues, not that we knew of, and he was only sixty-nine. Sixty-nine! That's young these days. Well, it certainly is looking from my current perspective of sixty-five.

Funny, isn't it, the way people say so glibly, 'A heart attack in his sleep – oh yes, please, that's the way I'd like to go.' Sure, it's fine for the deceased, but what about the one who's left behind? Poor Mum.

I sometimes wonder if it's not kinder to have the warning of a terminal illness. To be given the time to adjust, to prepare emotionally, to care for your partner and share the prospect of impending death. Shock and grief is a terrible mix.

Joe and the girls stayed in Sydney while I went to Perth for the funeral. My idea. Given the tyranny of distance, the girls hadn't known their grandfather all that well, so they were experiencing no deep-seated grief, and I didn't believe there was any need for them to feel duty-bound. Plus, they were still in their early teens, and what teenager enjoys a funeral? Besides, I intended to stay on with Mum for a week or so, which, thankfully, I managed to stretch to a fortnight because she really was a bit of a mess. Oh she was strong and determined not to go under, but she was rattled in a way I'd never seen her before. Lost. Unsure. Puzzled. Anxious. A whole cauldron of emotions just bubbling away.

'So sudden, Jac,' she said to me as we sat together in the lounge room the day after the funeral, both of us cried-out and empty. 'He was here one minute, gone the next. What's going to happen now? What do I do? How do I readjust?'

Shock and grief, you see? What can one say?

'Do you want to come to Sydney with me, Mum?' I suggested. 'Might be a good idea. I have a whole six weeks at home before I head off for a Melbourne-based production. You could spend some time with Joe and me and the girls.'

'Oh no, dear, no thank you. That would be running away. I'd only have to readjust all over again when I got back.' She looked lost as she gazed around the room, her eyes coming to rest on Dad's armchair parked in front of the telly. 'I have to start now. Right here and now. But it's hard, Jac' – no complaint, no bid for sympathy, just pure statement of fact – 'so very hard.'

The next jarringly big change came all too soon.
I arrived home from Perth to discover that Joe and Nat
were having an affair. No, not what you're thinking –
I didn't catch them *in flagrante*. Joe told me that very
night, and in the bluntest manner.

'I have something to tell you,' he said when the girls
had gone upstairs to bed, leaving us settled with the telly
and a bottle of excellent shiraz. He picked up the remote,
turned off the TV and then dropped the bomb. 'Nat and
I are having an affair.'

Flabbergasted, gobsmacked, flummoxed, dumbfounded
. . . All those gloriously antiquated terms applied, and I
sat there jaw agape, unable to feel anything but disbelief.
Silence followed.

'For how long?' I finally managed to stammer. And
I did too – stammer, that is. I don't remember ever having
stammered. Nothing's floored me enough to make me
stammer. But *really?* My mind was doing the maths. We'd
met Nat when Rosie was five and starting school at Bondi
Primary. Rosie was thirteen now. *Eight years?*

My incredulity was readable, and Joe shook his head.

'Last week,' he said. 'It would have happened sooner –
we actually came pretty close when you were off on that
South Australian production last year, but Nat knocked
me back. Out of deference to you, of course.'

Well bully for you, Nat, I thought, perhaps cynically but,
still suspended in a state of disbelief, vaguely aware that I
felt no anger. Surely the timing was a bit off though – I'd
just buried my father.

Once again Joe appeared to read my thoughts. 'It does
seem a bit rough,' he went on apologetically, 'that it

happened while you were away at your dad's funeral. But it was going to happen sometime, Jac, and in six weeks you're heading off to Melbourne, so I decided the time was now. We have to make plans.'

'What sort of plans?' *This sounds ominous,* I thought. *So they've had a fling, but we can get over it, surely. I'm prepared to forgive and forget. Well, forgive anyway – sort of.*

But Joe had clearly decided from the start that brutal was the way to go.

'Nat and I are in love,' he announced boldly. 'We probably have been for quite some time, but neither of us was prepared to admit it, even to ourselves let alone each other. We just pretended to ignore our feelings, but now we have to face up to the fact and make plans for the future.'

I could tell his resolve was weakening, and for the first time since he'd embarked upon this confrontation, which he'd obviously determined to meet in a full head-on collision, he looked guilty.

'I'm sorry, Jac,' he said. 'I really am sorry. I never meant to hurt you, and neither did Nat. It just happened . . .' A miserable shrug. 'Over a period of time . . . A *very long* period of time . . . It just . . .' A hopeless shake of his head. 'I dunno . . . It just happened. Nat and I are right for each other.'

He was struggling so hard to explain something he couldn't understand, but as he went on *I* could.

'I love her and she needs me,' he said. 'I love you too, Jac, and I always will. But you don't need me. You never have.'

There was no accusation in his tone, just the declaration of a long-observed truth. 'You've never needed anyone. And somehow that makes a difference. At least it does to me.'

Oh *yes*, I understood implicitly. How could I not? Once again, and after all these years, my choice in men had proved disastrous. Not disastrous for me, but disastrous for him. Poor darling Joe, what a rotten wife I'd been.

I downed the remains of my shiraz and poured myself another.

That particular change should have been a massive one, wouldn't you agree? But somehow it wasn't. Joe just shifted three doors down the street – tastefully six weeks later when I was in Melbourne – and the girls split their time between the two homes. As they had for the past eight years anyway.

The divorce eventually went through, quite amicably. Joe and Nat married the year after that, and everyone was happy. How bizarre can you get? I felt no animosity towards Nat, although I tried hard at first. She was still the same lovely person with the same lovely nature (still homely looking), and she was so right for Joe.

The next big change came another eight years later when Mum died. (In numerology, my destiny number is eight, so that may have had something to do with the scheme of things.) Her death brought with it that jarring sense of my own mortality. Surely it's the same for everyone, isn't it? The moment when you realise you're the next cab off the rank? A sobering thought.

We had preparation time, though, Mum and I; time enough to say our goodbyes. She'd been diagnosed with cancer – pancreatic, stage four, inoperable, two months at the most. She didn't accept the offer of chemo, which might have bought her extra time.

'What's the point?' she argued, 'I'll opt for quality not quantity, thank you very much. Should they become necessary, painkillers will do.'

I cancelled everything and moved to Perth to be with her, and I cannot tell you how precious our time together was. I treasured every minute of it, and do to this day. The memories we shared! And, oh, how we laughed.

She didn't make the two months – she barely made five weeks – but I'm convinced she willed things that way.

'I'm not going into hospital, Jac,' she announced the moment I arrived. 'I'm going to die right here, in my own bed, in my own home. That's important to me dear. You do understand, don't you?'

'Yes, Mum.' It sounded distinctly like an order that I was to obey under all circumstances, but what if I couldn't? What if she became so incapacitated she *had* to be hospitalised?

I needn't have worried. Mum looked after everything herself, dying in her own bed, in her own house, just as she'd said she would. I regretted at first that I hadn't been there with her, holding her hand right at the very end, until I realised she'd wanted to be on her own. She'd said her goodbyes that very same evening as I'd sat on her bed and we'd chatted away. I hadn't realised they were goodbyes at the time; I'd just thought she was being reflective.

'You never really did understand Margaret, did you, dear?' she asked out of the blue, taking me completely by surprise. 'You considered her the aunt from hell.'

'Yes, I did,' I replied, thinking this was going to become one of our jokey reminiscences. 'But with pretty good reason. You've got to admit she was the most terrible tyrant.'

'She was the closest thing I ever had to a parent,' Mum said in that distant way that signalled she was somewhere else. 'Margaret was mother and father all in one. A truly good person devoted to her siblings, particularly me, being the youngest.' She jumped back to the present. 'You couldn't see that, could you?'

I felt it essential I back down at this stage – just a little anyway – although I wasn't prepared to lie. 'No, I couldn't, Mum. I couldn't see that at all, I'm afraid. But I didn't view things from any perspective other than my own in those days. I was young and selfish. All young people are selfish.'

'Yes, that's true. You've always been selfish. You still are. And yet you're no longer young.' In typical fashion Mum was making no accusation, merely voicing an observation, but I couldn't help wincing at the remark.

'Oh don't be hurt, dear. It's pointless. You are who you are, and I wouldn't want you any other way. You've always chosen to live life on your terms, and if on occasion things didn't turn out for the best, you can't be held entirely responsible.'

We both knew exactly what she was talking about, and her frail hand reached out to pat mine.

'Joe was fully aware of what he was letting himself in for, you should never have felt guilty the way you did all those years ago. It was your strength he fell in love with, after all. And you know what your greatest strength is, Jac?'

I shook my head. I really had no idea.

'Your honesty. You've been true to yourself for the whole of your life. Ever since you were a little girl, you've never been afraid to say what you think and be who you are.'

I wonder where I got that from, I couldn't help thinking.

'That sort of honesty is to be respected, Jac. I'm proud of you and I love you.'

'I love you too, Mum.' I leaned down and kissed her.

'That's nice, dear.' Her smile was one of sheer bliss, and although her face was weary and worn, emaciated even, I thought she'd never looked prettier. 'I'm going to sleep now.'

'You don't want me to read to you?' I usually read until she nodded off.

'No thank you, dear, not tonight. I'm very tired.'

'Right you are.' I stood. 'Night-night then, see you in the morning.'

'Goodnight, Jac.'

They were her last words to me. I hadn't realised that she was saying goodbye, of course, but I knew the moment I saw her the following morning, lying there so serene, so peaceful. She'd said her goodbyes and slipped away quietly on her own, just as she'd planned. Oh god how I loved that woman.

Life's changes continued in relentless and unpredictable fashion. The girls graduated from university. Mandy became a lawyer and Rosie an architect – our funny little Rosie designing grand buildings, just fancy that! I'd pictured her more as a stand-up comic. Then Mandy got married and had a baby. Good grief, I was a grandmother!

'Do you want to hold him, Mum?' Mandy asked, thrusting her newborn at me.

'No thank you, dear. I'd rather not.'

The laughter that followed. They all thought I was joking. Oh my goodness, how Mum continued to live around every corner.

Joe and I had long since sold the little semidetached in Bondi. This was around about the time the girls finished school, and Joe was by then a father all over again. He and Nat had a baby. And guess what? It was a boy! I was genuinely happy for him. When I called around to congratulate them, Nat didn't offer the baby up for a cuddle though. Joe had obviously warned her.

When I turned sixty I 'sort of' retired and moved up to the Central Coast, a couple hours north of Sydney. I mean it when I say 'sort of', because I hadn't really retired at all. By that time my work was mostly done on computer anyway – not only the drawing up of budgets and schedules, but a great deal of communication and meetings were conducted online. God, the poor actors were expected to film their audition pieces and email them to the production company. Who would ever have thought things would come to that! Having spent the whole of my existence maintaining the line that 'work is who I am', retirement was hardly something I was eager to embrace anyway, and the 'sea change' wasn't all that difficult.

My move north brought with it the greatest and most unpredictable change of all. After the disastrous choices of men I'd made throughout the whole of my life, I finally met another partner! Ronnie. The same age as me.

And no, Ronnie's not short for Ronald. Veronica's her name.

I never knew I could be attracted to a woman – sexually, I mean. Plenty of my straight female friends have been over the years. Good grief, in the world of film and show business in general I think I was one of the few who'd never been tempted to experiment with their sexuality. I don't quite know why – it had simply never occurred to me.

Not so Ronnie. She'd known she was a lesbian from a very early age, and she told me it's her greatest thrill to 'turn a straight'. She just loves the challenge, she said. Always has and still does.

'What?' I asked. 'Even now when you're over sixty?' I was shocked. 'You're surely a bit beyond that, aren't you?' I'd had no idea she was doing a line for me at the time. My shock lay in my personal assumption that people over sixty didn't have sex.

'You're never past it if someone's the right person,' she said, her black-currant eyes beaming holes into mine. The power of Ronnie's full focus can be pretty overwhelming. 'And age is never a barrier for anything,' she added with her contagiously wicked smile, 'unless perhaps you're aiming at the Olympics.'

That's when I recognised this was a line, and that the line was aimed directly at me. It was very effective.

I didn't fall for it immediately, of course – a period of adjustment was necessary – but I did allow us to become friends.

Ronnie's an extraordinarily attractive human being. Not beautiful, not in the least, and she wouldn't have been even in her youth. I know this for a fact – I've seen the photos. But she's highly intelligent and outrageously funny with an energy impossible to ignore. Above all, Ronnie is fearless. And I've discovered that fearlessness is a quality to be admired in anyone – male or female. Little wonder it wasn't long before I succumbed.

'You know what I like most about you, Jac?' she asked that first time as we lolled around on a late Saturday afternoon.

'No idea,' I said, still dazed and lost in wonder at this latest turn my life had taken.

'You're so readable.'

'Oh.' I was disappointed, and more than a little hurt, but I covered the fact. 'How insufferably boring of me.'

'Not at all. It's refreshing. You don't play games. You are who you are and you're not afraid to admit it.' (Why did Mum spring instantly to mind?) 'I like that. I like that a lot.'

Ronnie and I have been together for nearly five years now. The girls are totally accepting of our relationship. They were from the very start, which I suppose was to be expected – they're young and they're modern.

'We're happy for you, Mum,' they said. Which pleased me.

Joe, too, was accepting, and that came as more of a surprise because Joe's a conservative man at heart, even bordering on the old-fashioned.

'You've always known what you wanted, Jac,' he said. 'I'm happy for you.' Which also pleased me.

But even if none of them had been accepting, I'd still be with Ronnie. Because that's who I am, as both Ronnie and

Mum would say. Living life on my own terms. Selfish to the very end.

Ah well, this concludes my ramblings, although as I said from the outset I've no idea who they're intended for. The girls perhaps? I don't think so. The girls know me far too well; they'd find no surprises here. For the grandchildren maybe, when they're of an age to be remotely interesting to me, that is. Yes, possibly. I'll give Ronnie a look, of course – bound to raise a smile there. But I think ultimately this will be for me – I'll read it ten years from now and see what further changes may have occurred.

Life is so interesting, isn't it? You never know how things are going to pan out. I must say, though, at this stage in my journey it's very nice having someone to grow old with.

A WORD FROM JUDY

I recently came upon a mysterious folder in my computer files that bore the title 'General Notes'. As I have a sea of folders in my computer, each relating to specific books or short stories, I wondered which particular one these notes might belong to, but I called it up only to discover it didn't belong anywhere. The file contained just a series of observations I'd made over the years – bits and pieces jotted down in sundry notebooks that at some stage I'd decided to file away then promptly forgot I'd done so. And now here they were.

The discovery was quite a treasure trove really, this collection of musings and memories. I decided to use some of my 'General Notes' in a story written from the perspective of an older woman reviewing her past, and that's how 'Changes' came about.

THE HOUSE ON HILL STREET

Timothy Drew lived in Hill Street, West Hobart, a pleasant street in a pleasant, middle-class suburb in the postcard-pretty capital of Tasmania. Timothy's house was one in a line of a half dozen or so terraces built at the dawn of the twentieth century, which now, in 1983, were regarded as fashionable. Brick-rendered and identical, the cottages were not as picturesque as the stone terraces that were a feature of 'old Hobart town', but they were attractive nonetheless.

Timothy didn't actually own his cottage, he rented it from Henry Jervis, a real estate investor whose passion for restoring old houses had made him a wealthy man, but Timothy *felt* as though he owned his cottage. He'd lived there quite happily for the past decade and, apart from a biennial raise in the rent, he'd had no interference whatsoever from his landlord. It was not surprising – Henry Jervis only wished that all of his properties could be leased to introverted pharmaceutical assistants like the grossly overweight, meek and malleable Timothy Drew.

Timothy took great pride in his house and his garden, and the community in general. He considered it a privilege to live in Hill Street – such a respectable neighbourhood. Good heavens, there was even a scientist a few doors up the road. Professor Jameson and his family had moved into the end terrace just the previous year. The professor was a biochemist, employed by the CSIRO no less. In Timothy's opinion, a person of such standing was a credit to the community and, although he hadn't dared attempt to cultivate the great man's friendship, he always kept a packet of sweets in his pocket for those times when he bumped into Mrs Jameson and the children. This was usually during the weekends when she took the boys to the park – always on her own. The professor was rarely to be seen, he was clearly a busy man.

Eileen Jameson seemed a very nice woman – late thirties Timothy guessed, quite a deal younger than her husband, who appeared in his early fifties. Good-looking, brunette and stylish, as befitted the wife of a scientist.

Lately, Timothy had taken to accompanying Eileen and her children on their stroll to the park. For Timothy it was more of a struggle than a stroll as he waddled beside them trying to keep up. When they got there he would push the swing for the youngest boy, Thomas, who was six. Nine-year-old Robert, fiercely independent, would eschew any form of assistance, swearing he could swing himself higher than anyone could push him. Eileen, seated on a bench, buried her head in a book and ignored the lot of them. Ten minutes later, when the swings had lost their appeal, the boys would gravitate to each other's company and Timothy, his supply of sweets by then demolished, would be redundant altogether. That was when he would make his departure.

'Cheerio,' he'd say, and Eileen would look up from her book and give him a wave.

Timothy loved his visits to the park.

One chill autumn day, emboldened by the dreadful knowledge that, with the advent of winter, the park would soon be out of bounds, Timothy made a move that surprised even himself. He joined Eileen Jameson on the bench.

Clasping a knee with both hands, he heaved one hefty thigh over the other and crossed his legs in a clumsy attempt at nonchalance. 'I'd be happy to babysit,' he said a little too loudly.

Eileen glanced up from her book into the currant-brown eyes of his doughy face and the desperate plea that lay there.

'You could drop the boys off at my house any time during the weekend,' he said. 'Or, if you like, I could call by and collect them. And I'm free in the evenings too . . .' He tailed off lamely as he noticed that she did not appear particularly receptive to his suggestion.

Eileen Jameson supposed there was nothing sinister in Timothy Drew's offer. He was just the lonely man she'd always presumed him to be, she told herself. But she found his bid for her children's company repellent nonetheless. Her response was polite, but unequivocal.

She appreciated the offer, she said, but her mother would never forgive her if she accepted it. Her mother had shifted interstate to be near her grandsons and lived only ten minutes away in Lenah Valley. 'Mum can't get enough of the boys, I'm afraid,' Eileen said apologetically.

'Of course, most understandable,' Timothy hauled himself to his feet, 'just thought I'd make the suggestion. Well, cheerio then,' he said.

Eileen waved goodbye and returned to her book.

The subject was not mentioned again.

Over the ensuing weeks, there were two more visits to the park, after which Timothy saw little of Eileen and the children. Winter came unseasonably early, as it so often did, icy winds sweeping up from the Antarctic, and parks became the realm of only the hardiest Hobartians. But by that time Timothy had lost sight altogether of Eileen. He occasionally saw the professor arrive and depart the house at the far end of the terraces, but there was no evidence of Eileen or the children. He wondered whether there may have been trouble in the marriage – perhaps she'd left her husband and taken the boys to her mother's. Timothy worried about Eileen.

Then, in August, he was confronted by something far more worrisome than a neighbour's possible marital problems.

It all started upon a visit to the bathroom.

Timothy's bowels had never performed well, but he'd come to accept constipation and a painfully chronic haemorrhoid condition as a way of life.

On this particular morning, after a more or less successful evacuation, he followed his customary procedure. He flushed the toilet, washed his hands and turned to check that the bowl had cleared – he was a fastidious man. But upon gazing down at the lavatory, he froze in horror. A sickening sight met his eyes. The bowl was a mess of blood. There were even pieces of something floating about that looked like intestines. He felt the bile rise in his throat. This was not the result of ruptured haemorrhoids.

Something shocking was happening to his body. His very insides were falling out. He was a dying man.

He staggered from the bathroom to the lounge and sat sucking in air, trying not to faint. Then, when he felt strong enough, he took himself directly to the emergency wing of the Royal Hobart Hospital.

Over the next day or so there were others in Hill Street who suffered similar unnerving experiences. The common plumbing system shared by the conjoined houses produced alarming results in a number of lavatories. People were understandably terrified.

As the fretful residents of Hill Street wondered what on earth was going on, workers in the nearby sewage plant made a gruesome discovery. A severed finger was found amongst the sewage. They reported their find to the police, and a fingerprint of the digit was telexed to the Bureau of Criminal Investigation in Canberra. A match was found on record and the finger was identified as that of a woman who'd been convicted of a drink driving offence in Queensland in 1980. The woman's name was Eileen Elizabeth Jameson. Further investigation revealed that she and her husband, Professor Bradley John Jameson, currently resided in Hill Street, West Hobart.

The inexplicable mystery of the bloody lavatories was about to be revealed.

Lucas Matthews, just turned thirty, had recently been promoted to Detective Sergeant. His senior partner, CIB Inspector Max 'Curry' Carruthers considered the promotion

well-deserved: young Luke was a good cop, diligent and
reliable, albeit a little overly academic when it came to
the interrogation process. Luke was of the new breed who
believed in the psychological approach. Curry, who had a
good ten years on his partner, belonged to the old school.
'Frighten the shit out of them,' he'd say, 'no point trying to
reason with crims.'

Max Carruthers had always been a tough cop. The
running gag amongst his colleagues for the past twenty
years had been 'give 'em Curry', and they weren't altogether joking. But Curry himself was the first to admit
that he and young Luke made an excellent team. They had
the 'good cop, bad cop' interrogation routine down to a
fine art.

It was late afternoon as the two plain clothes detectives approached the house on Hill Street. The street was
deserted and, having parked their car around the corner
out of sight, they made their approach on foot. Their
demeanour was casual – people could be watching from
nearby windows.

There was no sign of movement within the house –
the front door was closed and the curtains drawn – so the
officers made their way down the side path to the rear
of the property, their plan being to check the layout of
the place.

Away from prying eyes, they took stock of their surrounds. They were in a small garden with a potting shed;
a head-high fence separated them from the adjoining terrace
house. There were windows either side of the back door
and, creeping to the nearest one, Curry peered into what

was obviously the kitchen. The room was deserted, but there had clearly been a great deal of recent activity.

'Holy shit,' he muttered.

Luke joined him and, gazing through the window, his gasp was audible.

Both men drew their weapons.

They glanced at each other. The look in Luke's eyes spoke multitudes, and Curry's responding look said exactly the same thing. In all his years as a police officer, he too had seen nothing like this.

They crept to the back door. Very slowly, very gently, Curry tested the old-fashioned knob of its handle. He expected to find the door locked, but it wasn't. The knob turned, the door opened, and the two men stepped into the carnage.

The walls, the benches, the floor, even the ceiling – all was awash with blood. Strewn about on surfaces were weapons and tools of every description, each bearing evidence of recent use: knives, meat cleavers, an axe, a hacksaw, and, most repulsive of all, sitting in a corner by the power outlets, an electric blender as bloodied as its surrounds.

Luke wanted to throw up, but he couldn't – he was too terrified. The adrenalin was pumping through his body at an alarming rate. Who was responsible for this massacre?

Curry jerked his head towards the open door opposite that led to the hallway and the rest of the house. Revolvers at the ready, they started towards it.

Then, to their right, they heard the flush of a lavatory.

They whirled to face the sound, their .38s trained upon the door to the side, which they now realised led off to the bathroom. The seconds ticked heavily by, a full minute that felt like an hour. Then the door opened and a man appeared. In his early fifties, of average height and build, with thinning grey-brown hair, there was nothing remarkable about Bradley John Jameson.

'Good heavens, what on earth are you doing here?' he demanded. Nothing remarkable, that is, except his demeanour. Bradley John Jameson was not only unperturbed by the weapons trained upon him, he was plainly affronted by the presence of two strange men in his house.

'Police,' Curry barked. 'Are you Bradley John Jameson?'

'I am indeed.' The professor's face was a picture of outraged innocence. 'What is the meaning of this invasion? I take it you gentlemen have a warrant?'

Word sped via the grapevine in typical cop fashion. The more grisly the case, the quicker news of it got around, and this case was undoubtedly one of the grisliest.

'He what!'

'He flushed his wife down the toilet.'

It wasn't long before Bradley John Jameson became the talk of every police station in Tasmania.

'You've got to be joking!'

'Nope, it's a fact. He chopped her up, boned her out, fed the meat through a blender and poured her down the bog.'

'What did he do with the bones?'

'They haven't been found yet, but he put her head in the oven.'

Having immediately established that the children were safely ensconced with their grandmother, the police had interrogated Professor Bradley John Jameson. He had then been charged with the murder of his wife and incarcerated in Risdon Prison while a full investigation was mounted.

Police were brought in from across the state and a special task force was assigned to the case. The residents of Hill Street were interviewed, backyards were dug up and plumbers ordered to dismantle the common sewerage system linking the terraces.

During the days that followed, police reported to the morgue on a regular basis with pieces of human tissue in small plastic bags. Each offering was examined by the chief forensic pathologist and, once identified as a particular part of Eileen Elizabeth Jameson, it was pieced into the outline of the female body that had been drawn on the mortuary slab. An intensive search of the surrounding area was underway in an effort to find other remains of the body, most particularly the bones. The backyard of the Jameson terrace having revealed no evidence, the whereabouts of the bones remained a mystery.

Throughout the investigation, minimal information was released to the press, and the general public remained unaware of the gorier aspects of the case. There were enough civilians in the know for word to get around locally, however – the Hill Street residents and the plumbers were only too quick to spread the news – and the grisly story met with a common response.

'You wouldn't believe it possible, would you?' Timothy said to old Mrs McGraw from number 95. 'Not *here*.'

'It's absolutely unheard of, Timothy,' Mrs McGraw agreed. 'This sort of thing doesn't happen in *Hobart!*'

Curry Carruthers was aware of the locals' reaction, and he found their incredulity both naive and irritating. *This is exactly the sort of thing that* does *happen in Hobart you dumb shits,* he thought. Perhaps not in such a spectacularly grotesque fashion, he'd have to admit, but pretty little Hobart town had a very black underbelly. It always had. Christ alive, this town had seen madness and evil unlike any other – in its day it had been one of the most brutal convict colonies the world had ever known. You never got rid of a past like that. You could cover it with a veneer of respectability, but every so often the shit would rise to the surface – just as it had now.

The naiveté of the locals was not the only element of the Bradley John Jameson case that Curry found irritating. Bradley John Jameson himself was proving an ongoing cause of intense irritation and frustration to his interrogating officers, who happened to be Curry Carruthers and Luke Matthews.

Despite the recent discovery of new evidence, which had allowed the detectives further interrogation of the prisoner, no fresh progress had been made. For two days now, in the interview room assigned them at Risdon Prison, they had taken turns at the Olivetti, painstakingly typing up – in triplicate as required – a further record of interview with Bradley John Jameson, but they remained at a stalemate. It was driving Curry to distraction. Christ alive, he thought, the case was cut and dried. The man was as mad as a hatter. He'd murdered his wife. The evidence was irrefutable.

He'd been discovered at the scene of the crime surrounded by bloodied weapons all bearing his fingerprints, and the woman's blood had been under his fingernails, for God's sake! So why the hell didn't he admit to the murder, as advised? Tell them the whole story and engage a lawyer who would obviously plead insanity? But Bradley John Jameson had refused a lawyer and insisted upon sticking to his own ridiculous form of response throughout the seemingly interminable interrogation process.

'Where are the bones?' Curry barked for what must surely have been the one hundredth time. 'Did you bury them? Tell us where they are.'

The professor answered as methodically as he had on each previous occasion. 'I don't know, and I didn't, and I can't,' he said. He even smiled an apology at Luke, who was seated nearby, tapping away at the Olivetti. The smile intimated he would be only too happy to help if he possibly could. Curry ached to hit him. But the bastard was mad. You didn't belt the mad ones, much as you wanted to.

Curry had initially found the mad professor interesting. Following Jameson's arrest, the interview they'd conducted at the police station had taken a fascinating turn.

'Why'd you murder your wife?' Curry had launched into the interrogation with his customary belligerence. Legs astride, fists planted on the table, he'd leaned forward threateningly.

'I didn't murder my wife.'

'Oh, come on, you mad prick. We found you in a fucking bloodbath – she was splattered all over the kitchen. Why'd you do it?'

'I didn't. It was not my doing.'

'Not your doing? Her head was in *your* fucking oven, her flesh was in *your* fucking blender, and her blood was under *your* fucking fingernails.' Despite his aggression, Curry spoke methodically so that Luke could keep up on the typewriter, although Luke's censored version was substantially reduced. 'Stop mucking us around you crazy bastard. Why did you kill her?'

'I didn't kill her.' Unlike many a hardened criminal before him, the professor had refused to be daunted by Curry's bullying tactics. He'd remained unruffled and obdurate. 'I am being wrongfully accused.'

Things could have gone on like that for some time, but Curry, realising his antagonism was making no impact, wisely passed the baton to Luke. They might as well try the 'good cop' approach.

Curry seated himself at the typewriter while Luke drew up another chair and sat opposite the prisoner, propping gently on his elbows, his body language conveying no menace.

'Tell me, Professor Jameson ...' He spoke calmly and respectfully and, despite the bizarre circumstances, his suddenly seemed the true voice of reason. 'If you're being wrongfully accused, as you say you are, would you have any idea who might have killed your wife?'

The professor's mild, grey eyes met his, and in them was a look of gratitude for the show of courtesy. 'Oh yes, Sergeant. Yes, indeed I would.'

'Ah.' Luke didn't turn to Curry but kept his full focus upon Jameson. 'And who might that be?'

'Bad Bradley.' There was an *of course* implicit in the professor's reply, as if Luke should have been able to come up with the answer himself. 'It was Bad Bradley who did this terrible thing.'

'Bad Bradley?' Luke maintained focus, his eyes locked into Jameson's.

'Most certainly. Good Bradley would never commit such a crime. This is the work of Bad Bradley.'

'I see.' Finally allowing himself to break eye contact, Luke glanced over to his partner.

Curry nodded congratulations and resumed the reins. 'So where did Bad Bradley bury the bones?' he demanded.

'I would have no idea,' the professor replied coolly. 'Bad Bradley would never tell Good Bradley such a thing. They rarely communicate.'

Realising congratulations had been a little premature, Curry signalled Luke to continue and returned his attention to the typewriter.

Luke paused long enough for the previous question and answer to be typed into the report. 'Professor Jameson,' he said, 'do you know why Bad Bradley killed his wife?'

'I'm afraid not, Sergeant.' The professor seemed sincere in his apology. 'Bad Bradley chooses not to share his personal life with others.'

'Ah. Right.' Luke nodded slowly as if he quite understood, then, choosing his words with care, he continued, 'I have a favour to ask, Professor. I wonder if it might be at all possible for you to put a question or two to Bad Bradley on our behalf.'

'Oh, good heavens above no – I couldn't do that.' Jameson's blanket dismissal was so peremptory that Luke, sensing his partner's annoyance, dived in before Curry could explode.

'May I ask why?'

'You certainly may, Sergeant.' The professor seemed to be rather enjoying his exchange with the polite young policeman. 'I avoid Bad Bradley. I don't like him one bit. Bad Bradley and Good Bradley have nothing at all in common.'

'Why is that?'

An expression something akin to pity crept into the professor's eyes, as though he suspected Luke might be slightly retarded. 'Bad Bradley is evil,' he said, *of course* once again implicit in his tone. 'Surely you must have gathered that fact. Bad Bradley is in league with the devil.'

Having spelled out the problem, Jameson sat back in his chair, indicating the conversation was over. 'I'm sorry I can't be of more help to you, Sergeant.'

The conversation was certainly not over as far as Curry was concerned. He stood, signalling another change in the interview. As Luke took over the typewriter, he launched into a further attack, this time choosing a different angle.

'Listen, you smug prick, we know bloody well why you did it. Your mother-in-law's been interviewed and she couldn't wait to talk. We know the whole fucking story.' Fists on the table, he leaned over Jameson and spat the words into his face. 'Your wife was pissing off with the kids, wasn't she? She shifted in with her mother a month ago and was planning to take the kids back to Queensland.

So you asked her around for a chat, didn't you? And then you fucking well killed her, right?'

Curry's bullying tactics finally produced a reaction, although it was hardly the one he'd hoped for. Jameson displayed neither fear nor guilt that his motive was known to them. He just looked extremely annoyed.

The only sound was the clatter of typewriter keys as Luke recorded the shorthand version of Curry's question.

'Come on, you bastard, admit it,' Curry growled. 'That's why you killed her, isn't it?'

'I have killed no-one,' the professor said icily. 'Good Bradley is innocent. He has no further comment to make.'

And that was it. The stalemate had been reached. Jameson had refused to budge and, unable to detain him any longer without charges, the detectives had been forced to conclude their interrogation. Bradley John Jameson had been charged with the murder of his wife and taken to Risdon Prison where he'd been examined independently by two psychiatrists. Their reports had immediately confirmed that the man was insane and that he suffered a dual personality disorder. The news had come as little surprise to the detectives.

Then, three days later, Eileen Jameson's red Austen Kimberley was found abandoned on the outskirts of town. Upon examination, the boot was discovered to be heavily bloodstained. And tucked into one corner, neatly stripped of all meat, was a shinbone.

'New evidence,' Curry had triumphantly announced to Luke. 'We can have another go at him. We'll nail him to the wall this time.'

They'd visited the prison and resumed their interrogation with new vigour, but Jameson had remained
intransigent, despite Curry's bullying and Luke's cajoling.
The two continued to practise their 'good cop, bad cop'
strategy, but no longer for purely tactical reasons. Each
now firmly believed that his own particular approach
would bring about the breakthrough.

'We know you transported the bones in your wife's car,
you mad bastard, so tell us where you buried them.'

Curry refused to acknowledge Jameson's 'Good Bradley'
alter ego. He was convinced he could wear the man down,
that eventually Jameson would snap and 'Bad Bradley'
would be goaded into existence.

Luke continued to practise patience. He avoided con-
frontational questions and drew the man into conversation
in the hope that 'Good Bradley' might inadvertently let
drop some vital information, or even agree to help them
with their enquiries.

There was a moment when he felt on the verge of
discovery.

'Tell me about Bad Bradley, Professor. You say he's
evil . . .'

'Or insane, Sergeant – there's always that possibility,
isn't there?' Having weathered the inspector's aggression,
Jameson appeared in the mood for a pleasant chat with
the respectful young sergeant. 'Surely, for a man to do the
things Bad Bradley has done he would have to be insane,
wouldn't he?'

'Yes. Yes, I suppose he would.' Luke didn't dare glance
at Curry. Despite the clack of the Olivetti, the professor

seemed to have forgotten that his aggressor was still in the room. Wondering whether this might be the moment of breakthrough, Luke nodded encouragingly. But no encouragement was necessary.

'Evil and insanity can become so easily confused, can't they,' the professor blithely continued. 'Perhaps it's simply a matter of perception, or perhaps the interstice between the two is so minimal that people really can't tell the difference.'

Luke remained silent. He didn't dare move. The normally mild, grey eyes now gleamed with a steely and fierce intelligence. Surely Jameson was trying to tell him something, but what?

'Sometimes they can't see what's staring them right in the face. But then that's typical of human nature, isn't it? People are blind to so much. It's little wonder that occasionally they can't recognise the infinitesimal difference between evil and insanity.'

The infinitesimal difference between evil and insanity, Luke wondered, or the infinitesimal difference between Bad Bradley and Good Bradley? Was that what Jameson was trying to tell him?

'Who am I talking to?' he asked. The steely eyes didn't leave his, but they looked a query. 'Am I talking to Bad Bradley?'

There was a moment's pause. Then the professor leaned back in his chair, crossed his legs and laughed, as if Luke had just come up with the most wonderful joke.

'Oh dear me, Sergeant, how very fanciful of you. I was merely making an observation.'

No you weren't, Luke thought. *You were teasing me, you lunatic bastard, you were playing a bloody cat and mouse game.* He felt a surge of anger and for a moment, like Curry, he wished they could just belt the prick's lights out. Then a thought occurred to him, a chilling thought. He studied the professor, who'd lost interest now and was gazing distractedly into the distance. It wasn't possible, surely. It couldn't be. He looked over to Curry, who met his glance with a comical roll of the eyeballs that said, 'serves you right for trying to converse with a loony'. *He'll howl me down,* Luke thought. *He'll probably even laugh at the notion but, what the hell, I can't keep it to myself.*

'What if there's no Bad Bradley?'

Back at the station, over polystyrene cups of coffee, he brought up the subject.

'Come again?'

'What if there's no Bad Bradley?'

Curry gazed at him blankly. 'Sorry, mate, you've lost me.'

'What if the whole "Good Bradley versus Bad Bradley" scenario's a set-up? What if there's no split personality?'

'What the fuck would it matter?' Curry remained puzzled. 'Of course he's schizo, but even if he isn't, who gives a shit? He murdered his wife, that's all that counts.'

'No, you're missing my point. What if the man's *sane*?'

There was a second or so of incredulous silence before Curry let out a hoot of laughter. 'Jesus, Luke, give us a break. You reckon a sane bloke'd bone out his wife and flush her down the bog?'

It was the reaction Luke had expected, but he refused to be daunted. 'That's more or less what Jameson said.'

'Eh?'

'You were the one at the typewriter, don't you remember? "For a man to do the things Bad Bradley has done he would have to be insane, wouldn't he?" That's what Jameson said.'

'Well, he's bloody right there, isn't he? I mean what *sane* person would commit a murder as grotesque as that in the first place? And what *sane* person would hang around at the scene of the crime surrounded by murder weapons and bits of his wife?'

'Perhaps a *sane* person who wants to be considered *in*sane,' Luke replied dogmatically.

Curry dropped the scornful tone but remained dismissive. 'No way, mate,' he said. 'I can't buy that, not for one second. Besides, you're forgetting – the shrinks said he's schizo.'

'Yes, but they couldn't come up with Bad Bradley, could they?'

During his psychiatric examinations, Jameson had regularly referred to himself in the third person, just as he had with the police, but neither psychiatrist had been able to make direct contact with the alter ego known as 'Bad Bradley'.

How typical of Luke, Curry thought, to over-analyse something that was basically simple. And now, like a dog with a bone, he wouldn't let it go. But you had to give him points for trying. He was a bloody good cop who cared about his job. You had to respect him for that.

'I'll grant you Jameson's a smart bastard, Luke, but the truly whacko ones often are. I've come across criminally insane killers with massive IQs.' Curry downed the dregs of his coffee before clinching the argument. 'But I tell you what, even if Jameson *is* playing a game with us – and you might well be right – it doesn't mean he's sane. A crime like his isn't the act of a sane person. It couldn't be.'

Luke studied his partner thoughtfully. 'So it's beyond all human comprehension that one of our own kind could commit such a crime without being insane. Is that what you're saying?'

'That's precisely what I'm saying. And so are the shrinks.' Curry had had enough now; it was time for the pub. 'Besides, when it all comes down to it, who gives a shit? Get the bastard behind bars and get the crime off the books. That's what we're here for.'

'Yeah, I suppose you're right. I mean, yeah, of course you're right. Heck,' Luke shrugged, 'it was just an idea.' An idea that, despite Curry's eminently sound reasoning, Luke knew he could not altogether dismiss.

'Knock-off time.' Tossing his polystyrene cup into the wastepaper basket in the corner, Curry stood. 'Let's grab a beer.'

The following morning's breakthrough came as a huge surprise to them both. There had appeared no particular defining moment the previous day that may have led to Jameson's overnight change of heart. Luke later concluded that the professor had merely become bored with the proceedings.

'Right, let's start from the top, shall we?' Curry launched into his customary attack. 'Your wife was about to piss off with the kids, so you murdered her, right?'

The professor responded with his customary silence.

'You chopped her up, put her head in the oven and fed pieces of her down the bog, correct?'

Silence, except for the chatter of the typewriter.

'We have the head, we have most of the meat, but we're lacking the rest of her. Where did you bury the bones?'

Still nothing but the Olivetti.

'Did you hear me, arsehole? Where are the *fucking bones?*'

'Cornelian Bay Cemetery.'

This time the silence was absolute as Luke's fingers froze above the typewriter's keys. The detectives exchanged a look. Was the man joking? A *cemetery?* Was this another game?

'One of the older plots. One of the ones covered with pebbles, or so he told me.'

'Who told you?'

Jameson ignored Curry and looked over to Luke. 'Good Bradley would rather talk to the sergeant.'

The detectives quickly changed places.

'I made some enquiries as you requested, Sergeant,' the professor said as Luke pulled up a chair and sat opposite.

'You spoke to Bad Bradley?'

'Yes, just last night. It was not a pleasant experience. Bad Bradley can be very rude. He doesn't like Good Bradley. But then the feeling's mutual. Good Bradley doesn't like him either . . .'

'And you asked him where he'd buried the rest of the body?' Luke gently steered the professor back on track.

'I did indeed. He told me in great detail. Would you believe, he actually boasted about it. "A *cemetery*," he said, "isn't that *apt*? Where *else* should one bury the dead?" Those were his exact words and that was his exact tone. He was extraordinarily arrogant. Apparently the pebbles made it easy to disguise the fact that the plot had recently been dug up. At least that's what he told me. "They won't find her in a million years," he said. He was very boastful, very proud of himself.' The professor gave a moue of disapproval. 'Evil, you see. Evil or insane, either or, take your pick. Or perhaps both, or perhaps even neither, all a matter of perception . . .'

Curry had stopped typing and the look in his eyes was murderous. Any moment he'd roar *where are the fucking bones,* Luke thought. He interrupted the professor's rambling as delicately as he could.

'Was Bad Bradley in any way specific about the location, Professor? We wouldn't want to find ourselves digging up every one of the older plots in the cemetery, would we?'

'Oh good heavens above no, Sergeant, there'll be no need for that. Bad Bradley was most precise.' Producing a neatly folded sheet of notepaper from the breast pocket of his shirt, the professor laid it out with great care on the table. 'He drew me a map. There, you see. Fourth plot from the end, second last row, X marks the spot.'

Luke gazed down at the pencil-drawn map. It was meticulous in every detail, even to the name on the tombstone, which was clearly printed beside the circled 'X'.

'I presume that more or less concludes these interviews,' the professor said, folding the map up and handing it to him. 'There really isn't much purpose in their continuance, is there? I shall miss our chats, Sergeant.'

As their eyes met, Luke found himself unable to look away.

'You're a very bright young man. Oh yes, yes. A very bright young man indeed.'

He's congratulating me, Luke thought. *Why?*

'Perhaps in another place, another time, you and I could have become friends.'

The approval in the grey eyes suddenly changed to mockery. Or perhaps it was triumph. Luke couldn't be sure.

'Good Bradley would have liked that,' the professor said.

Three months later, Bradley John Jameson was found not guilty of murder on the grounds of insanity. The findings were read out to the court. He was to be remanded in custody under psychiatric observation at the Governor's pleasure until such time as he was deemed mentally fit to rejoin society.

As the findings were read out, the professor looked across the sea of faces to Luke. Then, just as he was about to be led from the dock, he winked.

A WORD FROM JUDY

Although a work of fiction, 'The House on Hill Street' was inspired by a real event, which did indeed take place at a house on Hill Street, West Hobart, Tasmania.

In 1983 Rory Jack Thompson, a scientist employed by the CSIRO, murdered his wife, Maureen, dismembered her and attempted to flush her body parts down the toilet. He was found not guilty on the grounds of insanity.

My characters are fictional, but the gruesome facts are quite true, I can promise you! Why and how do I know this? Because I had the story 'straight from the horse's mouth', as they say. Police inspector Lee Renshaw (Rtd) was the investigating officer, and he and my husband Bruce (also an ex-copper) were best mates at the time, and still are. Lee's been tremendously helpful, as I'm sure you can imagine, and he doesn't mind my dropping his name as proof of the story's origins.

However, outlandish as this story seems in all its hideous truth, there was one element I dared not include, because I would have been accused of writing something not only frivolous and designed to raise a cheap laugh but utterly beyond belief.

At various stages during the trial of Rory Jack Thompson, his two major legal representatives were Stephen Chopping and Pierre Slicer. Yes. This is true! Lawyers Chopping and Slicer were assigned by the court for the defence of this gruesome case – surely proof without doubt that fact is stranger than fiction.

JUST SOUTH
OF ROME

'You must go to my friend Wendy's restaurant. It's just south of Rome. By the lake. Near the Pope's summer palace. You'll love it.'

That's what Roland had told me. 'Truly, Janie,' he'd said in that rich, fruity BBC voice of his (despite being fourth generation Australian, Roland is a thorough Anglophile), 'it's heaven.' Then he stretched out his legs and leaned back in the sofa, his hands clasped behind his head of impressive silver-grey hair. 'Oh how I envy you the magic of your first European encounter – the enchantment of Tuscany seen for the very first time through youthful eyes!' Roland is so theatrical I've always thought that it was he who should have been the actor, not me.

Ours is a bizarre friendship. Not only is Roland twice my age, he is a romantic. He is flamboyant in every sense of the word, and a confirmed monarchist. I am efficient. I am practical to a fault, and an ardent republican. On occasions we find ourselves in fiery debate, but there's never any real harm done; we always end up laughing. And that, of course, is the true basis of our friendship. We find each other hugely amusing.

'Ah, Janie,' he'll sigh, 'where's your sense of romance; you're far too pragmatic for an actress.' (He deliberately uses the old-fashioned term 'actress' when he knows I prefer 'actor' – I mean, this is 2013 for God's sake!) 'You would have made a very good pharmacist.' Bitchy as such remarks sound, I know he actually respects my work. In fact, it was through a feature article he wrote eight years ago about 'the rising new breed of classic actors in the Australian theatre' (flatteringly including me in my first major role after leaving drama school) that we met. Since then we've agreed to disagree on many aspects of my work, however, most particularly my performance of Hedda Gabler two years ago.

'A thoughtful interpretation, Janie,' he said, 'intelligent and perceptive as always, but too young, my darling, altogether too young.'

'Too young?' I was a little mystified. 'In what way was my Hedda too young?'

'Not your Hedda, darling, *you*. *You* were too young. The great classic roles are the preserve of actresses in their thirties. Hedda needs more *weight*, more *depth*, more *maturity* . . .'

The superior way he hammered his nouns home irritated me, and that infuriating reference to actresses! Does he do it simply because he's old-fashioned or because he knows it drives me mad? I have often suspected the latter, although Roland's views on casting are so distinctly old-fashioned I do begin to wonder. Twenty-seven is hardly too young for Hedda – perhaps in his time, but certainly not these days. In fact, twenty-seven is the perfect age for Hedda. I didn't retaliate, of course, knowing I'd only be offering him further ammunition and that he'd smile condescendingly and accuse me of being 'a tad on the defensive'.

Maddening though Roland can be, he has continued to have a profound effect on my life, probably because in the face of my occasional negativity, he can be so damned positive – as he was just two months ago.

'It's the opportunity of a lifetime, Janie,' he urged. 'It's a gateway to the career you've always dreamed of, treading the boards of the finest theatres in the world.'

'It's a pantomime, Roland,' I said drily. 'It's *Snow White and the Seven Dwarfs* at the Pavilion in Bournemouth.'

'And Bournemouth is a train ride from London and the West End,' he replied, exasperated, 'and you now have an English agent!'

'I somehow doubt that an agent who books Australian soap actors for British pantos is likely to land very many West End contracts,' I said, this time with a distinctly cynical edge.

Roland took a deep breath. I could be as maddening to him as he could be to me. 'Now you listen to me, Janie. You'll be thirty next year,' (he simply had to remind me, didn't he?) 'and the British theatre is not as obsessed with extreme youth as is the Australian theatre. This is the decade when you're destined to come into your full strength as an actress,' (no comment) 'and you owe it to yourself to seize such an opportunity with both hands.'

The panto offer had been the direct result of a six-month stint I'd done in a highly successful soap opera (which the network always referred to as a 'drama series', but which was a soap opera nonetheless) that was even more popular in Britain than it was in Australia, and don't ask me how, but after a further ten minutes' haranguing, Roland's enthusiasm started to make inroads. I actually found myself excited by the prospect of what might lie ahead if I chose to go to London after the panto closed. I'd been well-established in the Australian theatre for the past five years, but thirty was looming and perhaps Roland was right. Perhaps now was the time to make my bid for a career on the London stage, the Mecca of theatre for any serious actor.

Over the ensuing weeks, Roland had further advice. Indeed, reliving his youth, he never let up. 'Travel,' he urged. 'Devour the riches of the world, Janie! Drink your fill of life while you're young!' On and on he went, fanning the flames of my own longings. Why not? I asked myself. Why not leave Sydney six weeks earlier than planned, hire a car and drive around Italy? The whole boot – from the Alps to Naples.

Then finally . . . 'You will promise me, won't you?' His parting words at the airport. 'Castel Gandalfo, just south of Rome. Wendy's restaurant is near the palace, by the lake, you can't miss it . . .'

For two weeks now I had travelled the Italian countryside in my little Hertz Honda. I had braved the terrors of high-speed alpine motorways where everyone drives on the wrong side of the road. I had plunged without warning into black tunnels carved through the hearts of mountains. I had negotiated the narrow laneways of medieval villages and dodged the bee-like swarms of Lambrettas in the messy, lane-less streets of cities. And for the whole two weeks I had stopped dutifully to visit every duomo, every castle, every Roman ruin.

I would finally take Roland's advice, I decided. I would visit his friend Wendy's restaurant. I had earned it. Wendy was English. She had married an Italian and they had run the restaurant for seven years now. Wendy would know the area thoroughly, I told myself. Wendy would direct me to a nearby hotel, a comfortable one where I could rest up and gather my forces before the assault on Rome. Merely circling Rome from the north had been confusing enough. To plunge deep into the very core of the city was a terrifying prospect. But I would do it. Alone. Armed with nothing but my dozen or so Italian words and my, by now, well-refined talent for mime, I was determined.

But, in the meantime, I would find Wendy and her restaurant. I would finally talk English and exchange stories of mutual friends, and regardless of budget I would spend two nights in a highly recommended hotel where I would soak in my own ensuite bathtub and have my breakfast delivered by room service at eleven o'clock. No pensione with the bathroom up a flight of stairs and three doors to the right. No gathering at the communal table for seven o'clock breakfast and enquiries as to the whereabouts of the nearest architectural wonder.

*

'*No parla Inglese.*'

It was a bit of a surprise but, undeterred, I soldiered on. 'Your *moglie,* Wendy, *si?*' I knew the word for wife.

'*Si, mio moglie Wendy. No parla Inglese.*'

Damn. I knew I should have rung first. I knew I shouldn't have just landed at the restaurant. But I'd become so proud of my prowess at finding my way around that I hadn't been able to resist the challenge. I hadn't even known the address – Roland had given me Wendy's name and phone number only. So I'd headed for the Pope's summer palace, parked the car, walked for half an hour or so and bingo, there it was, '*Ristorante del Lago*', a cosy little trattoria with a vine-covered balcony that overlooked the lake. Everything had gone beautifully to plan. I'd eaten bruschetta, sipped a glass of wine and waited comfortably among the vines, savouring the smell of fresh garlic and admiring the view, until Wendy's husband, Bruno, had arrived. Wendy wasn't coming to the restaurant today, the waiter, who spoke a little English, had informed me. But Bruno would be here soon.

Now here was Bruno. '*No parla Inglese,*' he insisted a third time.

'Oh. Well . . . *Mio amico* – Wendy *amico,*' I said, miming 'old pals'.

'Ah.' He nodded but didn't look remotely interested and, before I could dredge up another word or two of my abominable Italian, to my utter horror he walked away.

I was starting to feel distinctly embarrassed. Also a little confused. Wendy had been married to her Italian for over thirty years, Roland had told me, how come Bruno didn't speak English?

'I've never met the husband,' Roland had said. 'Can't remember his name, but I'm sure he's very nice. Wendy's adorable – you'll love her.'

Roland and Wendy had been pals in London in their early twenties when he'd made the mandatory trip that all Australians of artistic persuasion did in those days. They either headed to Paris to paint or to London to break into the theatre (which was exactly what I was doing, so I suppose some things don't change) or to Italy to write. Roland was a writer. At least he is now. Those early days in London I think he was a jack of all trades. Wendy was an English actor – well, an aspiring one anyway – who was waiting tables in a Soho restaurant, and I suspect that's how they met. I have a distinct feeling that Roland was waiting tables too, although he prefers to paint that period of his life with a little more bohemian colour.

'Oh how Wendy and I knew London,' he went on with a wistful sigh. 'The London of the seventies, the hub of the world, ours for the asking . . .'

I didn't enquire too deeply into what they asked for or what was returned upon request. It sounded a little overly idyllic to me. Roland is a product of the fifties with a baby-boomer mentality, and I've always found baby-boomers' romanticism of the seventies a touch suspect.

'Now don't give me that cynical look of yours, Janie. Wendy and I may be twenty or so years older than you,' (thirty, actually – Roland will be sixty next year) 'but we "did our thing" just as you're about to do yours. And we certainly didn't have the luxury of cruising around Europe in cars.' (Luxury? Cruising?) 'We couldn't afford to hire cars. We backpacked and hitchhiked and hopped trains when we had the money.'

As usual, just when he started sounding like my father, Roland stopped. 'Honestly, sweetheart, you'll love Wendy. She may be approaching sixty but underneath, like me, she's really twenty-nine. And you may be twenty-nine but underneath you're really approaching sixty, so the two of you are bound to get on.'

He studied me for a second. 'You even look a bit alike. I suppose it's the fair hair and the good legs.' Then he added, 'Mind you, Wendy was a true beauty when she was young.'

I barked a laugh by way of reply, but he continued unperturbed. 'Oh, "interesting" is a much better look, believe me, and you're far more talented than Wendy ever was. You'll adore her, I promise. Do look her up.'

Well, I'd done my best, I thought, as I watched Bruno at the front desk chatting animatedly to a departing guest. At least I'd met the husband. Or had I? A horrifying thought occurred to me. Was it possible there were two restaurateurs in Castel Gandolfo, each with a wife named Wendy?

'*Il conto per favore.*' (One of the only Italian phrases I could muster in full.) The waiter nodded towards Bruno and I approached the front desk with money in hand.

When Bruno shook his head, my minor embarrassment turned to utter humiliation. 'No, no, please,' I insisted. Had he thought I was seeking special favours? Had he pinned on me the worst possible label for an Australian? That of 'bludger'.

'*Mio amico* Roland from Australia – he tell me Wendy and he . . .' I was getting desperate, gesticulating hand to heart, pointing somewhere in the direction of Australia and generally carrying on like a demented clown.

'*Si*. Wendy.' Bruno nodded. 'Wendy *domani*.' And he turned to greet the arrival of a fresh group of noisy guests.

My face crimson, I pocketed my money, fled the restaurant and, while I walked the kilometre or so to the car, cursed Roland every step of the way. Why, oh why, had I decided to stop off at his friend Wendy's restaurant just south of Rome! Why, oh why, hadn't I kept on driving! I knew it was my own fault for having arrived unannounced, but there was no way I was coming back '*domani*' to address the problem. What if they thought I wanted to freeload again? What if she really wasn't the right Wendy?

So much for my 'highly recommended' local hotel – I must find my own.

Castelvecchio, a kilometre down the road. Four star, very grand-looking. Yes, I'd drown my humiliation in a hot bath and a stiff gin and tonic there. No rooms. '*Hotel complete*,' I was told.

Miralago Hotel further down the road. Not so grand but I told myself 'picturesque' was good enough. No rooms. '*Hotel complete.*'

Out of Castel Gandalfo. The next town. Albano. Two more hotels. No rooms. '*Hotel complete.*' It's late afternoon. A touch of desperation. The next town. Genzano di Roma.

And that's when I find it, the Hotel Visconti, a once-proud villa on a hill less than a kilometre from the town's central piazza. Upon the discovery of the Hotel Visconti, the Wendy-Bruno mystery paled into insignificance.

~

As I drove my Hertz Honda through the large, stone, arched entrance and parked beside the blue Mercedes that sat in the centre of the gravel courtyard, I wondered whether I could afford the Hotel Visconti. The sign above the arch had four stars beside it (my absolute limit), but it looked suspiciously five to me, a grand hotel – the sort that Roland visited every now and then.

Beyond the courtyard was a rambling garden, complete with fountain and statues, and, to the side, marble steps led up to the ornate doors of an impressive villa I judged to be mid-eighteenth century.

What the hell, I thought. I was desperate and I was booking in. It was after five o'clock, I'd been searching for a hotel for nearly four hours, and damn it I was going to have my two nights of luxury.

'*Buonasera signora*,' I said in my best Italian.

'Good evening. Welcome to the Hotel Visconti.' A woman in her mid-forties, short dark hair, a stocky figure in a well-cut suit, glasses and an intelligent face bordering on handsome smiled efficiently across the reception desk.

'Do you have a room? Preferably with a view of the gardens?' Forget the Italian, the woman's English was excellent.

'You are lucky. We have left one room. Large. A double room. Very beautiful.' She had already produced the reg-istration form and was thrusting a pen at me. 'We have a party of Americans staying. It is our last room. You are very fortunate. Your passport?'

I wanted to ask the price of the room but, as I was so very fortunate, it didn't seem in the best of taste. Besides, the woman's manner, brisk and authoritative, had momentarily daunted me, so I did as I was told and handed over my passport.

While she flipped through it, I glanced about. The grand staircase was gilt-finished and opulent, and the dining room, glimpsed through glass doors to the left, was spacious and elegant. I also noted, however, that the carpets had seen better days and that the gold frame of the huge mirror behind the reception desk was flaking a little here and there. Perhaps it wouldn't be too expensive after all. There was no-one else in sight and, as I filled in the registration form, wondering vaguely where the Americans were, my eyes strayed around the counter trying to find the tariff list. There it was. The woman had turned away to select a collection of leaflets from the shelves behind her, and I edged down the counter. 'Suite €350,' it read. Hell! Then underneath: 'Double Room €300.' Damn! It was still fifty euros over the absolute limit I had allowed myself for the odd night of indulgence.

'Tear it up,' the voice of thrift said to me. 'Tear up the registration form, grab your passport, say "so sorry, made a mistake" and get the hell out of here.' But a voice that sounded suspiciously like Roland was telling me 'Let go! Give in! Abandon yourself!' Finally, it was neither Roland nor thrift that won. It was the voice of reason that told me I was in no situation to do anything other than give

in and that Rome would have to be the cheapest pensione
I could find.

'I have here for you some information.' The woman had
turned back and was spreading a number of leaflets out
before me. 'This is a beautiful part of Italy, many pretty
towns. Nemi is very famous for its straw berries.' She gave
equal emphasis to the two words, which confused me for
a second until I glanced down at the leaflet sporting a big,
fat, red strawberry above the name 'Nemi'.

'But our town of Genzano is the most beautiful,' she continued without drawing breath, it was obviously her sales
pitch. 'Our town of Genzano is famous for its flowers.
You see?' She picked up the leaflet that read 'Genzano di
Roma' and, above the name, was a photograph of a street
completely blanketed with floral displays of the most intricate design. 'The festival of the flowers,' she said proudly.
'So beautiful. The flowers, they cover the main street, from
the piazza all the way up the hill to the church. For two
days of every year we have the festival. For two days of
every year people they come from everywhere to see. You
have just missed it.' She thrust a key at me. 'Room 22
at the top of the stairs. Welcome to the Hotel Visconti.'
Another efficient smile, a brisk nod, and she picked up a
mobile phone and disappeared.

I looked around the deserted reception area. Had she
gone to get a porter? I waited for a few minutes, decided
she hadn't and, when the lift didn't work, lugged my
suitcase up the grand staircase.

Room 22 didn't overlook the gardens as I'd hoped – it
overlooked the main street. I pushed open the wooden

shutters and leaned out as far as I dared. To the left, the road turned a corner and dipped out of sight behind a Shell petrol station. To the right, it stretched a kilometre or so into the town and beyond. Up the hill, at the very far end, I could just see the church, its white steps glinting in the last of the late-afternoon sun. This was the street featured on the front of the leaflet, I realised. This was the street that, for two days a year, was decked in flowers from the piazza to the church. I squinted into the distance. It didn't look at all the same without the flowers.

Plenty of time to explore the town tomorrow. I closed the shutters and turned my attention to the room. It was a nice room, painted cream, big and light and airy, with a high ceiling and a large brass bedstead, but it was somewhat characterless compared to the rest of the Hotel Visconti. The ensuite bathroom was adequate, but I certainly would have expected more for €350 a night. There was no shower recess, just a curtain on a circular railing so that one showered on the floor. The whole setup was clean and fairly new-looking, so I gathered that they had recently refurbished the place and done it as cheaply as possible. A pity, really. Were the other rooms as bland as this, I wondered. What about the €400 suite?

There was a tap at the door. I opened it. '*Buonasera signorina*, you wish to see my suite?'

A short, middle-aged Italian man in a three-piece pin-stripe suit stood there. He had incredibly black hair, a little moustache and looked like Charlie Chaplin's 'tramp' gone badly to seed. I was shocked. See his suite? Had he read my thoughts?

'I beg your pardon?'

'Welcome to Hotel Visconti. I am Umberto Visconti, I own this hotel, you wish to see my suite?'

'Umm . . .' Was it a proposition? He certainly looked like an aging roué.

Sensing my confusion, he added 'Annita say you are from Australia.'

The efficient woman materialised behind him at the top of the stairs. 'From Sydney,' she said. 'She is an actress from Sydney.' The mobile phone was pressed to her ear and she carried a pile of fresh towels under one arm. 'I am sorry,' she said to the mobile phone as she disappeared down the corridor, 'there are no more rooms, we have a party of Americans staying.'

'You will like my suite,' Umberto promised. 'It is very grand.'

I was irritated that Annita was broadcasting the contents of my passport (which said 'actor', not 'actress' anyway) and my reply was a little snappy. 'I'm quite happy with my room, thank you, Signor Visconti.' There was no way I was forking out €400.

'Umberto, please. I am Umberto.' He beamed bonhomie, offered his hand and shook mine effusively.

'Jane,' I was forced to respond. 'Jane Prescott.'

'You no hire the suite. Is *my* suite. Come, I show you.'

He took my arm and bustled me across the landing to the lift. I didn't even have time to close the door to my room but, as there didn't seem to be anyone about, I supposed it didn't matter. I was confused: If he didn't want me to hire the suite, why did he want to show it to me? And if it was his personal suite, what was his motive? But, despite his extraordinary appearance, there didn't appear to be anything particularly threatening about him, so I allowed myself to be led into the lift.

'It doesn't work,' I said, a trifle sullen, as he pressed the third floor button and nothing happened.

Umberto appeared not to hear me. He bashed the button hard. Twice. The lift shuddered, gave a slight cough and started grinding upwards.

'I like Australia,' he was saying. 'I have a cousin, he live in Melbourne. My cousin, he write for *Il Globo*, you know *Il Globo*?' I shook my head. The speed at which Umberto spoke was alarming and his accent was so thick it was difficult to follow. 'Is a newspaper for Italians, I write an article about the festival of the flowers and I send it to my cousin, it is published in *Il Globo*. Is very good,' he said proudly. 'I have a copy, I show you.'

All the while, I was studying him as discreetly as possible. What was it that made his appearance so extraordinary? Certainly the thatch of dyed black hair, which sat on his head like a large dead cat, contributed. Then I realised that not only was his hair dyed, but his eyebrows and moustache were as well. Clumps of pitch-black hair sat above his eyes and his upper lip as if they'd been pasted on. The man was a caricature.

The monologue continued as we stepped out of the lift. 'I inherit this hotel from my aunt, she is very beautiful, si?' I realised he meant the hotel as he stroked the railings of the grand staircase. 'This. The original gilt, you know?' His fingers lovingly traced the golden leaf design. 'Is beautiful, *si*?'

'Yes, very beautiful.'

'Now you see my suite.' He produced a key from his vest pocket and proceeded to unlock the door at the top of the stairs, the same position as mine two storeys below. 'Is even more beautiful.' He stepped in and held his arms out wide. 'Venezia design!' he announced loudly. Then he sighed and wandered about the room, caressing the sideboard and the mantelpiece and the four-poster bed with a lover's touch. 'Ah, so beautiful.'

I stood at the door, still a little unsure as to whether I might need an escape route, but Umberto's performance was so unashamedly theatrical that I was not alarmed. He was an atrocious actor, I decided. I had known a number of atrocious actors, all of whom were harmless, so I relaxed and looked around the 'suite'.

It wasn't a suite at all. It was a room, of exactly the same dimensions as mine downstairs, but where mine had been stripped of all character, here every intricate detail had been painstakingly preserved. The ceiling was pure rococo, a swirling pattern of leaves in aqua and gold. In fact, everywhere was aqua and gold – the carved mantelpiece and sideboard and dressing table, the four-poster bed with two gold cherubs above the bedhead. Even the lace curtains were trimmed with aqua and gold. There was a central crystal chandelier, and other gold cherubs leaned out from the walls holding imitation candles in their chubby hands. It looked like a garish movie set and reminded me of pictures I'd seen of the interior of one of Mad King Ludwig's castles in Bavaria, a museum piece, nothing out of place and not a shred of evidence as to its occupation. Did Umberto really live here?

He turned on the light switch and the cherubs' candles glowed. 'Is beautiful, *si*?'

'Yes,' I found my voice. 'Beautiful.' Then I noticed the utterly incongruous picture on the wall beside the bed. It was a framed photograph, in colour, of Omar Sharif as Doctor Zhivago.

'Ah, you see my old friend Omar,' Umberto said proudly, crossing to stand beside the photograph – he'd quite obviously been waiting for me to notice it. 'He come here whenever he want to get away from the world. He ring me and he say "Umberto, I want your suite."'

Umberto patted the photograph. 'Omar, he a famous man,' then he patted his chest, 'and my friend. My friend the famous actor, *si*?'

He was grinning like a Cheshire cat by now, and I realised that he was simply an incorrigible show-off. He probably didn't live in the suite at all, I thought. He probably just showed it off to all his guests, together with his picture of Omar Sharif, a publicity shot from a film made close to fifty years ago.

I grinned back. It was all so ridiculous I couldn't help it. 'Very impressive,' I said.

'Come. You see my suite, now we have a drink before dinner.'

I found myself warming to Umberto – it was impossible not to – and after begging off for half an hour to unpack and freshen up I met him in the downstairs bar.

It was a poky little bar. The glass counter displaying bottles of wine, the several Laminex-topped tables and the little wooden chairs completely out of keeping with the general ambience of the Hotel Visconti. But then I was rapidly realising that the Hotel Visconti was a series of contradictions. Had they run out of money halfway through refurbishing?

It was cosy, nonetheless, and Umberto was determined to make me feel at home amongst the several people gathered there.

'You meet Annita.' He rose from his table and waved at the efficient woman, who stood behind the counter. Annita gave one of her brisk smiles and continued to hurl Italian invective at whoever was on the receiving end of the mobile phone still attached to her ear.

'And here Rosella,' Umberto placed a proprietorial hand on the shoulder of the young woman seated beside him, 'my beautiful Rosella.' He beamed a mixture of lechery and pride.

'I'm Jane, how do you do.' I offered my hand.

'You are Australia,' she said, shaking my hand, bobbing her head, wriggling in her seat and flashing me an electric smile all at the same time. 'From Syd-en-ee.'

'Yes, that's right.' She did look like a rosella, I thought. The multicoloured silk cocktail dress she wore reminded me of the vivid crimson-and-green lorikeets and rosella parrots we used to feed by hand during my childhood holidays on the Central Coast.

A young girl of about seventeen, wearing a maid's cap and a frilly apron, was wiping down the table and replacing the ashtray. 'This Sarina,' Umberto said, 'she speak no English.'

The girl smiled a brief, apologetic smile and ducked as quickly as she could behind the bar. My gaze followed her involuntarily, as anyone's would – Sarina was a true beauty, a young, radiant Ingrid Bergman.

'She is shy,' Umberto said and the girl flushed with embarrassment, 'but she work hard and she is learning from me good English, yes Sarina?' The girl nodded and lowered her glorious eyes to wipe a non-existent stain from the counter. 'You see? She understand English, she just no speak it.'

'How do you do, I'm Jane.' I offered my hand to the remaining person seated at the table in order to divert the attention from Sarina. He was a rather good-looking man in his late twenties, but his handshake was disappointingly weak.

'This Rosella's husband, Natale.' Umberto's tone was rather dismissive, and Natale half-rose and sat again. Rosella's husband? I was surprised, I had assumed that Rosella was Umberto's exclusive property. His hand still rested on her bare skin, one arm of the low-cut lorikeet dress having slipped provocatively off her shoulder.

'What you like to drink?' Umberto demanded, and I looked around the table to see what the others were having. A demitasse coffee cup sat in front of Umberto, Natale was drinking a beer, and Rosella sipped at something bright green.

'A gin and tonic would be lovely. Thank you.'

'Annita!' he called loudly, although she was only several yards away, 'a gin and tonic for my good friend Jane,' and he pulled up a chair, settling me in between him and Natale.

Rosella leaned over the table, displaying a handsome cleavage. 'You are famous?' she asked, her kohl-blackened eyes wide with excitement, '*Si?*'

'No,' I said.

'*Si*, I think so.' She didn't believe me and gave a con-spiratorial wink to prove it. 'You are . . . how you say? . . . "*modesto*". You are actress. All actress is famous.'

'I prefer "actor", actually.' I knew I sounded unfriendly and cursed myself, but Annita's broadcasting of my personal details once again annoyed me, and Rosella's girlish sex-kitten act aroused a further flash of irritation.

Neither hurt nor insulted, Rosella waited for me to go on in breathless anticipation. My remark had clearly been of great interest.

'That's a very pretty dress, Rosella.' It was my gauche attempt at an apology. 'Lovely colours.'

'*Si*, very pretty.' She wriggled and giggled and glowed at the compliment. 'Is silk. You touch.' She hitched the fallen sleeve back onto her shoulder and leaned across the table so that I could feel the fabric.

'Very sexy.' I smiled. She wriggled and giggled and glowed again with a delight that was obviously genuine, and I realised that perhaps I'd misjudged her. Perhaps it wasn't an act at all. But then I'd always been awkward with overtly feminine women.

Annita put my gin and tonic on the table in front of me. The tonic was flat and there was no ice, but I decided not to say anything. As I raised the glass to my lips, she said, quite loudly, 'You wish me to put it on your bill?'

'Oh.' A little nonplussed, I glanced at Umberto, who had quite obviously heard her. But Umberto grinned his inane moustache-twitching, eyebrow-raising grin and lifted his demitasse cup in silent salute. 'Yes, of course,'

I said to Annita, 'put it on my bill.' Then, as she turned to go, 'Do you think I could have some ice?'

'Ice.' She froze, staring at the glass I held in my hand. 'Oh, *si*.' She came to life. 'Ice, yes, of course. Ice.' She headed back to the bar. 'Sarina, *ghiaccio*.' Sarina looked equally stunned. '*Cucina*,' Annita hissed, '*cucina*,' and Sarina hurriedly left the bar.

'To my friend, Jane, the famous actress from Sydney.' Umberto clinked his coffee cup against my glass. 'Welcome to the Hotel Visconti.' The others followed suit – 'welcome to Genzano di Roma', 'welcome to Italia' – and we clinked glasses around the table.

'Thank you. Thank you very much.' I sipped the gin and tonic. It was warm.

Something was very odd, I thought, as the others chatted in rapid-fire Italian and I was left to take in my surrounds. Rosella and Natale were obviously friends of Umberto's – well, Rosella was anyway – so where were the hotel guests? Given that the party of Americans were off doing whatever a party of Americans did in Genzano di Roma, where were the other guests? There *were* other guests, surely? And staff. Annita the receptionist and Sarina the maid were the only hotel staff I'd seen. Annita kept disappearing with her mobile phone and Sarina, having returned to deposit a saucer with two small cubes of ice before me, had also disappeared.

'*Grazie*,' I said just before she darted off.

'*Prego*.' She bobbed a curtsy and was gone.

It was weird, and I was about to query Umberto when there was a commotion at the front door. People arriving.

A lot of people. A woman's voice. Very loud, very brash. 'My, my Father Ralph, that was some day. That was some day. My, my!' Then other female voices reverberated until there was nothing but a hen-like babble as the women surged into the reception area.

'The Americans!' Umberto jumped up from the table and vanished in a second. '*Signoras!*' I heard him call before his voice was swallowed up by the babble.

'The Americans.' Rosella looked at Natale and they, too, rose and left.

I sat alone in the little bar with the remnants of my gin and tonic and wondered what I should do.

'Ladies!' A strong male voice with an American accent. 'Ladies! Ladies!' And the babble died down. 'Umberto informs me, dinner at half past seven. The dining room in a half hour, if you please!' It started again, the babble, rising to a crescendo as the women made for the stairs.

I decided I'd wait for ten minutes then duck into the dining room before they came downstairs. That way I could order my meal in peace before the onslaught. That was probably what the other guests were doing, I thought. Yes, of course! That would explain it. The other hotel guests were dining early to avoid the Americans.

I rose and studied the bottles of wine on display behind the glass counter. Maybe I'd treat myself to a really good red with dinner. I could drink half, have the waiter re-cork it and save the rest for tomorrow night. It was an impressive-looking collection. Mostly French. ''78 Burgundy,' I read. ''82 Bordeaux'. I knew nothing of European wines, only the wonderful Australian reds Roland had introduced me to, but wine with an age like that would have to be magnificent, surely. Magnificent price too, I assumed, chastising myself. I'd look at the wine list and settle on a bottle of local red instead.

The hubbub had died down. The last slamming of upstairs doors. Silence. Time to go to the dining room.

〜

The dining room was as elegant as I'd imagined it would be from my glimpse through the glass doors. A big room with high ceilings, a sea of white-clothed tables beneath a vast crystal chandelier, an impressive floral display on a central pedestal and, here and there, large terracotta tubs with lush green plants.

To the left, a small dance floor and three long banquet tables, I presumed for the Americans, and to the right, tables set for smaller parties. Also to the right, adjacent to the swinging doors which I presumed led to the kitchen, was a servery table with huge bain-maries and baskets of bread.

Two sets of French windows on the opposite wall opened out onto the terrace. They were closed now, as the night outside was gloomy and overcast, but the floodlit view beyond of the garden's fountains and statues and vines was enchanting.

It was a beautiful dining room. Only one thing was wrong. It was deserted. Deserted and silent – not a sound from behind the swinging doors, no sign of movement at all. I stood there, uncertain. Should I tap on the doors to the kitchen? No, I decided, I would commandeer the table closest to the French windows and enjoy the view until somebody noticed me. But, before I could do so, the swinging doors opened and a young man in a white apron and a large chef's hat appeared.

'Ah. Good evening,' I said, relieved, 'may I have the table there by the windows? I know it's set for four, but . . .'

He looked at me blankly, took off his chef's hat, folded it and put it in the large front pocket of his apron. Then, without a word, he left, undoing his apron strings as he went.

Very odd, I thought as I positioned myself by the windows.

I studied the menu. It was comprehensive and tantalising. By now I was starving, having eaten nothing since the lunchtime bruschetta at Wendy and Bruno's restaurant in Castel Gandalfo. I looked for the wine list but there wasn't one, and I must have sat there for a full five minutes before the doors once again swung open and Sarina, the maid, appeared. She didn't see me as she scurried towards the main doors of the dining room.

'*Scusi*,' I called.

'Oh.' She turned, startled.

'Sarina, *buonasera*.' I smiled encouragingly. I was about to ask her if she could send the waiter when I noticed that she'd changed. She was wearing a black skirt and white blouse, and a small white apron was tied around her waist. She scuttled over, taking an order pad from the pocket of her apron.

'*Si?*' she asked as she stood nervously beside me, and I realised that she was the waitress.

'May I have the wine list?' I knew it would confuse her so I picked a wine glass up from the table and mimed sipping from it. 'Wine ...' I said and tapped the menu with my other hand, 'list.'

'Ah. *Si*.'

She scuttled off again. She always scuttled. Someone so startlingly pretty really shouldn't scuttle, I thought. And two minutes later she was back with a carafe of water, which she placed on my table.

I realised she'd misunderstood. Time to muster my abominable Italian. '*Acqua ... bene ... grazie*,' I said. 'But, *vino* ...' I tapped the wine glass, 'list.' I tapped the menu again – I had no idea what the word for 'list' could be – '*per favore*.'

'Ah, *vino, si*.'

She disappeared once again and I wondered what to expect next. She'd probably reappear with a glass of house wine, but by now I didn't care. By now, my stomach was rumbling and food was the most important thing – I must get my order in before the Americans arrived.

But Sarina didn't reappear. It was Annita who bustled efficiently out from the kitchen.

'Wine,' she said. 'You wish to have some wine.'

'Yes, thank you, Annita. If I could see the wine list.'

Again, that blank look. 'The wine list?'

'That's right, the wine list.'

'Ah. The wine list, yes, of course.' She started to go but I called her back.

'Perhaps I could order first.' She turned and stared at me. There really was something daunting about the woman. I smiled apologetically, 'If that would be all right, I'm very hungry.'

I opened the menu and she leaned over me, her eyes focussed on my finger as I pointed out my choices. 'I'd like the *bistecca*, please . . .' I hadn't had a steak once since I'd been in Italy; '*bistecca*' was always the most expensive item on Italian menus. Now on my night of luxury, having decided to satisfy my Aussie red-meat lust, I was positively drooling at the prospect, 'And I'd like the *spinaci*.' The perfect meal. I adored the way Italians did spinach, rich and creamy.

I looked up expecting one of her brisk, no-nonsense nods, but her eyes were still focussed on my finger.

'The *bistecca* with *spinaci*,' I said firmly, closing the menu. 'Thank you.'

'The chef . . .' she said uncertainly, and it was the first time I had seen a chink in her efficient armour. 'The chef is sick.' I was at a loss for words. I stared back at her and I think my jaw gaped a little. Then she stood to attention, her armour back in place.

'But everything is good,' she announced. 'One moment please.' And she marched off.

Only seconds later, Umberto himself arrived from the kitchen.

'*Buonasera, bella signorina* Jane!' It was the full performance. He beamed, clutched his heart, took my hand in his and closed his eyes in ecstasy. '*Ah bella, bella signorina.*' He bowed low, pressed my hand to his lips so that I could feel the tickle of his absurd moustache and kissed it.

'Good evening, Umberto,' I said pleasantly, withdrawing my hand. 'I'd like to order my meal and see the wine list.'

'Ah, for you I have special.' He winked and the opposite eyebrow shot up alarmingly. 'For my famous friend Jane, actress from Australia, I have special wine from my very own cellar. You like a beautiful *vino rosso*, eh? Very good, very old, *si*?'

'Well . . .' Of course I would, but what was he going to charge me?

Umberto read the reason for my hesitation in an instant. 'Special price for my friend Jane. Other people €30, for you €25 only.'

What the hell, I thought, extravagant as it might be by my normal budget standards, forty dollars for a bottle of red the likes of which I'd seen behind the glass counter was an excellent price. 'Thank you, Umberto,' I said, picking up the menu, 'and I'd like to order the *bistecca* and . . .'

'No, no, no . . .' He winced as he took the menu from me. 'You no want the *bistecca* . . .'

'Yes, I do . . .'

'No, no, no, for you I do Umberto special. I create for you my special dish. My pasta al –'

'No thank you . . .' I was going to stand firm. I'd lived on pasta for weeks now, I was salivating for meat, and meat I was going to have.

'*Three* special dishes. All Umberto's secret recipes. I create just for you.'

'Thank you all the same, Umberto.' I didn't want to be hurtful but I was determined. 'I really do want –'

'Jane, my friend. Jane . . .' He sat beside me and clasped my hand in both of his. 'Never do I have in Hotel Visconti a famous actress from Australia.' Before I could interrupt, he held my hand to his chest and continued. 'I want I should create something special for you. Please you let me.' I could swear there was the glint of a tear in his eye. 'Then you go home to your country and you tell them Umberto he make the greatest dish you eat in the whole of Italy.'

For some unknown reason, I thought of the photograph of Omar Sharif in the upstairs bedroom and Umberto's proud boast of their friendship, and something in the ridiculous man's need to impress touched me. I heard myself say, 'Thank you, Umberto, I would love to try your special dishes.'

'Ah!' He kissed my hand again and jumped to his feet, overjoyed. 'Never will you taste such food. Never! I bring your wine.'

I cursed myself as he left but, dismissing the image of a succulent steak from my mind, I told myself that perhaps Umberto's special dishes really would be a sensation and that it was all part of the adventure and that Roland would approve. But I'd been manipulated nonetheless, and I didn't like being manipulated.

Several minutes later he returned with the wine. He showed me the bottle: French, a '98 Burgundy. It looked impressive. But it was already open. And there was no cork. Surely he should have opened it at the table, I thought, but I didn't say anything as he poured me a full glass. No taster. I was surprised that the flamboyant

Umberto wasn't making a more showy presentation of the special wine from his private cellar.

'Do you have the cork, Umberto?'

'Eh?' The bottle remained poised for a moment.

'The cork, do you have it? I'd like to save some of the wine for tomorrow.'

'Ah, the cork. *Si*, sure, sure.' He finished pouring, placed the bottle on the table and clapped his hands together in delight. 'You enjoy, is beautiful, is –'

Loud voices. Heavy footsteps on the stairs. The herd was approaching. As Umberto made a dash for the main doors, I sniffed my wine and took the first reverent sip, preparing myself for the ultimate sensation.

I sipped. I put down the glass. I stared disbelievingly at the bottle. The wine was thin and bitter and instantly reminded me of the cheap cardboard cask reds we used to buy when I was a student at drama school.

I looked at the bottle. '98 Burgundy? Impossible, surely. Perhaps it had been badly corked. Perhaps it had gone off. Perhaps ... Umberto had brought the bottle to the table already opened ... perhaps ... No, of course he wouldn't do such a thing. I sipped the wine again; it was certainly no worse than the cardboard cask reds and, face it, I wouldn't know what a '98 Burgundy tasted like anyway.

I took a large mouthful (I was paying for it, I might as well drink it) and studied the Americans as they thundered through the doors. All thirty-eight of them as I later discovered.

I had never seen so many big women. The two or three tiny ones amongst them only emphasised the heftiness of the others. Predominantly in their late fifties and early sixties, they were healthy, beefy, bosomy and loud, and looked for all the world like a convention of amiable truck drivers in drag. And they were having a whale of a time. I wondered who they were and what had brought them to Genzano di Roma.

'*Signoras*, welcome. Welcome.' A beaming Umberto stood by the door, waving them in and kissing a hand here and there.

'You come sit next to me and Amy-Lou, Father Ralph.' It was the same voice I'd heard bellowing from the reception area a half an hour ago. The first woman through the doors, one of the biggest of the group and obviously the leader of the pack, plonked herself at the top of the banquet table nearest to me and pulled out the chairs on either side. 'Come along now, come along, Amy-Lou.'

The only young member among them, a pretty-faced, huge girl in her mid-twenties sat beside the woman, and it was obvious at a glance that they were mother and daughter. They were joined by a handsome, sixty-something clergyman who looked Italian but spoke American. 'Happy to, Mary-Jane, happy to . . .' The other women took it as their cue and, with much good-humoured jostling, the scramble for seats was on.

Umberto disappeared into the kitchen and there was a flurry of activity in and out of the swinging doors. Sarina and Annita kept reappearing with huge plates of food, which they placed under the silver-domed lids of the bain-maries on the servery table.

I continued to study the women, fascinated as they ripped into their bread rolls, laughed and hollered from table to table.

'For you.' Umberto was beside me, a steaming bowl of pasta in his hands. He placed it ceremoniously on the table. 'Umberto special, for my famous friend Jane.'

'Thank you, Umberto. It looks delicious.' It didn't. Not to me anyway. It was a marinara dish, and I've never liked seafood with pasta. But I couldn't tell him that, I didn't want to hurt his feelings. I wondered how I could get rid of it without his knowing.

Umberto smacked his lips around his fingers, blew a kiss into the air and disappeared once more into the kitchen.

I managed to catch Annita's attention as she placed a giant bowl of salad on the servery table. I called her over.

'You wish for something?'

'Yes, thank you, Annita. I wonder ... um ... you see, Umberto is preparing two more of his special dishes for me, and if I eat this,' I gestured at the marinara, 'um ... well ... I won't have room for –'

'You do not want the marinara?'

'Well, I'm sure it's lovely, but –'

'I take it away.' Unperturbed, she picked up the dish.

'I don't want to offend Umberto,' I said. 'Don't –'

'Of course.' And she was gone.

Several moments later, Sarina stood beside my table, another steaming bowl of pasta in her hands. 'Umberto *specialita*,' she announced, as she'd obviously been instructed. Damn, I thought, Annita must have told Umberto I'd returned the marinara and now he didn't want to serve me himself. How tactless of her. I felt embarrassed.

'Thank you, Sarina.'

It was a ravioli in a cream sauce. Bland and tasteless, I discovered. I downed my wine, poured another glass, and hoed into the pasta regardless. I'd be drunk if I didn't. Besides, by now I was starving. So much for Umberto's special creation. I could only hope the third dish would be an improvement.

Annita was dolloping out great bowls of pasta from the servery table and the women roared their approval as Sarina scurried about delivering their food. 'More bread please, dear.' 'Could we have some more butter, thank you.' Then the first voice of complaint. 'Marinara? We had marinara last night.' Good-natured banter was bellowed across tables. 'It's probably the same stuff; they've probably recycled it.' But the women laughed and got stuck into it anyway.

'Hey, Umberto!' Mary-Jane yelled in between shovels. 'What's for seconds? Ravioli again?' And the others laughed and clinked glasses of water. I noticed that there was no wine on their tables.

Umberto appeared from the kitchen. He strutted about, grinning and bowing and acknowledging their friendly heckling as if it were a standing ovation. 'Is good, eh? For my American *signoras* I make my special. *Molto benne, si*?'

I was slowly starting to burn inside. Marinara? Ravioli? Umberto's special dishes? It all made sense to me now. The chef wasn't 'sick' at all. The chef had obviously gone home after he'd prepared the mass fodder for the Americans.

One stray Aussie in the place didn't warrant à la carte service. I'd been dumped with the set menu and I was feeling angry. Very angry.

Despite their good-natured grumbling, the women devoured their pasta with a passion. Food was obviously serious business to them and the talk died down until the last bread roll was wiped over the last empty bowl. It started up again as the plates were collected and the next course set before them.

'Ravioli! Wow! What a surprise!' Mary-Jane exclaimed. 'More bread rolls, thank you, dear.' And relative silence once more prevailed as they attacked the second course.

Sarina collected my plate. Well, of course Umberto would send Sarina, I thought. He wouldn't have the nerve to come near me himself. She gave me a quick, nervous smile before scuttling off – the poor girl hadn't stopped scuttling all night. She was desperately overworked.

'You like the ravioli, eh? Is good, *si*? This even better. Is my masterpiece! *Si!* Umberto's masterpiece!'

I couldn't believe the audacity of the man and I sat, silent, dumbfounded, as Umberto placed the bowl before me. 'My very special bolognaise, for my friend Jane.' He grinned triumphantly, kissed his fingers – 'You like, is very, very good' – and left.

I stared down at the spaghetti bolognaise. It looked suspiciously like the spag bol I made at home – stick a jar of Paul Newman's sauce into a half kilo of mince – and it tasted suspiciously the same too.

I ate a few mouthfuls and toyed with my food, still fuming, while the Americans caught up.

'Spaghetti bowl-of-nails, my, my, my.' The others laughed loudly, it was obviously Mary-Jane's running gag.

'Is the best bolognaise you ever taste, *si*?' Umberto was prancing about amongst the tables. 'Is my very special bolognaise for my American *signoras*.'

'Which jar'd you get the sauce from Umberto?' a beefy brunette called from the far table, and the others roared with laughter. Yells of 'Prego' and 'Paul Newman' resounded around the room.

'*Signoras, signoras,* please.' Umberto positioned himself on the dance floor, his hands in the air, desperately calling for their attention. 'Is my special recipe that I give the chef.' A few disinterested cries of 'sure, sure' went around the room, but Umberto continued. He looked genuinely hurt and his voice quivered with emotion. 'Is a secret family recipe,' he said, but the women weren't paying him attention anymore as they piled salad onto their plates.

I couldn't help myself, I actually felt sorry for him. 'Is a secret family recipe, I swear to you.' Umberto looked about to cry. 'Handed down from my mother's mother to –'

'Give us Charlie, Umberto!' It was the beefy brunette again and the others backed her up – 'Yeah.' 'Charlie Chaplin.' 'Come on, Umberto, give us Charlie.'

I watched, appalled. The man was being humiliated. How could these apparently humorous, good-natured women be so cruel?

But, even as I watched, Umberto's face cracked into his inane grin. He leapt to the sound system beside the dance floor, flicked a switch and grabbed the bowler hat and cane that were sitting on top of the adjacent speaker.

'Smile, though your heart is aching,
Smile, even though it's breaking . . .'

A scratchy old recording of the famous Chaplin song emanated from the two speakers, and Umberto went into his act. He shuffled, Chaplinesque, between the tables, doffing his hat right and left, smiling, winking, over-using his eyebrows and twitching his moustache. He kissed hands here and there and leered at one and all. He leaned on his cane and fell over in slow motion. He mimed something in his ear, put his head to the side and butting his temple with the pommel of his hand took out the imaginary offending object and ate it. Then finally he shuffled back to the centre of the dance floor, pretending to trip and glaring back at the invisible object that had tripped him, took off his hat, gave a final facial contortion and bowed to thunderous applause. It was obviously his nightly performance and the women loved it.

This, I thought, is the most bizarre evening I have ever spent.

'He is good, Umberto, *si*?' It was Rosella. She fluttered into the seat beside me, the feathers of her bright silk dress taking a moment or two to settle. Without a word, Natale sat beside her. There was a third person with them. 'This Stefano,' Rosella said, 'he is tour guide for the Americans.'

Stefano had remained standing. 'Do you mind if we join you?' he asked.

'No, not at all,' I heard myself say, 'would you like a glass of wine?' Not that there was much left – dear God, I hoped I wasn't slurring my words.

'No thank you.' As he sat he held up the beer he was holding and I noticed that Natale, too, had brought his drink in from the bar. Rosella had another green concoction in her hand.

'I'm Jane,' I said.

'Yes,' he shook my hand, 'I know, the famous actress from Australia.'

'I'm not at all famous, I'm afraid.' I smiled apologetically. 'Just a working actress, that's all.' Had I really said 'actress'? Well, it didn't seem important anyway, the night had suddenly picked up. Here was a normal person. One who was sane, civilised and spoke perfect English.

I suddenly wished that I'd dressed for dinner instead of throwing on a fresh shirt. Stefano was more than normal – sane and civilised. Stefano was devastatingly attractive.

'Umberto is good actor, *si*?' Rosella was clapping her hands with glee as Umberto took the last of his bows, Chaplin-style, the strains of 'Smile' crackling to a finale, leaving only the hiss of the speakers.

What could one say? 'Yes,' I replied, 'very amusing,' and I shook my head to Sarina, who was offering me a dessert dish of stewed pears as she collected my barely touched bowl of spaghetti bolognaise.

'How long are you here in Genzano?' Stefano smiled and made polite conversation while Rosella and Natale chatted in Italian.

'I leave for Rome the day after tomorrow.' The man's attention was wholly centred upon me, as if every word I uttered was of the utmost interest, and I was a little disconcerted. It was his eyes that made him so extremely attractive, I realised. They crinkled humorously at the corners, as if sharing a very special joke with the person upon whom they were focussed. And that was me.

'Your English is excellent.' I realised I sounded brittle and rather patronising, but I meant to. I didn't like feeling disconcerted and told myself that he knew how attractive he was, that his interest was an act and that he was a suave Italian womaniser flirting with a tourist.

'My mother is English.' He didn't appear in the least offended. 'I have spent a lot of time in London over the years. What is Sydney like? Is the harbour as beautiful as they say?'

'Yes.' Damn it, I wasn't falling for it. 'And you're the tour guide for the Americans?' I'd keep the conversation focussed on him, I decided. Besides I was dying to know what the American women were doing in Genzano di Roma. 'What sort of tour is it?'

'It is a religious pilgrimage.'

'Oh.' I was surprised, I don't know why – it certainly explained Father Ralph. But, as I glanced at the American women devouring their stewed pears, it was somehow difficult to associate pious devotion with such healthy appetites and robust energy.

'Yes, there are many sacred sites in this area,' he continued. 'We spend four days here and then we travel north to Assisi.' He looked at the Americans. 'They're nice women, mostly from New Jersey. All except Mary-Jane, that is – she is from Arkansas.'

As if hearing her name, Mary-Jane had heaved herself out of her chair and was heading for our table.

'Dessert's over, sing-along time,' she announced as she arrived. 'Hallo there dear.' She beamed at me. 'I'm Mary-Jane.'

'Hallo.' I shook the hand she extended to me. 'Jane Prescott.'

'Jane, my, my, we have something in common. That's nice.' It was a beefy handshake. 'Would you like to join us, dear? Father Ralph is going to lead the sing-along.'

Stefano, who'd risen from his chair, noted my hesitation and rescued me. 'Perhaps another time if you don't mind, Mary-Jane.'

'You always say that, Stefano, you always say that,' she grumbled pleasantly.

'Jane is going to tell me all about Sydney.' He sat again.

'Sydney, Australia?' Mary-Jane looked impressed. I nodded. 'My, my, such a long way. Come along, Rosella, we need our little sparrow.'

But Rosella had been on her feet the moment she'd heard the word 'sing-along'. She bent and whispered excitedly in my ear, 'I am singer. Music is my life.' I watched as she flitted off after Mary-Jane, the faithful Natale at her side.

'Thanks,' I said gratefully when they'd gone. 'Are you sure you don't want a glass of wine? I really can't finish the bottle.' I was beginning to feel a little ashamed of my rudeness. Stefano might be a womaniser, but he was an extremely polite one.

'If you insist. Thank you.' He poured himself a modest half-glass.

'You didn't eat with the Americans,' I commented. 'You're not staying at the hotel?'

'No, I am a local. When I work in this area I stay with my parents, it saves money. Gospel Tours are not the biggest of payers.' The eyes crinkled. 'Besides, the food here is terrible.'

Again, as if by cue, Umberto bounded up to the table. 'You like my food, is good, *si*? The wine, is good, *si*?'

I was at a loss for words. Outrage burned, but I simply didn't know what to say in the face of his audacity. Stefano winked at me, a devastating wink, which confused me even further.

But Umberto didn't wait for a reply. 'You do not join the sing-along,' he urged. 'Come. You must. You must.'

'No thanks, Umberto.' Again, Stefano took over. 'We're going to take our drinks into the bar.' He stood and picked up the bottle of wine.

'Ah, the young, the young.' Umberto clasped his hands and looked dotingly at us. I rose, feeling myself flush with embarrassment. I wanted to hit the man.

As if announcing our departure, forty voices burst into song. I'd expected hymns but, led by Father Ralph's impressive baritone, the women were all singing *'Funiculi Funicula'*. They knew every word.

'Jammo, jammo, ncoppa jammo ja!
Jammo, jammo, ncoppa jammo ja!
Funiculi funicula funiculi funicula,
ncoppa jammo ja, funiculi funicula.'

The Italian lyrics, with a strong American twang, resounded boisterously about the dining room.

'He's a rogue,' I said as we entered the bar, more to cover my embarrassment at Umberto's parting remark than anything, although I was still fuming about the entire evening.

'Who?'

'Umberto. He's a rogue.'

'Yes, he probably is.' We sat and Stefano poured the remains of the wine into our two glasses. 'But he's a harmless one.'

'Like hell,' I protested, 'he's a conman.'

Having drunk nearly the entire bottle, I was well and truly feeling the effects of the wine by now, and for the next ten minutes I loudly voiced my outrage about the 'sick chef' and the 'special dishes'. So carried away was I that I forgot I was sitting with a drop-dead gorgeous thirty-something man who looked like an Italian movie star and had Ryan Gosling eyes. I even found myself leaping into Umberto impersonations.

'"I create Umberto special for my very good friend Jane".' I closed my eyes in ecstasy, kissed the air with my fingers, wiggled my eyebrows and generally gave it the full performance. '"When you go back to your country, you say to everyone is the best meal you eat in the whole of Italy".'

Stefano was laughing loudly, which only encouraged me all the more. '"Never will you taste such food! Ah, *bella, bella, signorina* Jane ..."' I noisily kissed my arm from hand to elbow.

Stefano applauded when I'd finished. 'You are obviously an actress,' he said.

'He's an appalling man,' I insisted, trying to maintain my outrage, although by now I'd relaxed and so enjoyed my own performance that my anger was spent. Stefano merely smiled and shrugged.

'He's a liar and a conman, surely you agree?' I demanded. I get a bit belligerent with a few drinks in me, or so Roland tells me, and I wanted Stefano to acknowledge I was right. 'You said yourself, the food is terrible, and what about this wine? Is this honestly a '98 Burgundy?'

He shrugged again. 'I am no connoisseur . . .'

I knew he agreed with me but his refusal to join in my assassination of Umberto's character only brought out my fighting spirit.

'Well, I'm not going to let him get away with it,' I said. 'He has a menu and tomorrow I'm going to order a la carte, and I'm going to demand to see the wine list and –'

'There is no wine list.'

Stefano laughed as I stared back at him, my tirade halted midstream. 'Umberto has a cellar full of wine left him by his aunt. He sells bottles for whatever he thinks a guest might pay. Some are good and some are bad, but Umberto would not know – he drinks nothing but coffee.'

He took a sip of his wine. 'You are right, this is terrible,' but he drained the glass nevertheless. 'It works both ways, however. Sometimes you will get a real bargain. Sometimes Umberto will sell a truly magnificent wine for very little.'

'It wouldn't be out of the goodness of his heart,' I grumbled, 'that's for sure.'

'Oh no, it is out of ignorance, I agree. But then that means he is not a true conman, surely.'

A rousing rendition of 'O Sole Mio' emanated from the dining room and, above the voices of Father Ralph and the women, I could hear Umberto giving it all it was worth.

'If he was a good conman,' Stefano insisted, finally forced into debate, 'the Hotel Visconti would attract more than the odd cheap package tour. But Umberto knows nothing of business. He simply likes to play the host. Annita keeps the villa functioning on a basic level and Umberto pretends that he is running a five-star hotel.'

'Exactly. He pretends. That makes him a conman.'

'All right,' Stefano said, acceding that 'pretend' was the wrong word. 'He *believes* it. He believes that his Hotel Visconti is a grand hotel and that his food is special and his wine is special and that he is host *extraordinaire*.'

'Well, he's certainly that,' I muttered.

I was intrigued. Had I misjudged Stefano? Was he one of those 'good' people who refused to think ill of anyone? No, he was too suave, too good-looking to be 'nice'. Perhaps, like Rosella and Natale, he had simply fallen under Umberto's spell. Surely not, he was far too intelligent. Perhaps, and this was the most likely scenario, I decided, Stefano was a conman himself, a conman who recognised another conman.

'I have an excellent idea,' he said, changing the subject. 'Will you join me for dinner tomorrow night?'

'Oh.' I was jolted back to reality by the Ryan Gosling eyes.

'At my parents' place.'

'Oh,' I said again. (His parents?)

'No, no,' he laughed, my surprise at the suggestion was readable, 'not their home. They have a little restaurant in

Castel Gandalfo.' He was waiting for me to say something but I didn't. 'The food is good,' he added.

Still I was silent, my mind rapidly adding up the data. His mother is English, I thought. She's married to an Italian. They have a restaurant in Castel Gandalfo. Oh my God . . .

'The food really is very good,' he promised again, 'and there are lovely views of –'

'The lake.'

'What?'

'The lake. You said there were lovely views.'

'Yes. Of the lake. That's correct.'

I was right. I had to be. Stefano was Wendy and Bruno's son. 'Um . . . that would be lovely, Stefano, but . . .'

I was curiously deflated. Stefano's mystery was diminishing before my very eyes. His relationship with Wendy made him somehow 'family'. Good God, if I went to the restaurant, not only would Bruno think I was freeloading again, we'd all end up talking about Roland and the good old London days, I could just see it. And much as I loved Roland . . .

'No thank you,' I said firmly. 'I intend to eat at the Hotel Visconti.' I was stubborn in order to hide my disappointment. 'I'm determined to put Umberto to the test. I shall order a la carte, a huge steak, and I shall choose my own wine, which he will open at the table.'

Stefano looked at me for a moment and shook his head, either in admiration or exasperation, I wasn't sure which. 'In that case,' he said, 'may I join you?'

What could I say? Disappointment flew out the window. 'Yes, I'd like that.'

A few minutes later, the Americans rounded off with 'Quanto e Bella' and Umberto raced into the bar.

'Come, come,' he said, grabbing my arm, 'the Americans go to bed. You listen to Rosella. She sing.'

I was tired with travel, heady with wine and knew I should go to bed, but Stefano was following us into the dining room, so I decided to stay for a further half hour of his company.

As the last of the Americans trudged up the stairs, however (I noticed none of them used the lift), and as Umberto settled me back at my old table, Stefano made his apologies.

'I must talk to Father Ralph about the morning's itinerary, please excuse me. I shall see you tomorrow, Jane. Seven o'clock, in the bar?' There was a wicked twinkle in his eyes – he knew he'd left me stranded.

'Yes, fine.' I glared back. 'Seven o'clock's fine.'

The indefatigable Sarina was scuttling in and out of the swinging doors, collecting the dishes that Annita was methodically and efficiently stacking. The night was clearly over and I longed to go to bed.

Rosella and Natale joined me at the table. 'But I thought you were going to sing for us, Rosella,' I said. The sooner we started, the sooner we could get it over with.

'Yes, yes!' Umberto exclaimed. He took a CD from his pocket and flourished it at me. 'Here, she sing. You listen, you listen.' He dashed over to the sound system.

'They play this song on the radio,' Rosella said, glowing with pride.

'Umberto has friend in the radio.' It was Natale. I was surprised to hear him speak at last. 'He ask for his friend to play this song.' Natale glowed with a pride that equalled

Rosella's. 'He say he will make Rosella a star. Umberto is good to Rosella.' The two of them nodded, held hands and smiled fondly at Umberto as he returned to the table.

The speakers started to hiss . . . Then came the sound of a third-rate band playing disco music . . . 'Is good, *si*?' Umberto pulled his chair up to the table. 'I have friend with studio. He has band . . .' Natale put his finger to his lips . . . Then, finally, there was Rosella, twittering faintly and prettily in the background:

'*Ah, ah, ah, ah, stayin' alive, stayin' alive.*

Ah, ah, ah, ah . . .'

It took me a while to discern the fact that she was singing in English. When she wasn't being drowned out by the ghastly backing, her accent was so appalling that it sounded like a different language altogether.

Rosella herself was leaning on the table, hands clasped beneath her chin, eyes staring radiantly up at the ceiling, lips mouthing the words of a song that had been a hit nearly forty years ago. Natale and Umberto were both beaming at me and I was left with nowhere to look. I fixed my sights on the nearest speaker, painted on a smile and nodded along to the rhythm, although even that part was difficult to discern every now and then.

The song seemed to last forever. Just when I thought it had finished, off she'd go again:

'*Ah, ah, ah, ah, stayin' alive, stayin' alive.*

Ah, ah, ah, ah . . .'

And I'd have to go back to my nodding. Finally, the sounds faded to the hiss of the speakers and I realised that it was over.

I applauded. There was nothing else I could do, they were all waiting expectantly. 'Very good, Rosella, what a pretty voice you have.'

'You think?' she asked, breathless with excitement.

'Yes. Very pretty.' The sound system was making some ugly noises and Umberto left to rescue the CD. 'Do you sing songs in Italian?' I asked, trying to make it sound innocent.

'Oh no,' the answer was most definite, 'is not fashionable.'

'You take this,' Umberto was back, thrusting the CD into my hands. 'You take this and you make Rosella a star in the Sydney radio, *si*?'

I looked into his beaming, asinine face. It was in full contortion, eyebrows and moustache working overtime and, again, I wanted to punch him. But then I looked at Rosella, the breathless expectation, the pathetic hope in her eyes. And I knew I couldn't make a scene.

'I'm going to London.' I handed the CD back to Umberto.

'You take it to London.' He thrust it at me once again.

'I don't know anyone in London.' This time I placed the CD on the table in front of Rosella. 'I wish you every success with your career, Rosella.' I knew I had to leave before my temper got the better of me and I let Umberto know what I thought of him in no uncertain terms. But, as I rose to leave, I saw the shadow of disappointment in Rosella's eyes. I couldn't leave her like that.

'You have a very pretty voice, Rosella.' The shadow departed, she glowed once more. 'And you have the looks to go with it too.' I smiled. 'Goodnight.' As I left, she radiated happiness, it was that easy. Bloody Umberto, I thought, how dare he delude her with such false hope?

I was still angry when I got to my room. A hot shower before bed, I decided.

Naked, I stepped into the bathroom and fumbled for the light switch. There it was. I flicked it on. But there was no light. Instead, an animal scream ripped the air. Dear God, what had I done? I groped about frantically in the dark, trying to turn off the hideous noise. I hit the light switch by mistake. Thank heavens, at least I could see. The noise was coming from above, a high-pitched, pig-like, angry squeal. Then I saw it. The extractor fan churning and screaming like something demented.

I found the switch and turned it off. I leaned against the wall, breathing heavily, heart pounding. Just the fan, that's all, I told myself, just the fan. Then I pulled the shower curtain around me and turned on the taps.

The pressure was useless but at least the water was good and hot, and I must have stood there for a full ten minutes waiting for my shattered nerves to settle.

I was so tired that it was only when I turned off the shower that I realised I was standing ankle-deep in water. I pulled aside the curtain. The bathmat was floating. The whole bathroom was flooded and water was starting to seep over the doorstep into the bedroom.

Wet and desperate, I ran around collecting all the bath towels and handtowels I could find and, when I'd dammed up the bedroom door, I realised I hadn't left one with which to dry myself.

The flannel. There was a dry flannel sitting beside the washbasin. I waded through the bathroom and back and, when I'd dried myself with the flannel, sat down on the bed and wondered whether to scream or sob.

I was tired and defeated and sick to death of the Hotel Visconti. I couldn't take any more. I'd book out first thing in the morning, I had no other choice.

Then I thought of Stefano. I'd been so looking forward to tomorrow evening . . .

No, damn it! I wasn't going to let Umberto and his rotten hotel win. I'd wait until everyone was at breakfast, then I'd sneak out and explore the town. I'd sit in a chic little outdoor cafe and have hot bread rolls and cafe latte and, by the time I got back to the hotel, if they hadn't fixed my shower, I'd demand another room, Umberto's 'Venezia design' suite if necessary.

Furthermore, I'd dress for dinner. My designer-label, pinstripe power suit that made my legs look fantastic, and I'd order my steak and my wine and . . .

Battle plans laid, I went to bed and slept like a baby.

A noise woke me. It reverberated through the room. Thunder? The floorboards seemed to be shuddering. A minor earthquake? Where was I? Morning light filtered through the wooden shutters. Yes, of course, I recollected, the insufferable Hotel Visconti. Then I heard the women's voices and realised it was the Americans thundering down the stairs.

The bathroom had more or less drained itself during the night, but still I had to splash my way across to the basin in order to wash. I dressed and waited until I was sure they were all at breakfast, then quietly I stole downstairs.

There was no-one in sight. Good. The sounds of healthy eating from the dining room. The scrape of spoons in bowls, the clatter of cups on saucers. I halted momentarily at the reception area. Annita was there, but she was engrossed with her mobile phone and gave me only the briefest of nods as I walked purposefully out the main doors.

It was a grey day, not cold, but the threat of a storm imminent. I turned right and strode down the hill towards the town, spirits lifted, glad that I hadn't succumbed to last night's frustration. I was looking forward to exploring Genzano di Roma.

Not far from the Hotel Visconti I passed another villa. Beyond its huge wrought-iron gates was the stone statue of a woman, her strong, splendid face gazing up at something she was holding aloft in her right hand. As the hand itself was missing, one could only guess at the object of her attention. Weeds and wildflowers had successfully found their way through the many cracks in the paving stones of the circular driveway and, here and there, the outer layer of the villa's walls had crumbled away to expose vulnerable patches of white plaster beneath the terracotta stain. The whole was surrounded by a tumble of overgrown gardens where the hardiest of weeds and vines vied for survival. There was no sign of human presence, all the windows were cracked or broken, and I presumed the place was derelict. The sight of such picturesque decay was somehow sad. This was once the grand part of town, I presumed. The nobility had lived in these wealthy villas on the hill.

As I neared the main town square, the shops and cafes I passed were drab and listless. Business was slow. It was now nine o'clock in the morning, but there were surprisingly few people in the street.

Then I arrived at the piazza, the hub of the town. Of course, I told myself, this was where the action was.

It was a big, open square surrounded by outdoor cafes, with public benches and tables in the centre, a gathering place for the people of Genzano di Roma. To the left, another main street, to the right a park, and ahead, the wide road that led up the rise to the church.

Half a dozen young people were lounging at the kerb side as I rounded the corner into the square. The boys wore leather jackets and leaned carelessly against lamp-posts. One of them sat astride his motorbike, nonchalant, arms crossed, the bike declaring him the alpha male. The girls, overly made-up, thrust their young breasts out under tight sweaters and, hands tucked in back pockets of tight jeans, shifted their weight from one high-heeled boot to the other, tough and cool, yet sexy and appealing. It seemed a complicated business to me, and very early in the day to be playing such games. They couldn't be more than seventeen or eighteen – didn't they have anything better to do?

People were sipping coffee in cafes, sitting chatting on benches and generally wandering about the piazza, but there was no bustle, no sense of the energy I'd come to expect from Italian meeting places. The town seemed languid, and I thought that perhaps, if there really was nothing better to do, the girls were right to play their image games. At least they had the stimulation of performance and flirtation.

I sat at a table observing the scene, had a very pleasant cafe latte and a hot bread roll with jam, and then set off up the road to the church. A slow, fine drizzle was starting to fall, but I refused to be daunted.

Although simple and basic in design, the church was attractive. Furthermore, it appeared to be the one building in town that didn't need either major restoration or at least a spit and polish. It gleamed pristine white in the sunlight that filtered through the gathering grey clouds. The wide expanse of steps leading up to its front doors was fastidiously swept and, inside, the burnished wooden pews and railings glowed with the love of devoted parishioners.

Beyond the church was the old quarter of Genzano di Roma. A mass of little laneways, buildings crammed together, steps leading to mysterious places. For me, the backstreets of a town always beckoned, but after fifteen minutes or so I reluctantly decided against further exploration. The rain was more than a drizzle now, heavy weather was setting in. I must get back to the hotel.

Forty minutes later, when I arrived at the Hotel Visconti, I was soaked.

The main doors were closed and, I discovered, locked. I tried my room key. It didn't fit. I rang the bell, which didn't appear to work, and bashed on the doors for a full minute or so before giving up. Damn it, someone must be in there! I walked around the side of the house, through the gardens, to the terrace and tried the doors to the dining room. They too were locked. I peered through the glass, tapped loudly, yelled loudly, and still no-one appeared. I circled around to the rear of the house where I presumed I would find the servants' and tradesmen's entrance, not bothering to duck for cover – by now I was saturated – and found a door surrounded by garbage bins. It was unlocked. I sighed with relief, opened it and stepped into the kitchen.

'Anybody there?' I called out. I didn't want them to think I was a burglar. No answer.

'Hello?' Through the swinging doors to the dining room, into the bar, then the reception area. All deserted. The television set in the small reception lounge was on and a cartoon was playing. *The Bugs Bunny Show*, I noticed.

I was dripping pools of water and starting to feel cold, so I ran up the stairs to my room, stripped and dried off, thankfully noting that the bed had been made, fresh towels supplied and the bathroom cleaned up. I wondered if the drain had actually been unblocked. I doubted it.

When I'd dressed, I returned to the reception counter. There must be somebody about, surely, I thought as I pressed the bell repeatedly. There wasn't. I sat in the lounge and picked a magazine up from the coffee table. There was a fascinating article that I presumed to be about sex from the graphic pictures displayed, but I couldn't read it because it was in Italian. I watched Bugs Bunny. He was in Italian too.

Then I noticed the open door at the far end of the lounge. Where did that lead? I wondered, and got up to explore.

It was a small, messy office. Umberto's I assumed. The portrait of the woman in Edwardian dress that hung on the wall above the desk simply had to be his aunt. In the corner was an old-fashioned safe. The keys were in the lock and the door wide open. Inside, bound with elastic bands, were messy wads of money, together with boxes that I could only presume contained valuables.

Quickly, I closed the door, ducked back into the lounge and resumed my seat in front of the television, heart thumping a little. What if someone had come in and thought I was robbing the place! But as I sat mindlessly watching Bugs Bunny, I couldn't help thinking, What if I *was* a thief? I could have cleaned out that safe, headed off in my car and be miles away from the Hotel Visconti before anyone was the wiser.

This really is the most insane place, I thought, as an Italian Daffy Duck screamed abuse at an Italian Bugs.

It was an hour before Annita arrived.

'*Buongiorno*,' she said, taking off her wet plastic headscarf, her hair beneath immaculate, 'I thought you had gone out for the day.'

'Only for a walk,' I answered, 'and when I came back the doors were locked, I couldn't get in.' I waited for an apology but it wasn't forthcoming.

'Ah, but you did, didn't you. That is good.' Before I could answer she continued pleasantly, 'The dining room is not open for lunch, but I can prepare for you some sandwiches, or a chicken salad.'

I realised that there was nothing to be gained by complaining and that it was well after lunchtime and I was very hungry. 'Sandwiches would be fine, thank you.'

'I shall bring them to the bar in twenty minutes.' She picked up her mobile phone and marched off to the kitchen.

I sat in the bar reading my *History of the National Theatre*, which I'd discovered in a Paddington second-hand bookstore, and exactly twenty minutes later Annita arrived with a huge tray of what she called sandwiches. They weren't really sandwiches at all, not Australian sandwiches anyway. They were crunchy, white bread rolls stacked with ham and cheese and tomatoes and basil, and they were absolutely delicious.

'I make some for myself too,' she said, lifting two of the rolls onto a side dish. 'I may join you?'

'Yes, please do.' I was surprised. Her smile was friendly and for the first time I sensed warmth beneath the efficient exterior. It had probably always been there, I supposed, but not evident because the poor woman was too busy running the place. It was quite obvious that Annita was the only sane person in the Hotel Visconti.

'I am going to have a beer,' she said, crossing to the bar. 'You would like one?'

'Oh. Yes. Thanks.' I normally didn't drink alcohol during the day. Even one glass made me want to sleep away the afternoon, but what the hell, this was a holiday. Besides, it was the convivial thing to do, and I was interested in finding out a little about Annita.

She poured us both a beer and joined me at the table. 'I do not put this on the bill,' she said and smiled conspiratorially. I smiled back, I liked the woman.

We toasted each other with our beers and dived into the sandwiches. She ate vigorously and healthily, and I liked that too.

When I complimented her on the food, Annita nodded. 'Yes, it is very good,' she agreed and we munched together companionably.

'How long have you been at the Hotel Visconti?' I asked when I'd finished my first bread roll and decided that I couldn't possibly manage another.

'Four years. I like it here.' She took a swig of her beer and picked up her second sandwich. The woman could certainly eat.

'You work very hard.'

'Yes.' She smiled as her jaws worked overtime. 'What would Umberto do without me, eh?' My consensus was so obvious that she hastily added, 'Oh, I do not mind,' in case I had misunderstood. 'Umberto, he is so . . .' She searched fondly for the right words. 'Innocent . . . so . . . naive. He was left the villa by his aunt, and he knows nothing of hotels.' She shrugged modestly. 'I help him as much as I can.'

I decided it was better not to voice my views of her employer. Neither 'innocent' nor 'naive' were words I would choose to apply to Umberto.

'Have you lived in England?' I asked, safely changing the subject. When she looked quizzically at me, I added, 'Your English is perfect, I wondered whether perhaps –'

'Ah. Yes . . .' She took another large bite of her sandwich and kept talking. She was one of those women who could do so with style. 'Many years ago I was hostess for Alitalia. It was necessary that I speak good English.' Then she added, as if for my instruction, 'The hostess is now called "air steward".'

'Yes, I know.'

'I was senior hostess,' she continued. 'I was in charge of the cabin crew, I was very good.' It was no boast, simply a statement, and I wasn't in the least surprised. It certainly explained her air of authority.

'Why did you leave?' I asked.

She put down the remains of her sandwich and, in the silence that followed, finished chewing, swallowed, leaned across the table and announced solemnly, 'I was hijacked by terrorists.'

I didn't know what to say. 'Really?' I managed.

'Yes.' She was staring steadfastly at me and I found myself, mesmerised, staring back. 'Terrorists hijacked our aircraft. I was kept hostage for three days. It was terrible.'

Again, I didn't know what to say, but my eyes remained locked with hers.

'They let many people go, but not me. The pilot and the co-pilot and several of the crew, they would not let us go. They kept us prisoner. For three days and nights.'

I waited with bated breath for her to continue, but she looked away, glancing towards the door, as if she feared someone might overhear, and when her eyes returned to mine, they held a haunted look. 'For a whole year after, I had therapy,' she whispered and again she glanced away, this time in all directions, clearly fearing the walls may have ears, 'and now my personality is different.' When she looked back the haunted look had gone and there was sheer madness in her eyes. 'I like the Hotel Visconti. Here is safe for me.'

We sat in silence for a moment. Then she rose smartly from the table. 'You do not want another sandwich?'

I shook my head. 'I will clear the table.' The madness had vanished as quickly as it had manifested itself and, within seconds, Annita had efficiently cleared the table and disappeared.

I took the glass of beer up to my room, lay on the bed and tried to read *The History of the National Theatre*, but couldn't. In no time at all, I was sound asleep with Annita's hooded eyes burning in my brain. 'Now my personality is different,' she kept telling me over and over. 'I like the Hotel Visconti. Here is safe for me.' It wasn't a very restful sleep.

It was dusk when I awoke. I looked at my watch. Hell, twenty minutes to get ready for Stefano and I wanted to look my best. Dare I risk the shower? Yes, damn it.

The shower hadn't been fixed and three minutes later I stepped out onto the soggy bathmat. Oh well, what did I expect?

I applied a rather good stage make-up. A little more 'eyes' than usual – Italians liked 'eyes', didn't they? – and a lipstick a little bolder than my normal choice, one I kept for making that 'special impression'. I fluffed out the hair, donned the pinstripe suit with the miniskirt and checked that my one and only pair of silk tights was ladder-free. Yes, thank goodness.

The little gold earrings, the high-heeled black courts, a quick check in the full-length mirror on the wall and, yes, I decided, that was about as good as it got. For me, anyway.

I went downstairs.

'You look beautiful.'

It was exactly ten past seven and Stefano was leaning against the bar, chatting to Sarina.

'Thank you.' I was pleased at the ease with which I accepted the compliment. My reaction to flattery was usually rather gauche. 'I'm sorry I'm late. I fell asleep.'

Umberto, Rosella and Natale were at their customary table and Umberto leapt to his feet. 'Ah, *bella bella signorina* Jane.' He pounced on my hand, kissed it and dragged me over to the others. 'Come, come, you sit with us. What you like to drink?'

My look to Stefano said *Must we?*, and thankfully he came to my rescue. 'Why don't we take our drinks into the dining room,' he suggested, 'before it gets crowded?'

'Yes, that's a good idea. I'll have a gin and tonic, thanks, Sarina. Hello, Rosella, Natale.'

'*Buonasera*.' Natale half rose from the table and gave a bob while Rosella looked admiringly up at me.

'You are make-up,' she said. 'You eyes is beautiful.'

'Thank you, Rosella, what a lovely colour.' She was in peacock blue tonight.

Stefano handed me my gin and tonic, surprisingly cold with a generous serve of ice. We toasted the others, excused ourselves and left for the dining room.

There was a distant flash of lightning as we seated ourselves at the table by the French windows, then the faint rumble of thunder. 'There is going to be a big storm,' Stefano said. 'It has been threatening all day.'

'*Buonasera*.' Annita had materialised the moment we sat.

'*Buonasera*, Annita.' I smiled, but the smile and nod she returned was that of a subordinate awaiting orders. There was no trace of the warmth, or of the madness, for that matter, that I had witnessed earlier in the afternoon.

'Bring me several bottles of Umberto's wine, thank you, Annita,' Stefano said. 'We'll choose the one we want.'

'Of course.' And she marched away.

'She's a strange woman,' I said as I watched her leave.

'Yes. She was held hostage by terrorists in an aircraft hijack, that's probably why.'

'Oh.' I was taken aback. Annita had recounted her trauma to me in the utmost confidence, or so I'd presumed. 'You knew that too?'

'Of course. Everyone knows about Annita.'

I was going to say something, but decided not to pursue it and concentrated on the menu instead, although I knew exactly what I was going to have.

'What did you do today?' Stefano asked.

'I walked, for hours actually, to the lake and through the old quarter of town.'

'It is beautiful, isn't it?'

'The lake? Yes, lovely.'

'I meant Genzano.'

'Oh.' I thought of the decayed villa just down the street and the slum-like lanes and alleys I'd explored. No, I couldn't say they were beautiful; picturesque, evocative of bygone days, yes, but not beautiful. 'It was certainly a beautiful town once,' I said, which I thought was both honest and diplomatic.

Stefano was studying me closely, the same concentrated attention which had so attracted and confused me on our first meeting. 'It is beautiful still. Very beautiful, if you look at it through the right eyes.'

There was no rebuke in his tone but I wondered if I'd hurt his feelings; he was a local after all. 'I'm sorry, I wasn't criticising your town, it's very picturesque, I just meant –'

'It is not my town. I come from Castel Gandalfo.'

Those eyes again. They were too intimate, demanding something of me. I determined to keep the conversation light-hearted. 'Castel Gandalfo, yes, I know. And your father is Italian and your mother is English.'

Hah! I'd got him. He was confused by the change of topic.

'Yes, that's right.'

'And they have a restaurant with views of the lake.'

'Yes.' Still confused. Good.

'And their names are Bruno and Wendy,' I said triumphantly.

'No. Their names are Giovanni and Jill.'

'Oh.'

'I have the afternoon off tomorrow, why don't you stay another day and let me show you the town properly?'

My mind was still dwelling on Bruno and Wendy. Well of course there would be a number of restaurants with views of the lake, wouldn't there? It really didn't bear closer inspection, I told myself.

'I'm sorry?' I hadn't properly absorbed what he'd said.

'Stay another day.'

This time I heard. And there was a special invitation in his eyes, I was sure. I felt a resurgence of my initial reaction to the man. I'd been right, I thought. He was a suave Italian womaniser and I was a lone female tourist viewed as prime game.

'No,' I said tartly, 'that's not possible. I have a very strict itinerary, which I intend to keep.'

Stefano sensed the walls go up but he merely shrugged and said pleasantly, 'A pity. I have a friend with a boat; we could have gone rowing on the lake,' outside, the lightning cracked, 'but then perhaps not.' His smile was so amiable that once again I regretted sounding rude. God, the man was confusing.

Another crack and the gardens flared white as streaks of lightning forked the sky. 'It's almost overhead now,' Stefano said, both of us gazing out at the storm. 'Magnificent, isn't it?'

The rain was pelting down and there was an ominous rumble. It built and built until the thunder broke free with an angry roar, and we waited once again for the lightning. There it was, a maddened yellow serpent in the sky, and outside, the garden of ghostly white trees and vines and statues was frozen in time.

'Yes, quite magnificent,' I agreed.

Annita arrived with the wine. Stefano chose one of the bottles and insisted on paying cash for it.

'Well, dinner's going on my bill,' I said.

He shook his head. 'You cannot pay for my dinner,' I was about to interrupt, 'my meals at the Hotel Visconti are free.' Then he added with a mischievous smile, 'If you wish to take me out to dinner, you will have to stay another night.'

I laughed, feeling silly for having taken offence earlier. 'Really, Stefano, I can't.' It was true: I certainly couldn't at the prices Umberto charged.

As Annita poured the wine, I said very firmly, 'I'd like the *bistecca* with *spinaci*, thank you.'

'The *bistecca*?'

This time I refused to be deterred by the blank look. 'Yes, thank you, and the *spinaci*.'

'One moment.'

As she left for the kitchen, Stefano raised his glass. 'Good luck.' We clinked glasses and took our first sip. The wine was very good.

'Well, that's one step in the right direction,' I said. Then Umberto arrived at the table and the farce began.

'You no want the *bistecca* –'

'I do.'

'For you I have tonight my special . . .'

It went on for several minutes, and the Americans were stampeding through the doors when I finally said, very loudly, 'I take it you have no *bistecca*, Umberto.' At which point he halted and stood stiffly to attention, the proud and wounded host.

'Of course I have the *bistecca*. I have the best *bistecca* in the whole of Italy.'

'Then that is what I will have, thank you. Medium-rare.'

'As you wish. For you, Stefano?'

'Just the first course of the pasta, thanks, Umberto.'

Umberto clicked his heels, bobbed his head, sniffed disdainfully and left.

'You should have ordered from the menu,' I said. 'We're dining a la carte, remember?'

'You are,' Stefano replied wryly. 'I am not game enough.'

'My, my, just look at that!' The Americans were louder than ever as they yelled to each other above the crash of thunder. 'Will you look at that lightning, my, my!' Mary-Jane was the loudest of them all as they crammed around the windows ooh-ing and aah-ing each time the gardens flashed eerie and white.

As soon as the bowls of pasta appeared, however, the glorious Sarina once again scuttling from table to table, they sprang quickly to their seats to address the serious business of the day.

Annita delivered bread rolls and a salad to our table and returned moments later with an obscenely large steak and a bowl of pasta.

'*Bistecca*,' she announced, 'and salmon fettuccine.'

'And *spinaci*?' I queried.

'*Spinaci* is out of season.'

I didn't return Stefano's look. I had my *bistecca* and I had won, I told myself as I attacked it.

The meat was inedible. I hacked and sawed and could barely get my knife through it. Tough as boot leather, red and cold in the middle. 'It's still frozen,' I said incredulously.

Stefano simply laughed. 'What did you expect?'

There was a loud shriek. It was Mary-Jane. She lifted the tablecloth and peered beneath the table. 'We're being flooded!' she yelled.

It was true. The rain had seeped through both sets of French windows and was rapidly coursing its way under the tables. I looked down; any minute we'd be standing in centimetres of water.

The women jumped to their feet and started dragging their tables towards the main doors and the dance floor. Umberto, Sarina and Annita ran around with tablecloths and towels, damming up the doors. Stefano, strangely, was ripping open bread rolls and stuffing them with salad.

'I think we'd better move,' I suggested.

'Yes,' he said, wrapping the bread rolls in a napkin and draining his wine glass. 'Finish your wine.'

Automatically I did as I was told and he took both our empty glasses. 'Bring the bottle,' he said.

'Where are we going?'

'For a picnic.'

Mystified, I followed him through reception and into the hallway, where he grabbed a mackintosh from the hallstand.

'A picnic in the storm?' I queried as he threw the mackintosh over our heads and opened the front door.

'What better way to see it?'

'You're mad.' And together we raced out into the pelting rain.

Across the gravelled courtyard, past the fountain, between the statues, beneath the vine-covered trellises (damn, I felt the heel of a shoe snap) and finally to the pergola at the far end of the garden.

We were breathless when we arrived, and a bit giggly with excitement. Stefano plonked the food and glasses on the wooden table, shook the mackintosh out and draped it over a bench.

'Did you get very wet?'

'No, surprisingly. Busted a shoe though.' I took both shoes off. The heel of one had disappeared completely. 'Who cares?' I shrugged. 'They'd had it anyway.' They hadn't 'had it' at all – they were my very best black courts – but shoes seemed a petty consideration, standing there amongst the vines, the storm raging about us.

'I wonder how old they are,' I said, peering up at the vines, thick and impregnable, which formed the roof of the pergola. Barely a drop of rain escaped them.

'Very, very old,' Stefano replied, pouring the wine, 'possibly hundreds of years.'

We sat side by side on the wooden bench, sipping our wine, eating our bread rolls and admiring the storm. I wondered if, a hundred years ago, another young couple had sat under these vines watching a storm. And I wondered if, in a hundred years from now, yet another young couple would be watching yet another storm.

'This was a good idea,' I said, finishing my bread roll.

'I had to do something to get you out of there.' Stefano was enjoying the whole experience as much as I was. He looked very boyish in his excitement, I thought. 'You should have seen your face when you were attacking that steak.' He laughed. 'Poor Umberto, I feared for his safety.'

His laughter was infectious. I joined in.

He poured another glass of wine and we sat in silence while the storm rumbled its way towards the distant hills. Finally, its ferocity spent, we were left with nothing but the torrential rain and an occasional grumble of far-off thunder.

I don't know how long we sat there but, as the rain lessened, a wonderful sense of peace pervaded the garden. I couldn't help but feel surrounded also by a strange sense of triumph, as if this timeless space, in once again escaping the wrath of the elements, was claiming an age-old victory.

Possibly it was this sense of occasion or possibly I was cold, but I shivered a little.

'You're cold,' Stefano said and put his arm around me.

I was suddenly self-conscious. Was this the precursor to an embrace? Was he going to kiss me? I wouldn't have minded at all if he had, in fact I wanted him to, but his hand was gently and firmly massaging my right arm, a natural gesture to warm me. How was I supposed to react?

'I don't know how you can defend him. He's a dreadful man.' When in doubt I always talk.

'Who?'

The arm continued to harmlessly massage. Yes, he was only intending to warm me, I thought, feeling vaguely disappointed.

'Umberto. Do you know he leads Rosella and Natale on shamelessly? They honestly think he's going to make Rosella a star.' He was looking at me, and once again I was disconcerted. Keep talking, I told myself, keep talking. 'Well, I think that's terrible, don't you?'

'No.' He'd stopped massaging now but his arm remained around me. 'Umberto is very good for Rosella and Natale.'

I forgot my self-consciousness and stared at him, amazed. 'Surely you don't believe that. You couldn't!'

'There is little excitement in Genzano.' Stefano looked out at the rain, which was falling gently now. I recalled my morning's walk and the desultory air of the town. Well, he was right there, I thought.

'Rosella is a shop assistant and Natale works for the local post office,' he continued. 'Every evening after work, they dress in their finest and come to the Hotel Visconti.' He turned to me, his arm gently pulling me closer. 'At the Hotel Visconti they find a world of promise and excitement,' he was going to kiss me now, I knew it, 'a world of romance.' He gathered me in an embrace. 'What matter if it is fantasy?'

I returned his kiss – a long, lingering, beautiful kiss. I was a little breathless when we parted; my God but I'd never been kissed like that. More importantly, I'd never responded to a kiss like that. I desired him. He knew it too. And I knew that he knew it.

'The rain's stopped,' he said, 'shall we go inside? Your clothes are damp.'

If that wasn't an invitation what was? Oh, come along, Jane, I told myself, you're hardly a virgin, you've had one-nighters before. Well, two, neither of which had been particularly pleasurable, and I'd avoided them since. But this was my Italian adventure, wasn't it . . .? Well, wasn't it . . .?

'Um . . . yes . . . We'd better go inside.'

As we closed the front doors and he replaced the mackintosh on the hall stand, I still hadn't made up my mind.

'I'll see you to your room,' he said.

'Fine.' I smiled a trifle too brightly. 'Thanks.'

Did that mean I'd said yes? No, of course not, the voice of propriety insisted. There were still the stairs to go. Still time to say, 'Thank you for a lovely evening, Stefano. Goodnight.'

But I didn't.

I woke to find the touch of bed linen on my skin delicious and, for a moment, I wondered vaguely why I was naked and why I felt so sensual. Then I remembered.

It was morning and beside me the bed was empty. Stefano had gone. Naturally, he'd been discreet, I told myself in a drowsy haze. He'd left before the hotel awoke. It was the correct thing to do, it was to have been expected, it was for the best . . . I willed myself back to sleep, erotic images drifting behind my eyelids, before I could acknowledge my true disappointment.

The fact was, Stefano was the best lover I had ever experienced. Well, I'd only experienced three, and that included the two rebellious one-night stands after James and I had split up, so I suppose it meant I'd really only had one lover to speak of. But I had presumed that James's and mine had been a fully erotic relationship. We'd been partners for seven years, two of which we'd lived together during our student days at drama school, and our lovemaking had been mutually satisfying and adventurous enough.

Now, as I lay dreamily recalling last night, I realised that James and I had been as competitive in bed as we had been in our daily coexistence, that we had always been aware of the individual performances we were giving. Roland had said as much when we broke up. 'Dangerous for actors to live together,' he'd said in that peremptory manner that so irritated me, 'too much ego under one roof.'

Roland had been right, I thought, as I recalled the pure delight Stefano had taken in my body, and I in his. Not for one moment had I been conscious of my own performance. Not once had I thought, 'Am I giving him pleasure?' We'd both been lost in each other's sensuality and the eroticism of the night.

I lay, half asleep, half awake, recalling each touch of tongue and lip and finger, feeling myself becoming aroused at the memory.

'Do you know that your drain is blocked?'

Someone was calling out to me. I sat up groggily and looked around.

'The shower's flooded.' Stefano was standing naked at the bathroom door, brushing his teeth.

'Oh. Yes. I know. They haven't fixed it. Is that my toothbrush?' I asked lamely.

'Yes, you don't mind, do you?' He grinned through the froth and disappeared momentarily. The brief sound of gargling and he was back.

'Sorry about the shower.' He sat on the bed and kissed me. 'Good morning.' I was wide awake by now and a little unsure how I should react, but his complete lack of self-consciousness made it easy.

'Hardly your fault.' I kissed him back. 'It's been blocked since I arrived.' I was probably being unworldly,

I thought, but I couldn't help it. I felt a rush of pleasure that he was here with me, that he hadn't dissolved into the morning.

With the flat of his thumb he wiped ineffectually at the rings of mascara under my eyes. 'You should get rid of this make-up.'

I jumped brazenly out of bed, modesty seemed a secondary consideration with Stefano wandering around buck naked (besides which, no actor who has suffered the indignity of shared dressing rooms and backstage costume changes is coy about nudity), and looked at my reflection in the bathroom mirror. A sluttish owl looked back. Damn. I never went to bed with make-up on. How could I have done that!

'Won't be a tick.' I turned the shower on full bore – well, as full bore as it would go (let the bathroom flood, who cares) – and when I stepped out in a bathrobe several minutes later, Stefano was dressed and ready to leave.

He pushed my matted wet hair back from my face. 'You look lovely,' he said. 'I like you better without make-up.' And this time the kiss was not just a good-morning kiss. I opened my mouth to his, waiting any moment for him to open my bathrobe and run his fingers over my nakedness . . .

'I have to go,' he said. 'Father Ralph and the herd will be finishing breakfast.'

'Yes, of course,' I agreed, trying to sound sensible.

'You will stay another day, won't you?' Before I could reply, he continued, 'I'll be back soon. I take the Americans on a quick trip to the Pope's summer palace, and the afternoon they spend in church or preparing for tomorrow's trip to Assisi.' He started to nuzzle my neck. God, it felt glorious. 'I'll only be gone a few hours, wait here for me.'

'I'd love to. I would, really, but I can't.'

The nuzzling stopped. 'Your itinerary? Break it.'

'Oh, it's nothing to do with my itinerary, it's the Hotel Visconti,' I explained. 'I can't stay another night here.'

He laughed, assuming I was joking. 'We won't eat the food, I promise.' The lips started on my earlobe now.

'It's not the food, Stefano,' I laughed back, 'it's the hotel.' He left the earlobe alone and looked at me, mystified. 'It's too expensive, I can't afford it.'

'You can't afford the Hotel Visconti?' Now there was genuine puzzlement in his eyes. 'You are joking, surely.'

'No. I'm not.' I quelled the slightly sick feeling in my stomach. He didn't know the prices Umberto charged, I told myself, that was all. 'It's very expensive here, you know.'

'But you're wealthy, a wealthy actress from Sydney, Australia. That's what Umberto told me.'

There was no quelling the horror I now felt, rising from the very pit of my stomach. 'I'm afraid I'm not, Stefano.' I edged out of his embrace, although he didn't appear to notice, he was too busy staring at me in disbelief. He looked rather foolish, I thought. 'I'm a working actress. I told you that, if you remember.' My voice was sharp. I was angry, very, very angry. But I knew that it wasn't really anger I felt, it was deep humiliation.

'I thought you were being modest.'

'I wasn't. I was being truthful.'

I splashed my way through the bathroom and concentrated on brushing my hair, gazing at my reflection in the mirror above the washbasin, willing myself not to give in to the tears of disillusionment which threatened.

He followed and stood behind me, looking long and hard into the mirror, as if trying to discern some mystery.

'You're a struggling actress and you can't afford the Hotel Visconti,' he said eventually, as though he'd discovered the answer.

'Yes.' Why was he tormenting me? Why the hell didn't he go away? Beneath my humiliation, I felt a genuine stab of anger. Anger at myself, at my stupidity and naiveté, my dreamy, girlish assumptions of a shared eroticism – the man had played me for the fool I was. *Get out*, something inside me yelled. *What are you hanging around for? There's nothing in it for you!* But I remained silent.

Then he laughed. Loud and long. 'Poor Umberto,' he said, 'he is always getting it wrong.'

I stood, hairbrush poised, staring at him as he delighted in his private and delicious joke. Eventually he calmed down, put his hands on my shoulders and grinned at my reflection. 'Poor, poor Umberto,' he said again, shaking his head sympathetically. 'He has been winking at me and nudging me ever since you arrived.'

I couldn't believe it. Umberto had pointed me out and said, 'Go for it, mate,' and Stefano found it humorous! A joke to be shared! What was I supposed to do? Laugh along with him?

He continued to grin at me, entirely oblivious to the anger and humiliation that must have been mirrored in my face.

'Don't worry,' he said, 'I will sort out Umberto.'

'Oh yes? In which particular way?'

He failed to notice the iciness in my tone, or perhaps he merely chose to ignore it. 'He will charge you the tour rate, I will see to that.'

I watched the top of his head in the mirror as he pushed aside my towelling robe and bent to kiss my shoulder. I felt the warmth of his breath and the softness of his lips against my skin. 'Umberto will charge you the tour rate for the whole of your stay,' his mouth was against the curve of my neck now, 'it will be far less than you had expected to pay, so you see,' he turned me about to face him, 'you have no excuse. Now you *must* stay another night.'

He kissed me fully and, although I didn't return the kiss, I didn't resist. 'I will see you at lunchtime.'

Hairbrush in hand, feet in several centimetres of water, I watched him leave and, as I did, all I could think was . . . his shoes must be saturated by now.

He laughed again as he opened the door to the landing. 'Poor Umberto,' I heard him say, 'he is such a foolish man.' Then he was gone and I was left in a state of utter bewilderment.

I dressed, my mind numb. I didn't want to analyse the situation. Automatically, I had donned my walking gear, my light tracksuit and runners. Yes, that's what I'll do, I'll go for a walk.

The grinding of tyres on gravel. I looked out the window to see the Americans' tour bus pull out of the driveway. It turned right and I watched as it headed down the main street on its way to Castel Gandalfo.

When the bus had disappeared, I went downstairs and walked hurriedly through the reception area, hoping that Annita wouldn't ask me what time I was booking out, but she wasn't there. Once again the place was deserted, and I wondered whether it would be locked on my return and whether I'd have to steal in through the kitchen doors again.

This time I turned left as I walked out of the gates of the Hotel Visconti, past the Shell garage, down the hill and into the countryside. Apart from a little white farmhouse way in the distance there was nothing but a narrow, hedge-lined dirt road winding across the valley amongst the olive groves. Strange to think that just over the rise behind me was Genzano di Roma where, for two days each year, thousands of people flocked to see the festival of the flowers.

I didn't make any decisions as I walked; my mind remained a blank. It was a glorious day and I wandered along the little dirt road, avoiding the muddy potholes, admiring the olive trees glinting grey-silver in the mid-morning sun, and simply drinking in the freshness of the countryside revived by last night's rain.

I made the little white farmhouse my target, but it was further away than it appeared, and by the time I stood looking at its walls of peeling plaster and the hens ferreting about the debris of the yard, I had been walking for well over two hours.

I hurried back to the hotel, hot and sweaty when I arrived, and vaguely disappointed not to see the tour bus parked in the driveway. Perhaps I had deliberately walked too far. Perhaps I had deliberately filled in my morning hoping Stefano would be there on my return, who knows? But I certainly was not going to sit in my room waiting for him.

Behind me there was an angry roar and I turned, startled, as a motorbike squealed through the gates and into the courtyard. A young man in a leather jacket alighted. Simultaneously, the main doors swung open and Umberto appeared with Sarina, who was wearing jeans and a silk scarf knotted about her head, turban-style. She looked more beautiful than ever.

I couldn't understand a word Umberto was saying, but the message was perfectly clear. His tone was loud and bossy, and he was pointing at his watch. Sarina nodded, agreeing meekly as she joined her young man waiting by the motorbike. Umberto kept repeating himself, calling after her and again pointing at his watch. Again Sarina nodded meekly. She climbed aboard the pillion seat and, even as the bike tore through the gates and she waved farewell, she was still nodding.

I fumed. I knew it was really none of my business, but the poor girl was desperately overworked. Was she not to have friends? Was she not to have a moment's respite from her slave labour? The man was a tyrant.

'Ah, *signorina* Jane.' As I walked up the steps to the main doors Umberto held his arms wide, as if to embrace me. I glared and strode past him, not daring to speak.

'You are booking out today.' Annita was at her post behind the reception desk.

'Yes,' I said without a moment's hesitation.

'There is no hurry.' Her smile was charming and her voice warm. God, the woman was mercurial. 'You would like to stay for lunch?' she continued before I could reply. 'We do lunch for the Americans on their last day. You would like to join them? They are dining now.'

'Oh.' So the tour bus had returned. 'No, thank you, Annita. I'll be booking out immediately.'

'As you wish.' She returned to her work. From the corner of my eye I had noticed Umberto crossing the foyer behind me. I avoided looking around until I sensed that he had entered his office, and then I turned briefly to make sure that he had closed the door after him. He had. I knew I was interfering but I couldn't resist.

'Annita,' I hissed, and she looked up from her paperwork. 'Is there nothing you can do about the appalling way Umberto treats Sarina?' Annita gave me one of her blank looks. 'He works her too hard,' I insisted. 'It's wrong.'

Annita merely shrugged. 'Sarina likes to work hard.'

I refused to be deterred. 'But he's rude to her. He yells at her –'

'Ah. I see you do not understand.' Annita's smile was warm but a little patronising as she interrupted me. I waited for her to continue. 'Sarina is . . . how do you say it . . .' She searched for the word. 'Simple.'

'Oh.'

'Yes. She has no family. Umberto is like a father to her. He cares very much for her. Without such discipline, who knows what would happen to a girl like Sarina.'

'I see.'

'Thank you for caring.' Annita smiled again, reached out, patted my hand resting on the counter, and returned to her work. I walked away feeling slightly foolish.

Passing the dining room and hearing the clatter of the Americans at lunch, I couldn't resist and popped my head through the door. The young man with the chef's hat, whom I'd met briefly on my first night, was scurrying about doing Sarina's job, but there was no sign of Stefano. So he had left with the tour bus. Well, that was my decision made.

Upstairs, I packed as quickly as I could. A brief glance around the room. Goodbye, Hotel Visconti, I thought, you've been an experience, there's no doubt about that.

I opened the door and gasped. Stefano stood there.

'I have a Lambretta.'

As I glanced out at the landing, vaguely expecting to see a motor scooter at the top of the stairs, Stefano took my suitcase from me, dumped it on the bed and started unzipping the sides.

'Do you have a bathing costume in here?'

'Yes, but –'

He threw open the top of the suitcase. 'I'll get some towels.'

He disappeared into the bathroom and, automatically, I dug out my bathers from the bottom of the case.

'Have you eaten?' he asked, reappearing with two bath towels, which he stuffed into the canvas bag slung over his shoulder.

'No.'

'Nor have I and I'm starving. My friend is going to cook for us.' He took my hand and marched me to the door, pausing briefly to glance back at the suitcase. 'You'll be glad you stayed.' He smiled, and it was only when we were walking through the hotel foyer that I realised I'd left both my room key and handbag upstairs.

'Wait.' I stopped. 'My handbag.'

'You won't need it.'

'My room key.'

'Leave it.'

'No, really Stefano –'

'I will lock your room for you.' It was Annita, smiling indulgently from behind her desk. 'The key will be waiting for you here at reception when you return. Have a nice day.'

'Thank you, Annita,' Stefano said, and the two of them exchanged conspiratorial smiles. Before I could ponder the sense of collusion, I found myself astride the pillion seat of the Lambretta, clutching on to Stefano for dear life as he revved the engine, churned up the gravel driveway and tore through the gates down the street towards Genzano.

It was a hair-raising ride. Along the main street, across the piazza, up the hill, a sharp right turn at the church, then into the depths of the town's old quarter. I clung like a limpet, feeling Stefano's ribs through his light denim jacket and shirt as the Lambretta sped down the steep hill, darting in and out the narrow laneways, a collision imminent around every blind corner.

When, at the bottom of the hill, we finally slowed down and pulled into a small stone courtyard not far from the water's edge, I realised I'd spent much of the journey with my eyes tightly shut.

'Sal! Gaby! We're here,' Stefano called up to the little iron-railed balcony above. His eyes were sparkling and his grin excited; he'd obviously found the ride exhilarating.

As I tried to get my breath back, calm my pounding pulse and tidy the windblown mess of my hair, I looked around. From the courtyard, stone steps led down amongst the bushes to the edge of the vast lake that shimmered silver in the sun. Above, heaped one upon the other like ill-stacked playing blocks, the tangle of houses wound its way up the hill. A colourful mixture of white and yellow and ochre, some with arched entrances, some with terraces or courtyards or balconies, they were a hive of activity. Washing flapped in the breeze, children played, people sunned themselves. Viewed from this aspect, Genzano di Roma was anything but listless.

A middle-aged couple stepped out onto the iron-railed balcony, and the man called out to Stefano in Italian.

'This is Jane,' Stefano yelled back. 'She is from Australia.'

'*Buongiorno*, Jane from Australia,' the man called. 'Come, come up.'

We climbed the steep steps from the courtyard to the door, which was opened by a matronly woman with abundant white hair tied up in an unruly bun.

'This is Gaby,' Stefano introduced us. 'My friend Jane.'

'*Buongiorno*, Jane.' She shook my hand warmly and we were joined in the small hallway by the cheerful, barrel-chested man from the balcony.

'And this is Sal,' Stefano said.

'He drive like a maniac, yes?'

'Yes,' I answered, still desperately trying to sort out my hair.

Gaby and Sal were older than I had presumed from my glimpse of them at the balcony. Mid-sixties I guessed, but a vital, energetic couple and clearly very fond of Stefano. Gaby spoke little English but, recognising my hair problem, she brought me a comb, for which I was grateful. Sal, who obviously relished his command of the English language, chattered on.

'One day he kill himself, Stefano. But more important, he kill my Lambretta, for that I not forgive him.' Sal punched Stefano on the arm and hooted with laughter, his forgiveness a forgone conclusion.

'It's your Lambretta?' I asked.

'*Si*. Whenever Stefano visit us he take the Lambretta.'

Gaby smiled and nodded, and she and Sal exchanged a fond look. As they did, I felt the same sense of collusion that I'd felt between Stefano and Annita. Did Stefano make a habit of borrowing the Lambretta and bringing women to their house? Gaby and Sal were not in the least surprised by my presence, and I recalled that when Stefano and I had walked through reception, Annita had nodded and smiled and said, 'Have a nice day,' as if Stefano regularly escorted women out the main doors and onto the pillion seat of his Lambretta.

Again, I was left little time to ponder the situation. Gaby and Sal were far too generous with their hospitality.

'Thank you.' I returned Gaby's comb.

'You keep, you keep.' She thrust it back at me.

'Oh. Thank you, Gaby. Thank you very much.' I thrust the comb into the bulging pocket of my tracksuit pants alongside my scrunched-up Speedo bathers.

'We eat, we eat.' Sal ushered us into the main room with its doors to the balcony and splendid views of the lake.

The room reflected an innate style that seemed at odds with Gaby's and Sal's homely physical appearance. Several small rooms had been gutted to form an open-plan, all-purpose living area, but none of the originality had been sacrificed. If anything it had been enhanced, the light bouncing off the ageless stone walls, giving them new life.

A huge wooden dining table, scarred, much-loved and laden with food, dominated the room. From its central position, it stood in the path of the welcome breeze from the open balcony doors and yet was within easy access of the kitchen area, complete with a wood-fuelled oven carved into the solid rock wall. Cooking and eating was obviously the focal point in this house, the aroma of freshly baking bread and garlic and lemon and olive oil attesting to the fact.

As it transpired, Sal and Gaby were highly successful, now retired, restaurateurs and close friends of Stefano's parents.

'It was on their advice that Mother and Papa bought the restaurant in Castel Gandalfo,' Stefano explained. 'I have known them all my life.'

Within minutes, large glasses of red wine had been poured from the two jugs on the table, and I was being plied with bowls of olives and salads, platters of salamis and cheeses, and a basket of slim bread rolls, which Sal had shovelled, piping hot, out of the stone oven.

'This you open,' he said, expertly breaking the crisp outer crust of one of the rolls, 'and you eat with the anchovy. Is excellent.'

With his fingers, he lifted one of the long brown fillets from the plate in the centre of the table, dumped it into the steaming bread roll, and handed it to me.

I'd been wondering what the dark, unidentifiable objects were, swimming in olive oil in the dish that held pride of place on the table. I'd presumed they were slices of eggplant. Anchovies. I loathed anchovies. To me they were the leathery strips of salty fish that I discarded from a caesar salad or, worse still, those gritty, inedible little circular things that came in flat tins impossible to open. I had always loathed anchovies.

'Thank you.' I put the roll onto my plate. Perhaps if I let it sit there long enough I could avoid it without their noticing. But all three of them were waiting expectantly. 'I'll just let it cool down,' I said.

'No, no,' Stefano insisted. 'The idea is to eat while the oil is warmed by the hot bread.' He was smiling. I had a feeling he knew I was avoiding the anchovy.

Realising there was no getting out of it, I bit into the damn thing, hoping I wouldn't gag.

To date in my life there have been four or five unforgettable taste sensations (of course I am hoping there will be more to come), but my anchovy at Gaby's and Sal's is, without doubt, the highlight of them all. Within the soft, doughy heart of the roll, the tangy taste of the sea mingled with the earthy warmth of olive oil and the bite of lemon juice and garlic.

'*Molto benne, si?*' Gaby said whilst Stefano applauded.

'*Molto benne*,' I agreed.

We ate and drank and dunked the bread in our glasses of wine.

'Pizza dough,' Sal explained, 'is good with red wine.'

Two hours later, Gaby and Sal left to do their shopping, and we waved goodbye in the courtyard as they took off on the Lambretta. They were a portly pair on the little motor scooter as it was but, with the large shopping basket attached to the handlebars and the backpack strapped to Gaby, they made a ludicrous sight.

'What a great couple,' I said as they chugged up the hill and out of sight. But Stefano's mind was elsewhere – he was already halfway down the steps to the foreshore of the lake.

'Come on,' he called. 'I promised we would go rowing.'

It was a wonderful afternoon. We rowed about the lake in the little dinghy, and we swam and laughed and dunked each other. I told myself that it didn't matter if Stefano had done all these things with other women. Like the anchovy, the day was unforgettable and I revelled in every moment.

It was dusk as we wandered up the hill and into town, and I was weary – the delicious weariness born of exhilaration.

We sat at an outdoor table in the piazza drinking coffee. A young man was playing a piano accordion, and the lights of the cafes and streetlamps glowed magic and festive. Families were dining in the open air, youths were lounging against lampposts, groups of elderly were gathered at park benches discussing their day. Good, honest people like Gaby and Sal, young people inventing their own excitement like Rosella and Natale. What a beautiful place, I thought.

'Thank you for the most wonderful day of my life, Stefano,' I said.

He leaned across the little table and kissed me. 'The best is yet to come,' he murmured, and I returned his kiss wholeheartedly. Perhaps he was a womaniser, and perhaps I was a tourist and fair game, but what did it matter? We were lovers and he was right. The best was yet to come.

We walked in the park and kissed and caressed and teased each other's growing desire, and it was late when we returned to the Hotel Visconti. I was glad. I wanted to avoid the querying looks of the Americans.

The reception area was deserted and there was no sound from the dining room, but as we passed the bar I heard the buzz of voices and paused to glance through the open doors.

Sarina was behind the bar. Umberto, Rosella and Natale were seated in their customary places and with them Annita, who, like Rosella, was leaning on the table, eyes glowing, gazing in rapture at the man seated opposite in the well-cut suit with the healthy head of silver-grey hair, which reminded me rather of Roland's. Umberto was chatting away full steam, the normally silent Natale offering agreement wherever possible. Annita and Rosella were giggling like schoolgirls (yes, Annita!). They were obviously thrilled by the presence of this mystery man whose face I couldn't see, as his back was towards me. From the elegant right hand that rested on the table, however, its fragile fourth finger impressively be-ringed, I could tell he was elderly.

Umberto and Natale wore dinner jackets, Rosella was in shocking pink silk with feathers in her hair, and Annita wore a tasteful black cocktail dress with diamante clips at the shoulder straps. Perhaps they had dressed for the Americans, I thought. After all, it had been the Americans' last night at the Hotel Visconti. Or perhaps they had dressed for their guest. Whatever the reason, the bar was redolent with a sense of occasion and Umberto was beaming with a pride fit to burst.

Then the elegant hand rose from the table and everything stopped. No sound, no movement. Umberto halted mid-sentence, the others froze, and a moment's breathless silence ensued.

'Excuse me, Sarina, I wonder would you mind . . .' The man's voice was silky. His English too well-spoken to be his mother-tongue. It was a voice strangely seductive and vaguely familiar. Then, as he turned and raised his brandy balloon in a gesture to Sarina, I saw him quite clearly in profile. The skeletal face of an old man certainly, but impressive nonetheless, and again eerily familiar. 'A little more cognac, if you would be so kind.'

My God, I thought, it's Omar Sharif. But is it? He sounds like Omar Sharif, or rather he sounds the way I assume Omar Sharif might sound. He certainly looks like Omar Sharif. Indeed, I might have been looking at an aged Dr Zhivago. But is he the real thing or is he an imitator? I wondered. Is anything real in the Hotel Visconti? I turned to Stefano, who was standing beside me. 'Is that . . .?'

'Yes,' he said. 'Umberto's great friend, Omar the actor. Do you want to meet him?'

I sensed reluctance in Stefano. Was it because upstairs was beckoning, or was it because he didn't want me to discover the man was a fake? I glanced back at the bar. The scene was surreal, like one of those old 'art' films that Roland so thrilled to, *La Dolce Vita* or *Last Year at Marienbad*.

'I will introduce you,' Stefano said. 'That is, if you really wish to meet him.'

'No,' I said, 'no I don't wish to meet him.'

We went upstairs instead.

⌒

I woke early the next morning. Beside me, Stefano was still sleeping. I studied his face on the pillow, boyishly beautiful. I touched his naked shoulder, silken smooth. And I wondered how to say goodbye, how to thank someone for an unforgettable experience, an experience that might possibly have changed my self-perception. Had it? I wondered as I studied the perfect curve of his eyelashes (any woman would kill for eyelashes like that). I was realistic. I knew that this had been what they call a 'holiday romance', an 'adventure', and that I must not make the mistake of believing I was in love with Stefano. But I had changed. Something inside me felt different, liberated, freed from some sort of constraint that I had always placed upon myself. I felt womanly, that was it. And possibly for the first time in my life I felt beautiful. For that I would always be grateful.

I crept out of bed, dressed quietly, and as I stole out of the room he was still sleeping.

Of one thing I was certain. I would not stand by while Stefano haggled with Umberto over 'tour prices'. Whatever the bill came to at the Hotel Visconti, I would pay it. I'd probably have to skip Rome and go directly to London, but I didn't care.

After I had settled my account I would return to the room and say my goodbye as briefly and with as much dignity as possible. But already I was self-conscious about how I should phrase it. 'Thank you for a lovely time, Stefano'? 'It's been wonderful, Stefano, thank you'? Every which way sounded glib and inadequate.

The reception area was deserted. Damn. Annita must be somewhere about, I thought. They'd be preparing for breakfast shortly. I gave the bell on the desk a quick tinkle.

Behind the counter, at the far end, was a cupboard, which I'd not noticed before. I noticed it now as the door slowly opened.

Staring out at me from amongst the mops and brooms stood Annita. Without moving a muscle she continued to stare at me balefully for several moments. Then, suddenly, she stepped from the cupboard, closed the door behind her and walked smartly up to the counter.

'You wish to book out?'

I looked at the cupboard door, baffled.

'I like small places,' she said, 'small places are safe.' Then, aware that I was still nonplussed, she continued, spelling it out to me patiently, as if I was a little dim. 'There is no-one behind you in small places. You understand?'

'Oh. Yes, of course.'

'You wish to book out?'

'Thank you.'

As Annita turned to her filing cabinet (I had noticed from the outset the distinct absence of computers in the Hotel Visconti) a voice whispered in my ear.

'Did you think you would escape me?' Stefano laughed as I gave a startled gasp. 'It is not as easy as that.' And he kissed me, oblivious to the fact that Annita had turned back and was watching us.

As I broke away a little embarrassed, Stefano gabbled something to Annita in Italian.

'Of course,' she said and tinkled the bell sharply twice. From nowhere, Sarina appeared. '*Caffe per favore*, Sarina.' Then to me, 'Sarina will bring you coffee in the bar.'

'But . . .'

Stefano put his arm around me, shepherded me firmly to the bar, refusing to listen to my protestations.

'Leave this to me, Jane,' he insisted. 'Please. Annita will have your bill ready in ten minutes. Now sit there and be a good girl.'

There was nothing I could do but obey. He deposited me in a chair, left, and several minutes later Sarina arrived with my coffee.

'Thank you, Sarina.' She was wearing a little sleeveless cotton dress, and I thought she was possibly the most beautiful young woman I had ever seen. 'Your *amico*,' I said, struggling to make conversation. I very much wanted to talk to the girl. 'He is . . .' Damn, I knew the word for 'handsome man', what the hell was it? Yes, of course, that was it. '*Un bell'uomo*.'

She smiled gloriously, then darted a quick glance back at the door to make sure we were alone. 'Yes,' she whispered. 'Verry 'andsomm.'

Had I heard correctly? 'Sarina,' I said, amazed. 'You're speaking English.'

'I spik much English.' Her smile was secretive and her eyes, normally downcast, met mine directly. 'When is my wish.'

I laughed. Her knowledge of English was obviously Sarina's form of rebellion, and it delighted me. 'Good for you,' I said. Did the girl also pretend to be 'simple'? There was nothing about her that appeared simple to me.

'I spik much English when is people I like,' she continued. 'I like you, Jane.'

I stood and embraced her. 'I like you too, Sarina.'

'Everything is sorted out.' Stefano was at the door. 'Annita has your bill ready.'

I looked at Sarina, expecting her eyes to be once more focussed on the floor and her shy demeanour back in place. But she was smiling broadly. 'I like also Stefano,' she said, and she kissed him on the cheek before sailing out the door.

Stefano watched me as I stared after her. 'Sarina is nobody's fool,' he said, and I didn't know what to say by way of reply. It was time I left the Hotel Visconti. I felt like Alice at the Mad Hatter's tea party – nothing was what it seemed.

I settled my paltry bill with Annita. 'What on earth did you say to Umberto?' I asked Stefano.

He laughed. 'We must look after our struggling actress from Sydney, Australia.'

I went up to the room and quickly packed while Stefano waited for me downstairs. I wanted to leave before the chaos of the Americans descended upon us.

The three of them had lined up to say farewell when I returned to the foyer: Sarina, Annita and Umberto. I was sorry not to be able to say goodbye to Rosella and Natale but, as Stefano explained, 'They only come to the Hotel Visconti at night.' I knew Rosella would like to be remembered in all her finery, so I told Annita to give her a message from me.

'There is a bird in Australia called a rosella,' I said. 'It is bright red and green and yellow, and it is very beautiful. Tell her it will always remind me of her.'

'I will tell her. She will be very proud,' Annita replied. 'I have a present for you.' From behind her back she produced a small wooden punnet. 'Straw berries. From Nemi.'

'How lovely. Thank you, Annita.' I kissed her on both cheeks and turned to Sarina, who was standing to attention staring fixedly at her feet. 'Goodbye, Sarina.'

As I kissed her, Sarina whispered, 'Goodbye Jane. I like spik with you.' We shared a quick and wicked smile before her eyes returned to her feet.

Then it was Umberto's turn. 'I too have present for my very good friend, *signorina* Jane from Australia,' he said, drawing from his breast pocket a worn and tattered newspaper cutting. 'You see? Is article I write for *Il Globo*. You remember I tell you about *Il Globo*? Is newspaper in Melbourne. My cousin, he work for *Il Globo* and I write article about the festival of the flowers, you remember I tell you.'

'Yes, I remember, Umberto.' I looked at the newspaper cutting, with its faded picture of the church and the floral display. 'But is this your only copy? I couldn't possibly take your only copy.'

'I have more, I have more. You take, you take. Then you always remember Genzano di Roma.'

'Oh, I'll always remember Genzano di Roma, I promise you.' I couldn't resist sharing a smile with Stefano, who was standing, patiently waiting. 'I must be going,' I said, 'the Americans will be arriving for breakfast soon and you'll all be very busy.' Stefano picked up my suitcase and we walked to the main doors.

'And you always remember the Hotel Visconti.' Umberto bustled along beside us whilst Annita and Sarina returned to their work. 'You tell everyone in Australia Hotel Visconti is most magnificent hotel in all of Italy.'

He kissed his fingers and the air as he pranced about me like a show pony. 'You tell them most magnificent food, most magnificent wine, most magnificent host.' Then he doffed an imaginary hat, twitched his moustache and wriggled his eyebrows, Chaplin-style, and I laughed.

'You tell them this, you promise me,' he insisted. He had stopped prancing now and I realised he was serious.

'Yes, Umberto. I promise.'

Umberto remained standing on the steps, watching as Stefano accompanied me to the car and put my suitcase in the boot.

'Do you have an address?' he asked. 'I can write to you when I am next coming to London.'

'No,' I said. 'I don't know where I'll be. I could write to your parents' restaurant when I know.'

'Good, that's excellent.' He took a notebook from his pocket and wrote down the name. 'Ristorante Guillietta,' he said, 'this is the way to spell it.' He smiled as he tore out the page. 'Papa wouldn't let my mother call it "Ristorante Jill".'

He slammed the boot shut and we stood together for a moment while I wondered what to say.

'Goodbye, Jane.' He kissed me gently. 'You are very beautiful.'

'Thank you.' It needed no more than that, I realised.

I got into the driver's seat, turned the key in the ignition, revved the engine and did a U-turn.

When I looked back through the open window, Stefano had joined Umberto on the steps of the hotel. Together they stood and waved. I waved back, and as I drove through the gates of the Hotel Visconti I could see them in the rear-vision mirror, each with his right arm raised in salute. They looked cocky, confident. Alike even. Were they conmen? I wondered. Were they tricksters and opportunists? Would I ever know? Did it matter?

I didn't write to Stefano.

I did go to Rome though. In fact, I spent a further week in Italy. I could afford to, given the 'tour rates' at the Hotel Visconti. And it seemed that I was seeing the country through new eyes. Oh, the motorways were as terrifying as they had been, and the narrow laneways as threatening, and the Lambrettas as cacophonous. But the countryside was different, the cities more welcoming and the people friendlier. Or was it me? I couldn't be sure.

I finished the panto and I've been in London for several months now, happily settled in a little bedsitter in Shepherd's Bush, and I've even landed my first West End job. Well, it's not exactly the West End, rather a small fringe theatre off St Martin's Lane, but close enough to the hub of things and very exciting. I often think of Stefano, and of Genzano di Roma and the Hotel Visconti. But I haven't written. Not yet anyway.

I did write to Roland though. His was the first letter to arrive after I'd sent my address to family and friends at home.

'At last,' he wrote in response,

I was beginning to worry. But you're there! In London!
The cornerstone of civilisation! Now you can become a
citizen of the world . . .

'Cornerstone of civilisation', my eye. Roland does so tend to live in his yesterdays, I thought as I looked around at the grey, dank London of today. Glorious, certainly, but to my eyes a city of the past. I thought of Sydney and the bright, exciting promise of its future. Suddenly I felt proud to be Australian, and I wondered whether, when I finally went home, I would see my country through different eyes. I had a feeling I would.

Lovely to hear of your fringe theatre job, and to know
that you're comfortably settled, but for goodness
sake, what of your Italian adventures? I want all the

> *details please. I am planning a trip there myself next*
> *spring. Did you go to my friend Wendy's restaurant*
> *just south of Rome, as you promised you would?*
> *I do hope so . . .*

I wasn't yet ready to detail him my adventures. Perhaps one day I might. Perhaps one day I might tell the world. Perhaps one day when I'm sixty, like Roland, I might end up boring some twenty-nine-year-old witless, regaling him or her with my romantic Italian sojourn.

No, that's not fair, I told myself. Roland is never boring. He's inspirational, in his own way. Perhaps I'll be an inspiration to youth in my middle years. That would be nice. But then perhaps not. Perhaps Roland's right, after all. Perhaps I'm too pragmatic and should have been a pharmacist.

Anyway, thinking about Roland always brings out the wicked in me, so I couldn't resist writing . . .

> *Dear Roland,*
> *Yes, I called in to your friend Wendy's restaurant*
> *just south of Rome. Very attractive, lovely views, but*
> *I discovered another gem of a place, which you really*
> *must visit on your forthcoming trip. Knowing your*
> *love of the picturesque, the exotic, the unusual . . .*
> *there is a hotel that captures them all. I believe*
> *Omar Sharif stays there from time to time . . .*

I wasn't being malicious, I decided. In fact, I was doing him a favour. After all, the Hotel Visconti is wonderful fodder for a writer. It might inspire in him a short story, a novella even.

It's called the Hotel Visconti, and you'll find it in a town called Genzano di Roma . . . just a little further south of Rome.

A WORD FROM JUDY

Amazing though it may seem, there is very little fiction in 'Just South of Rome'. By that I mean there's very little that didn't actually happen, and also virtually no characters who were not real at the time of my writing. With one exception on both counts: the love affair my leading character has, and the romantic young Italian with whom she has it.

The events of this holiday mirror the exact experience my husband, Bruce, and I had in a town just south of Rome – a town called Genzano di Roma.

The name of the hotel and its inhabitants have been changed, but, believe me, all is as real and unbelievable as it appears in the story. Umberto and his Charlie Chaplin impersonations, Annita and her terrorist hostage background, the bevy of large American women on religious pilgrimage, the food, the fraud, the flood, and the whole ludicrous series of mishaps ... it actually unfolded all around us, and I wrote the story by hand as it did, in the notebook that I carry on all my travels.

ACKNOWLEDGEMENTS

This collection of stories has been written over a period of time throughout which my husband, fellow author Bruce Venables, has been ever-present and supportive, so first thanks must go to him.

I am deeply indebted to a long-time dear friend of Bruce's (and now mine also) Lee Renshaw. In their younger days, the two were policemen together in Hobart, and Lee's vivid memories of the Rory Jack Thompson case, which he investigated, was my inspiration for 'The House on Hill Street'. Many thanks, Lee.

I have my mother, Nancy Nunn, to thank for 'Changes'. So much of her is there. If she were still around to read it she'd have a great laugh.

Thanks as always to my agent, James Laurie, and to those friends who offer encouragement together with practical assistance in their various areas of expertise: Sue Greaves, Colin Julin and Susan Mackie-Hookway.

Many thanks, too, to my publisher, Beverley Cousins; my editor, Brandon VanOver; my publicist, Karen Reid, and the rest of the hard-working team at Penguin Random House Australia.

Black Sheep

Judy Nunn

Judy Nunn's new blockbuster is a sweeping historical novel about a prosperous sheep-farming family and the enigmatic young man they let into their lives . . .

Black sheep – there's one in every family . . .

Orphaned at sixteen, James Wakefield was determined to be a gun shearer like his father. Now he's killed twice, changed his name, and is on the run from the law.

He had his reasons for both murders, and he felt no joy in taking life . . . Or *did* he?

Ben McKinnon, meanwhile, is heir to the vast Glenfinnan sheep property near Goulburn, New South Wales. He too has a secret that, if ever revealed, would shatter the privileged lives of his father, Alastair, and his sisters, Jenna and Adele.

When fate brings James and Ben together, a powerful friendship is forged, both men gladly becoming the keeper of the other's secret.

Then Ben insists his new friend come to work at Glenfinnan Station. Has James finally found the family he's always longed for? Or has the McKinnon dynasty just unwittingly adopted a black sheep?

From the Shearing Wars of Queensland to the exclusive gentlemen's clubs of Sydney, Melbourne and London; from the woolsheds of Goulburn, to the trenches of the Western Front, Judy Nunn once again brings Australian history vividly to life.

Showtime!
Judy Nunn

Judy Nunn's bestselling novel will take you from the cotton mills of England to the magnificent theatres of Melbourne, on a scintillating journey through the golden age of Australian showbusiness.

'So, Will, are you goin' to come with me and my team of merry performers to the sunny climes of Australia, where the crowds are already queuin' and the streets are paved with gold?'

In the second half of the 19th century, Melbourne is a veritable boom town, as hopefuls from every corner of the globe flock to the gold fields of Victoria.

And where people crave gold, they also crave entertainment.

Enter stage right: brothers Will and Max Worthing and their wives Mabel and Gertie. The family arrives from England in the 1880s with little else but the masterful talents that will see them rise from simple travelling performers to sophisticated entrepreneurs.

Enter stage left: their rivals, Carlo and Rube. Childhood friends since meeting in a London orphanage, the two men have literally fought their way to the top and are now producers of the bawdy but hugely popular 'Big Show Bonanza'. The fight for supremacy begins.

Waiting in the wings: Comedy, tragedy, passion and betrayal; economic depression, the Black Death and the horrors of World War One . . .

Khaki Town

Judy Nunn

A No.1 bestseller, *Khaki Town* is inspired by a true wartime story that has remained a well-kept secret for over seventy years.

It seems to have happened overnight, Val thought. How extraordinary. We've become a khaki town.

It's March 1942. Singapore has fallen. Darwin has been bombed. Australia is on the brink of being invaded by the Imperial Japanese Forces. And Val Callahan, publican of The Brown's Bar in Townsville, could not be happier as she contemplates the fortune she's making from lonely, thirsty soldiers.

Overnight the small Queensland city is transformed into the transport hub for 70,000 American and Australian soldiers destined for combat in the South Pacific. Barbed wire and gun emplacements cover the beaches. Historic buildings are commandeered. And the dance halls are in full swing with jazz, jitterbug and jive.

The Australian troops begrudge the confident, well-fed 'Yanks' who have taken over their town and their women. There's growing conflict, too, within the American ranks, because black GIs are enjoying the absence of segregation. And the white GIs don't like it.

As racial violence explodes through the ranks of the military, a young United States Congressman, Lyndon Baines Johnson, is sent to Townsville by his president to investigate. 'Keep a goddamned lid on it, Lyndon,' he is told, 'lest it explode in our faces . . .'

Sanctuary

Judy Nunn

In this compelling novel, compassion meets bigotry, hatred meets love, and ultimately despair meets hope on the windswept shores of Australia.

On a barren island off the coast of Western Australia, a rickety wooden dinghy runs aground. Aboard are nine people who have no idea where they are. Strangers before the violent storm that tore their vessel apart, the instinct to survive has seen them bond during their days adrift on a vast and merciless ocean.

Fate has cast them ashore with only one thing in common . . . fear. Rassen the doctor, Massoud the student, the child Hamid and the others all fear for their lives. But in their midst is Jalila, who appears to fear nothing. The beautiful young Yazidi woman is a mystery to them all.

While they remain undiscovered on the deserted island, they dare to dream of a new life. But forty kilometres away on the mainland lies the tiny fishing port of Shoalhaven. Here everyone knows everyone, and everyone has their place. In Shoalhaven things never change.

Until now . . .

Spirits of the Ghan

Judy Nunn

In this spellbinding No.1 bestseller Judy Nunn takes us on a breathtaking journey deep into the red heart of Australia.

It is 2001 and as the world charges into the new millennium, a century-old dream is about to be realised in the Red Centre of Australia: the completion of the mighty Ghan railway, a long-lived vision to create the 'backbone of the continent', a line that will finally link Adelaide with the Top End.

But construction of the final leg between Alice Springs and Darwin will not be without its complications, for much of the desert it will cross is Aboriginal land. Hired as a negotiator, Jessica Manning must walk a delicate line to reassure the Elders their sacred sites will be protected. Will her innate understanding of the spiritual landscape, rooted in her own Arunta heritage, win their trust? It's not easy to keep the peace when Matthew Witherton and his survey team are quite literally blasting a rail corridor through the timeless land of the Never-Never.

When the paths of Jessica and Matthew finally cross, their respective cultures collide to reveal a mystery that demands attention. As they struggle against time to solve the puzzle, an ancient wrong is awakened and calls hauntingly across the vastness of the outback . . .